THE WIDE HORIZON

The
Wide Horizon

Loula Grace Erdman

BETHLEHEM BOOKS • IGNATIUS PRESS
Bathgate   San Francisco

© 1956 Loula Grace Erdman

Cover illustration © 2007 Carol Phenix
Cover design by Ted Schluenderfritz
Back cover and title page decorations by Roseanne Sharpe

First Bethlehem Books printing September 2007

ISBN 978-1-932350-12-8
Library of Congress Control Number: 2007922980

Bethlehem Books • Ignatius Press
10194 Garfield Street South
Bathgate, North Dakota 58216
800 757 6831
www.bethlehembooks.com

Printed in the United States on acid-free paper

For
DOROTHY M. BRYAN
*who knew all along
that Katie would have her book*

Chapter 1

KATIE PIERCE was sure she must be the luckiest girl in the whole Panhandle of Texas.

Luckier even than her older sister Melinda who, after five years of waiting, was going to marry Dennis Kennedy in June and go with him to live in Amarillo. Dennis was a real doctor now, driving around the town and the surrounding country, looking after sick folks. Katie tried to imagine what it would be like for Melinda, living in the house Dennis had already bought for them, going to the store to buy what she needed, cooking meals, keeping things in order. Melinda would manage; she had always been the smart and capable one. She would have a wonderful time in Amarillo where exciting things were happening nearly every day.

But, fine as it all sounded, Katie would not want it for herself. Secretly she felt that hers was the much finer prospect. She was going back to East Texas to live with Grandmother and attend the Lewisville Academy for Young Ladies.

Six years ago Melinda had turned down the chance for herself, saying that Katie was the one to go when she was old enough. Now Katie was fifteen and this fall she would be going. As soon as the wedding was out of the way, Mama would start getting her ready to go. Two months, Mama said, was none too much time.

At first Papa was a little uncertain about the matter.

"How are you going to feel about giving up two girls at the same time?" he asked Mama.

"You'll have me," Carolyn reminded him.

"Of course I will," Mama said. And it wasn't until a long time afterwards that Katie remembered Mama really hadn't answered Papa's question.

Even so, it was in the back of Katie's mind most of the time. Underneath her own delight was a nagging little sadness. She would be leaving Papa and Mama and Carolyn; she would be leaving the twins, Bert and Dick, who, at seventeen, thought themselves men grown, but still acted like boys, teasing their sisters every chance they had. It was pleasant here at home, especially since Papa had built the new house in front of, but opening into, the dugout.

The old dugout was divided into two rooms now, one for the boys and one for Katie and Melinda. The girls slept in the bunks Papa had built for them at the time he first came to the Panhandle, before Mama and the children joined him. Katie still had the top one, because she was the younger. Carolyn slept in Mama and Papa's room, in a trundle bed that pushed under the big bed during the day. In this room, too, was the sewing machine. It was here that Mama and Melinda, Katie and Carolyn, sat now, one morning in early

June. They were working on the dress Katie was going to wear at Melinda's wedding.

Katie was going to be the bridesmaid at her own sister's wedding. When Melinda first began to plan, Katie had thought of course that she would want Annie Foster, who was her own age and her best friend— or maybe even Dennis' grown-up cousin from Kansas City. But Melinda took care of that quickly and completely, the way she always managed.

"I want Katie," she said.

"Oh, M'linda!" Katie gasped, overcome with surprise and pleasure. "Oh, M'linda—"

It had been a long, hard struggle for her to learn to pronounce her sister's name correctly. Mostly, by this time, she would say "Melinda" very properly. But she was so pleased with the honor Melinda was bestowing upon her that she slipped back into the old childish slurring.

"Oh, thank you—" she said, the words coming out like one long happy sigh.

"Don't thank me for doing what I want to do." Melinda laughed, and that was the way they settled things.

Mama seemed pleased, too.

"We'll get Papa to take us to Amarillo," she planned. "We'll buy the material for our dresses. Katie can have something that will look right for the wedding and still be nice for school."

Papa, when approached on the subject, was willing enough, although first he had to tease them a little.

"New dresses for all of you," he said. "What are you trying to do? Outshine Melinda at her own wedding?"

But he didn't mean that at all. He wanted them to look nice. He was as proud as they were over the selections— yellow for Carolyn, gray muslin for Mama, and pink flowered stuff for Katie. He even went to the store with them, insisted that Katie and Carolyn have hair ribbons to match their dresses.

As soon as Mama got home, she started making the dresses. She finished her own first, and then Carolyn's.

"I'll make Katie's last," she said. "It's the most important next to the bride's—I don't want the others on my mind while I'm doing it."

And now here was Katie's, ready for the final fitting.

"Come on, Katie," Mama said. "It's ready."

Katie went to her. She had already taken off her print dress and was wearing a white slip, her Sunday one, with a deep flounce trimmed in hairpin lace. She had made the lace herself—yards of it, enough for her own underwear and Melinda's and some extra to put on pillow cases and dresser scarves. She made it from thread, winding it around one of Mama's hairpins and then using a crochet needle to work out the pattern. She could do it as easy as anything; she loved watching the lacy lengths grow beneath her fingers. Melinda had scant luck with it—the thread always broke under her rebellious fingers, or she dropped a stitch and couldn't weave the crochet needle around to pick it up.

"You go too fast," Katie tried to explain, feeling embarrassed at the very thought of putting Melinda straight on anything.

"I don't like doing it." Melinda laughed, not minding her failure a bit. "I hurry so I can be through with the silly stuff."

But once it was finished, she liked it well enough, was glad to have it for all her underwear.

"Raise your arms, Katie," Mama said now, holding the dress up, ready to slip over her daughter's head.

Katie raised her arms obediently, stood still while Mama slipped it on. It fell into place, and Mama began to fasten the buttons. Katie's back was to the mirror; she did not know what the dress really looked like, could not know until Mama had fastened the last button and given her the word that it was all right to turn. The girl stood now in that delicious state of expectation, like Christmas, just before the sheet came off the tree; like birthdays, when all the gifts were still lying waiting to be opened. But this was a different experience, for it was a new one, never to be tasted again. To have one's first real look at the dress you were going to wear as the bridesmaid at your sister's wedding—ah, that was a joy almost too great for bearing.

But even as Katie waited, the complete delight of the occasion was marred by one ugly, nagging thought. What if she got scared, standing up there before all those people? What if her knees trembled so hard that everyone noticed? Just thinking of it now made her breath come quick and fast. She wondered how Melinda could be so calm about things.

"It's going to look fine on you, Katie," Mama told her, stepping back to get a full view. "Now you turn around toward the mirror and see for yourself."

"Yes, look quick," Melinda said.

Katie turned to face her image in the mirror.

Melinda was right. The dress was lovely, utterly lovely. The material—a soft silky white—had bunches of pink roses scattered carelessly over it, like flowers blooming on the surface of the prairie. Something caught at her heart when she looked at them. She wanted to paint them, to make a little poem about them. She wished she could tell Melinda how she felt, but words wouldn't come. Maybe she couldn't make her sister understand, anyway. Katie had rarely been able to tell Melinda exactly how she felt about things. Maybe it was because Katie was six years younger. Maybe it was because the twins laughed at her and teased her so much. Sometimes it seemed to Katie that people were always laughing at her, even when she didn't mean to be funny. She loved Melinda better than anyone in the world, after Mama and Papa, of course, but still she couldn't tell her how she felt about things—like when she saw a sunset or a field dotted with flowers, or heard a lark singing in the spring, or looked at the snow all white and cold and silent.

"Katie," Melinda broke in on her thoughts, "you look lovely. Like a doll on the Christmas tree."

"Oh, M'linda," Katie cried, so happy she slurred once more back into the old childish pronunciation. "Oh, thank you—"

"She looks *excruciatingly* pretty," Carolyn announced, putting her head on one side, the better to survey her sister. At eight, Carolyn was the great one for using big words, not always getting them in the right places. She didn't mind in the least when the twins laughed at her efforts.

"Thank you, Carolyn," Katie said with composure. The look in the mirror had served to steady her. She was fifteen years old; she had this beautiful dress; she was going to be a bridesmaid at Melinda's wedding and at the end of the summer she was going away to school. Maybe Papa was right when he said she was just about grown up.

"You do look pretty," Melinda assured her.

"Thank you, Melinda." Katie brought out the name correctly and distinctly.

"Mama," Melinda mused, looking at Katie thoughtfully, "I have an idea. Would it be all right for Katie to sing at my wedding, as well as be the bridesmaid? That way she would have two chances to show off her pretty dress."

Mama was silent, thinking the matter through. Katie was also quiet, torn between the great wish to sing and the fear that maybe she might have to choose between that and being the bridesmaid. Singing made her forget, for the moment, how scared she was of people and of things. The minute she heard music she could feel the sound of it creeping into her heart and then suddenly she could begin giving it back so that she ceased to be little Katie Pierce, timid and fearful, but an avenue through which song flowed. At such times, she wished she could go on singing forever.

"Well," Mama spoke at last, crisp and sure, now that she had made up her mind, "there's no real reason she shouldn't. She can sing before we start, and then I'll play the wedding march and you can come in on Papa's arm, just like we planned. When you are in your place, she can step over to your side."

"That's what I thought," Melinda agreed, sounding exactly like Mama.

"Oh, Mama—" Katie let out her breath sharply. Now she knew she would get along fine. If she sang first, she wouldn't mind standing up there before everyone while the preacher married Melinda and Dennis.

"Katie has a beautiful voice," Carolyn said, as if she were settling the matter, once and for all. "She sings 'stremely lovely."

"Of course she does," Melinda agreed absently. And then she added more firmly as if she had come to the real reason at last, "I want my wedding to be our family, doing things our way."

Mama looked at Melinda, her face bright with happiness. "That's a lovely thing for you to say, Melinda," she told her daughter softly.

Something—a fear, quick and piercing—caught at Katie's heart.

The family, doing things their way! This was the last thing they would ever do as a complete family. After the wedding, Melinda would leave. True, she would come back, but it would be for visits—like Annie Foster, or even Mrs. Kennedy, Dennis' aunt.

Melinda was leaving the family, to be in a home of her own. Katie wondered that she had ever thought herself lucky, being a part of the ceremony that would bring about the parting.

As Mama had said, there was much to be done in the three weeks before the wedding. In a way, this was fortunate, for it kept Katie from thinking too much about the fact that it meant Melinda's leaving. Sometimes she fancied that even Mama, for all she seemed so composed and sure about things, was also glad to be busy. She would miss Melinda, too, for she depended a great deal on her oldest daughter.

"All of us do," Katie thought. And even as she did so, she wondered how it would seem to have that knowledge—the realization that you were very necessary and capable about things.

Fortunately, there was no need to worry about making Melinda's wedding dress. When Grandmother Gaines, back in East Texas, had been told about the approaching wedding she had sent a big box to Melinda. In it was a dress, yellow with age and very old fashioned, but lovely anyway. There was a letter, explaining the gift.

"You are to wear this to be married in, if you want to," Grandmother had written. "It was your Great-grandmother Tillery's wedding dress, and I've always said you were more like her than you were like either your mother or me. So I want you to have it. I wish you much happiness. Thank you for wanting me to come. I would do so, but I haven't been feeling too well these last few months."

"Great-grandmother's wedding dress," Melinda said softly, feeling its delicate folds. "Grandmother's sending it to me—"

"I'm not surprised," Mama said. "She always mentioned the resemblance, in looks as well as ways. My—just see those little tucks, and every one put in by hand!"

Mama washed and ironed the dress herself, handling it as carefully as if it had been tissue paper. When she had finished, Melinda tried it on. In it she looked like someone in grandmother's picture album, out of another time—finer than she would have looked in something white and frilly like people were wearing now. Melinda was dark and slender —maybe not pretty, Katie had to admit, but having a quality better than prettiness. People stopped to look at her, disregarding far more beautiful girls who might be with her.

"She's interesting looking," Dennis once said. "She's regal. That's my Melinda. Regal, like a princess. Like an *Indian* princess."

"Don't you dare say that word to me," Melinda warned him.

Once she had given Dennis a good tongue lashing because he had laughed at her for being scared at what she thought was Indians. He could get her temper up any time just by saying the word. And yet, he admitted, it was this very tongue lashing which had started him thinking about making something out of himself. The desire had finally been realized by his becoming a doctor. Maybe Melinda didn't mind his teasing as much as she pretended. She and Dennis were always laughing together. Katie, watching them, thought it was wonderful to see two people enjoying each other the way Dennis and Melinda did.

When Dennis saw Melinda in this dress he would really be pleased, for she did look regal, as he had said. Tall and dark and proud, but kind and sweet and gracious, too.

"Take it off, Melinda," Mama said now. "I declare—it gives me a real start to see you in it. As if I were standing back in Mother's parlor, looking at

Grandmother Tillery's picture."

Melinda slipped out of the dress. Mama folded it, placing layers of tissue paper between the folds. This done, she put it into a pasteboard box with little rose-scented sachets. She tied the lid on carefully, handed the box to Katie.

"Put this in the chest under Melinda's bed," she said.

Katie took the box back to the bedroom, pulled the chest from beneath the bed. She opened the lid, remembering as she did so how Papa and the boys had made it for Melinda's birthday, the year she was fifteen. They had made nearly all the furniture in the room, and Mama had made the cretonne curtains at the window, the skirt for the dressing table. The Pierces were that sort of a family. Always they had done things for each other, making out with what they had. No wonder Melinda had wanted this to be a family wedding.

Katie placed the box in the chest, let the lid down quickly. She pushed it back under the bed. But even with it out of sight, she couldn't make herself forget that, after the wedding, when the family carried out some enterprise one of them would be missing.

Now with the dresses out of the way, Mama turned to cleaning the house. Every cupboard had to be put in order; every window had to be washed.

"You take the inside, Katie," Melinda said. That was the way they always did—Melinda washing the outside, Katie the inside. They worked together, looking out for spots.

"The very idea!" Mama cried, scandalized. "You stay inside, Melinda. Do you want to get all brown, like an—" She hesitated.

"Say it!" Melinda grinned, proving that she had long since got over minding being teased about the time she thought she saw the Indians.

"Brown as a gypsy," Mama finished, smiling too. "You keep out of the sun until after the wedding."

"Nonsense," Melinda retorted calmly. "Katie and I will wash the windows, like always. She couldn't get them clean by herself, and you know it."

So they worked together, as they had always done.

"That spot's on the inside, Katie."

Katie rubbed hard, but it did not come off.

"It's on the outside, Melinda."

"Oh—all right—" And she rubbed away until the window was clear as could be.

"She's thinking the same thing I am," Katie spoke the words only in her heart. "We'll never clean windows together again!"

All the curtains had to come down for a good washing and ironing. And every carpet had to be taken up, carried out into the yard and beaten with sticks until the last bit of dust was gone. This was the twins' job.

"All right, Mama," Bert grumbled, his red hair standing every-which-way, "now give me a couple of rags and some water and I'll go scrub the windmill tower."

He was the one who usually complained first, worked hardest for a while, gave up quickest. Dick, quieter, with Mama's dark hair and eyes, always grinned good naturedly at his twin's remarks. But that didn't mean he let him take the lead—not unless it suited him, he didn't. In some ways, the twins thought and acted just alike. But then, in others, they were as far apart as the poles.

"You wash, I'll wipe," Dick said.

But the pair didn't really mind. They were as anxious as anyone to have the place all clean and right for Melinda's wedding. And the whole family was proud that they could do things for themselves. Mrs. Kennedy, Dennis' aunt, had sent word she would be glad to help. Mama thanked her, but said they could manage. They were all glad that Mama knew what was necessary, even for a wedding like Melinda's.

At first, they had thought it would be very simple, with just the two families. But Mama had not reckoned with Melinda when she thought that.

"I want Annie," she said.

Annie was Melinda's best friend.

"Annie Foster," Mama wrote down.

"Manilla would want to come, too," Carolyn put in.

Manilla was the Foster girl nearest Carolyn's age.

Mama looked a little doubtful. "She couldn't come without the rest of the family," she reminded Carolyn.

"Ask the family," Melinda said.

"The family—?" Mama was more than doubtful. That meant eleven extras.

"And Nick and Herman," Carolyn went on. "They would be most terrifi-cully hurt if we did not ask them."

Of course they would. Nick and Herman were cowboys on the Kennedy ranch, and they had been almost like family ever since the Pierces came to Texas.

"I don't see how I can manage," Mama objected. "I don't know who to ask, who to leave out."

"Ask them all," Melinda said. She was so happy she was simply glowing. "Ask every single one of them, even Mrs. Lister."

They laughed at that, for the mention of poor Mrs. Lister always made people laugh. She was forever saying she had something terrible wrong with her, but she never missed anything—parties, church affairs, anything—even though she complained the whole time she was there.

"But we can't get them into the house," Mama pointed out.

"Don't try," Melinda told her. "Let them stay in the yard. The two families—and maybe Annie—can be in the front room. The rest can watch through the windows and the door. Then we can have the reception afterwards and everyone can see everyone else."

"We had planned a simple wedding, for morning," Mama reminded Melinda. "Remember how far some people will have to come, if you go ahead and ask the whole community. You can't expect them to get here that early, with the distances some will have to travel. Don't forget we were going to do it that way so as to give you and Dennis plenty of time to drive to Amarillo after the ceremony."

Amarillo was thirty miles away, and that was something to think about.

"We could have it in the afternoon," Melinda said.

"Say about three o'clock. People could get here easily by that time, and we'd still have time to drive to
Amarillo."

"Three o'clock, Melinda!" Mama's voice was filled
with protest. "You don't have big weddings at that
hour. You have them in the evening, eight o'clock, or
so. What would Mrs. Kennedy think!"

That was the real core of the matter. For all their
sakes, Mama wanted Mrs. Kennedy to see that her
nephew was marrying into a family that knew how to
do things right.

"It's not Mrs. Kennedy's wedding, Mama." Melinda giggled. "It's mine, and that's the way I want it."

"Oh, all right—" Mama gave in. "I guess it's the
best idea anyway. People would probably have come,
even without invitations. Nobody ever waits to be invited to things out here."

This was true. The word got around that someone
was having a party, and people came from everywhere.

Now, as soon as Nick and Herman heard, they
came riding over.

It was funny about Nick and Herman. They were
together so much that mostly when you thought of
one you thought of the other, like you did with the
twins. But they weren't twins; actually, they didn't even
look alike. Herman was shy and gentle and small; he
looked like a boy, really. He got along fine with children. Carolyn loved him, as did all the other homesteader children. Nick was really younger, but he was
larger. He usually took the lead. At heart he was just
as good and kind as Herman, but he was more likely

to tease. You could depend on both of the cowboys for help when you needed it.

"Hello, Sis," Nick said to Katie, who was out at the windmill, watering the zinnias.

"Hello," she said shyly.

"Ask your Ma if she has any errands in Amarillo. We're on our way and we thought, with all the neighborhood fixing to show up at the wedding, she might need some things."

With Amarillo so far away, it was downright rude for anyone to go there without collecting a list of errands from all the neighbors.

"I'll go ask her," Katie said.

She went in to tell Mama.

"Goodness, yes," Mama said, and bustled out with a list of things she wanted. Katie and Carolyn trailed her.

"Sure are getting things spruced up," Nick drawled. "That onery Dennis, he ought to be here helping."

"Oh, no," Carolyn told him primly. "It is not right ettikit for the groom to help with the wedding."

"Now ain't that just too bad," Nick declared, winking at Katie. "Maybe if he don't get here to help, he'll forget there is a wedding and not show up at all."

Herman grinned, though he took no part in the teasing.

"It is not proper ettikit for a groom not to come to the wedding," Carolyn explained patiently. "He will be here."

"Sure he will." Herman spoke up firmly.

The cowboys rode off, taking the list with them.

"It was nice of them to offer to help," Mama said,

going back into the house.

"Oh, they knew we'd be needing them," Bert told her. "Melinda's no good at all, mooning around the way she does. And Katie has to spend all her time doing her hair up in rags so it'll be curly enough to suit her." He reached out to pull one of his sister's curls.

He knew she never had to try to make her hair curl— never at all. Her hair was naturally curly. Sometimes she wished it wasn't. Her curls got all tangled and Mama had to help smooth them out.

"And Mama, you ought to speak to her!" Dick took up the chorus, not wanting to be outdone by his twin in anything, even in teasing his sister—especially in that. "I caught her rubbing red calico over her cheeks before we went to church last Sunday."

Katie smiled shyly at him. He knew she didn't do this. Mostly her cheeks were pink because she blushed so easily, and that was why he teased her.

"Katie's hair is very pretty," Carolyn spoke up. "She is most fortunate to have curls."

That was Carolyn, never lost for an answer. Maybe it came of being the baby, her ability to take petting or teasing with equal ease. Sometimes Katie thought it would be nice to be the baby, as Carolyn was, or the oldest, like Melinda, instead of the middle one, as she herself was. It put her in between—too young to be a real companion to Melinda, too old to find companionship in Carolyn. It made her feel stranded in the very middle of the family. Melinda had Annie Foster to talk to; the twins had each other. Carolyn made friends easily with anyone who happened along.

Katie did not want anybody to know it, but she felt

more alone than ever, now that they were all rushing around, busy with preparations for Melinda's wedding. Sometimes she suspected, though, that Papa guessed how it was with her.

"Well, Katherine," he said to Mama, "isn't it lucky we have another young lady coming on?"

"Me, Papa?" Carolyn asked pertly.

"Not yet," Papa told her. "You're still our baby. It's your sister Katie. After Melinda's gone, she'll be the young lady of the house—Mama's helper, Papa's comfort—and your big sister."

He put his arm around Katie's shoulders and suddenly she felt very proud. Yes, Papa knew how lost she would be without Melinda.

"Katie a young lady!" Bert snorted. "If you ask me, she's still our baby, too."

"She's no such thing," Dick retorted, in one of those rare times when he differed with his twin. "She'll be the young lady of the house. When Melinda's married, she'll be *Miss* Pierce."

He looked at Katie and there was only kindness, and maybe a little respect, in his eyes. That was the way it had always been. Mostly the twins stuck together. When they did differ, it was usually on some matter touching Katie and Melinda. Then it was that they showed very clearly, perhaps without even being aware of what they were doing, that Melinda was Bert's favorite, while Dick always sided with Katie. She gave him a quick, grateful look now, happy both at the prospect he had suggested and the fact that he had come to her rescue.

"Now Katie," Carolyn said, smoothing down her

skirts in a pleased, complacent gesture, "you hurry and get married, so I can be Miss Pierce. It would be a most scrumbumptious thing to happen."

"Just listen to her!" the twins howled in unison. "Where does she pick up those outlandish words!"

"I get them from the dickshumary," she told them. "You ought to read it yourself."

Melinda was busy ironing curtains the day Annie Foster came.

"Well," she said, "here I am. I've been wanting to come over and offer to help all along, but I was afraid if I did, you'd think I was fishing for an invitation, so I stayed home. The minute I got the word, I came right on over."

"You knew I couldn't get married without you here," Melinda said. "I was going to invite you, even if we didn't go beyond the family."

"Oh, get along with you!" Annie protested, all pink with pleasure. "Here, Melinda, you turn loose of that iron. I'm going to do these curtains. You mustn't wear yourself out before the wedding."

She took the iron firmly away from Melinda. That was Annie. She never seemed to give a thought to herself, just went around doing things for other people. Katie would never forget the first glimpse they had of Annie. She was fourteen then, just a little older than Melinda. But she was ragged and dirty and barefooted. And shy—too shy to speak when she was spoken to. Even Katie's shyness was as nothing compared with Annie's at that time.

No wonder she was shy, for not only was she dirty

and poorly dressed, but she couldn't even read! Melinda had taken care of that. Annie was smart. With Melinda helping her, she was soon reading like a streak. Then she taught her brothers and sisters. Sometimes she had to threaten them, and sometimes she bribed, but she wouldn't give up until they, too, were able to read.

Not only that, but she taught them to act more like other people. She kept at Mr. Foster until he built a new house—not as nice as the Pierces', but a better place than the old dugout the Fosters first had, which was no more than a hole in the ground. She made them learn table manners, after a fashion, and how to get along pretty well at parties and preaching and such things. Annie was wonderful, and no mistake.

And now here she was, taking over the ironing. She stood at the board, strong and dependable looking, making you feel everything was well in hand, now that she was here.

"Oh, Annie," Melinda told her, "I'm so glad you came."

Annie flashed her a quick, bright look. She seemed never to get over being grateful to Melinda. Now she was glad just to be here ironing curtains, as if it were a proof of Melinda's kindness to let her do it.

"Sakes alive, I wouldn't miss out helping." Swish, slurr—she pushed the iron back and forth across the length of curtain. "Looks like the whole neighborhood is wanting to be in on it. I met Nick and Herman on the way over and they said to tell you they'd be glad to barbecue a beef for the eats."

"Well," Mama hesitated delicately, "that's thought-

ful of them, Annie, but we've already planned the refreshments for the—er—reception. I'm baking ham
and making chicken salad and wedding cake, of course,
and so on—"

Her voice trailed off as she noticed the look on the
girl's face.

"My goodness!" Annie exclaimed, setting the iron
on a piece of paper to keep it from burning the cloth.
"My goodness—I might have known! You'd do this
wedding right, not like a Fourth of July celebration. I
might have known—"

She was humble and apologetic because she hadn't
thought to tell Nick and Herman on the spot.

"It's less trouble," Melinda explained gently. "We
can get things ready ahead of time."

"Now Melinda," Annie faced her, "that's not the
real reason, and you know it. Your Ma's doing things
that way because it's right and proper. With you marrying Dennis Kennedy, and Mrs. Kennedy knowing
all about manners and so on because they are Ranch
people, you just have to do it right. I'm real proud you
know how—"

It was still there, the differences between the
Ranch people and the homesteaders. The Pierces
were homesteaders; the Kennedys were ranchers.
Slowly the difference was narrowing, now that Papa
had more than one section of land and a nicer house
and a windmill, so that he didn't have to ask anyone
for water—but it was still there. Papa laughed and said
Melinda was the one who was bridging the gap.

"Well, you're doing it," he told her while they were
getting ready for the wedding. "You're joining the

homesteaders and the ranchers. It took my girl to get it done."

He was really joking, but all the same it was true.

Papa understood the resentment the ranchers had for the homesteaders who came in and plowed up the land that the cattle grazed on and built fences and settled close together so that there wasn't lots of room left any more. When the Pierces first moved to the Panhandle, they had to get their water from the Kennedy Ranch, which was embarrassing—but embarrassing or not, they had to do it, for people can't live without water.

Isn't it fine, Katie was thinking, that Mama knows this and can manage things right? Suddenly she felt a deep compassion for Annie, whose mother did not know any of these things—Annie, who had to learn for herself, even how to read, and then teach the rest of her family.

"Now I tell you what," Annie went on, "you're going to need somebody to keep things going in the kitchen that day, and you can just count on me."

That was Annie again. She would want to be watching the wedding more than anything else in the world, but if she was needed in the kitchen, she'd stay there.

Melinda looked at her quickly. "Kitchen, nothing," she said. She spoke quickly and impulsively, but with conviction. "You are going to be in the living room with the family."

Light flashed across Annie's face.

"And after the ceremony, I want you to—to preside at the punch bowl."

"Who, me—?" Annie gasped.

"Yes, you. Mrs. Kennedy is going to serve the wedding cake at one end of the table, and you can serve punch at the other end."

"Now Melinda," Annie said practically, "I wouldn't know the first thing of how to go about it. How to—well, serve—or anything. You just get that out of your head."

"You wouldn't be expected to know," Melinda told her. "I wouldn't either, if I had to. We'll get Mama to show us. You will, won't you, Mama?"

Mama said yes of course she would, although it was plain to see she hadn't thought of Annie in this role.

"I—" Annie began. Then she stopped. There was a mist in her eyes, but there was also a glow on her face. "I'd be proud," she finished simply. "I'd be just—real—proud."

Katie could understand how she felt. Annie Foster, standing across the table from Mrs. Kennedy, would know the greatest triumph of her life. All her family, all the neighborhood, would see her there and know she was taking her place with the best of them.

"Only thing, I don't know just how I'll come through." And then she looked at Melinda, quick suspicion on her face. "You aren't trying to be—well, to be good to me, are you? Because I'd not mind a bit helping in the kitchen."

"I asked you because I really want you," Melinda assured her. "After all, aren't you my best friend?"

It was nice of Melinda to put it that way—as if Annie would be doing her a real favor by accepting.

Katie wondered if maybe being happy yourself, the way Melinda was, didn't make you want to see the whole world happy. Some of the glow of that thought filled her own heart. Forgetting her own shyness, she spoke up with courage she seldom exhibited.

"You'll do it fine, Annie," she said. "You'll act just right."

"You'll be extremely gracious," Carolyn said primly.

"I'll probably bust the bowl and spatter everybody here," Annie said. "But if you want me, I'll have a fling at it all the same."

Chapter 2

"I DECLARE," Mama said, "I'm just not a bit satisfied about having zinnias for wedding decorations."

"Oh," Melinda consoled her, "they're awfully pretty right now, Mama. They'll work out fine."

They were, indeed, beautiful. Yellow and bright red and golden—all the glowing colors on the chart. The best of them grew around the windmill. It was a rule that everyone who went for water, whether for the house or for the stock, must slosh a little on them.

"We need white," Mama went on, a worried frown between her eyes. "I remember when I was married we used mock-orange. All over the parlor and the living room and twined up the stairway. We had a big bouquet on the dining room table."

She was lost in memory.

"Well," Melinda reminded her practically, "we don't have mock-orange blossoms out here—we don't have any white flowers. We have zinnias and that's what we'll use."

That was Melinda. She liked this country well enough not to regret the absence of white flowers.

She didn't mind using what it had to offer. Always she had been like this. She had been given her chance to go back to East Texas to school, and she had turned it down. She said it was because she wanted Papa to use the money for a windmill, but later on she admitted she didn't even want to go.

"I guess you're right," Mama agreed, "but I still wish we had white—"

"But we do," Katie broke in impulsively. "I mean— we can get them—"

"What do you mean, Katie?" Mama asked.

"Yucca—" she said.

Yucca. Down toward the breaks it grew, acres and acres of it. Not truly white, but a waxy, creamy color—tall spikes thrusting up from sword-like leaves. It was blooming now, unusually lovely because there had been a great deal of rain this spring.

"Why Katie!" Mama cried, warm approval in her voice. "Of course—that's the very thing."

"Well—" Melinda said, smiling all over her face. "In a way, I guess we couldn't have anything more appropriate—"

And then Katie remembered it was the tall spikes of the yucca plant which Melinda had mistaken for Indians, that day when Dennis had laughed at them for being afraid. The twins often teased Melinda about this, but never Katie. Her own fear at the time and her dependence on Melinda had been too great. She hoped her sister wouldn't think she was poking fun at her now when she made the suggestion that yucca be used for the decorations.

"I—I didn't mean—" she faltered uncertainly.

"Katie," Melinda said, "I think it would be lovely. What is it the Mexicans call those flowers? 'Candles of the Lord.' I'd like that—The Lord's Candles standing beside me while I am being married."

"She's right, Katie," Mama agreed, turning to her and speaking as if she were every day as old as Melinda. "Suppose you take over the decorations. I'll get the boys to bring you what you need. They'll help with the decorating, too."

"I—" Katie began, her face flushing with pleasure at the thought of the honor and the responsibility that was hers. "I—all right—"

So that was the way it happened. The twins, not without some grumbling and certainly not failing to go through some war-whoops to indicate they remembered the other long-gone occasion, made ready, two days before the wedding, to go harvest the necessary flowers.

"How many do you need, Katie?" they asked her.

It was strange and very wonderful, to have them coming to her for orders.

She hesitated, thinking hard. She shut her eyes, getting the picture in her mind. This was a tremendous responsibility that was hers. What if she didn't do it right? What if it looked awful, once she had the flowers in place?

"Oh, I don't know—" She hesitated. She could not get over the feeling that they wouldn't mind her anyway.

"Now that's a fine way—order us out to get the blamed things and not even know how many you want," Dick grumbled.

"Oh, maybe three or four dozen," she said, guessing desperately at the number.

"All right—want any other weeds brought back? Tumble weeds, or Russian thistles, or maybe cactus—" Dick asked.

"No—" And then she thought quickly. Those yucca stalks grow among green leaves. All flowers have green about them. She ought to have some green.

"I—I wish I had some cedar," she said.

"Wait a minute—" Bert protested, "It's not Christmas. You fixing to have a tree, or something?"

"I need some green stuff," she explained diffidently.

"She's right," Mama said. "When I was married, I had smilax draped up the stairway and looped over the doors. She does need greenery of some sort."

Mama had smilax. Out here there was no smilax, but down in the breaks, cedar grew. They could use it instead. Out here, you made out with what you had.

"Oh, all right," Bert agreed. "We'll get your cedar, Katie."

Even Katie, whose idea it had been, was unprepared for the lovely picture the cedar and yucca blossoms made together. As soon as the boys brought them home she put them into tubs of water. The next morning—the day before the wedding—she set about using them.

"I need something deep to put them in," she said.

"Deepest thing we've got is nail kegs," Bert told her, meaning to be funny.

"Of course!" Katie cried. "I'll wrap them in pieces

of old sheets, and they'll look like great big vases."

"My gosh!" Dick said. "Bert was only joking, and she takes him serious."

She had the boys put a nail keg on each side of the folding bed, so that they showed just a little in the glass. The folding bed sat in the front room. During the day, it was just a big rectangular piece of furniture, something like a tall chest, with a mirror in the front of it. At night, it could be let down, and there was a bed, the one they used for company. Now, with the two nail kegs in front of it, filled with the tall spikes of yucca and the trailing cedar, it looked perfectly beautiful.

"Like an altar, with tapers," Mama said. "My goodness, Katie, that was a wonderful idea you had."

They couldn't have asked for Melinda's wedding day to be any prettier. Warm, not hot, with an enamel-blue sky and those same white clouds to make it seem even bluer. Because of the rains, the grass in the yard was emerald green. The zinnias around the house and out by the windmill tower were blooming, bright jewels of color against the brightness of the day. Some of their loveliness was inside, in vases placed around the living room and the other rooms in the house.

The first thing Katie thought when she woke up was, "This is the day." She sat up quickly, looked down at Melinda's bunk. She was already gone! Katie sprang out of bed, dressed and went into the living room. She wanted to see for sure that the wedding decorations were as lovely as they had seemed when she left them last night.

They were even prettier. She put her head on one side, the better to look at them. It seemed to her she had never seen anything more lovely. She supposed she felt that way partly because it was her idea.

She could hear sounds of voices coming from the kitchen—Mama's and Melinda's. She made her way there quickly.

"Good morning, Katie," Mama said. She had on a fresh print house dress and was bustling around the kitchen, getting things in order.

"Well," Melinda laughed, "we just thought maybe you meant to sleep right through the wedding!"

Melinda had on an old, faded dress, one she had really outgrown. Her hair was hanging down her back in two pigtails. She looked like a little girl—maybe not any older than Katie.

"Papa and the boys have eaten and gone," Mama said. "You want to eat with Melinda and me? Carolyn's still asleep."

Mama poured a glass of milk, set it down by Katie's plate. She pushed a plate with bread on it closer to her. Then she reached back to the stove, got a dish of fried eggs.

"Now you try to eat something," she ordered. "Both of you."

Katie tried to take a bite, but there was something in her throat that would not let it go by. It was like a lump—a big, choking feeling that held food firmly and would not let it be swallowed.

Mama pretended not to notice. Usually, she was quite insistent that they eat everything on their plates. But this morning she sat there and said nothing while

Katie, and even Melinda, fiddled with their food.

"Well, hello!" It was Annie Foster, who had ridden on ahead of the family. "I thought I better get over early, with all there is to do."

"My, my," Mama greeted her warmly, "it's good to see you, Annie. We are certainly up to our ears."

Mama was right. There wasn't any time for feeling sad now; there wasn't any time for anything but work. Annie stood like a rock to lean on, mixing the salad, making the little sandwiches.

"Sakes alive, Mrs. Pierce," she marveled, "a body has to watch while he's eating these things, or they'll slip right through his fingers. And when I think how Nick and Herman fancied you might want a barbecued beef!"

She giggled at the very thought.

Finally things were ready, and it was time for Melinda to dress. Mama and Carolyn and Katie and Annie Foster went into the room to help. It seemed very crowded, that little room which had been half the house when first they came to the Panhandle. The tree had been right over in that corner for the Pierces' first Christmas here—the tree which had been made of chairs turned upside down and wrapped with green cloth. It was Melinda's idea, when the big storm kept them from going out and looking for a real one. And in that other corner the Bad Men had sat, the night they took refuge out of the blizzard and scared the family half to death. The whole room was full of memories.

Katie and Carolyn curled up in the top bunk, Katie's bed, in order to be out from under foot. Mama and Annie helped Melinda, doing things for her that she could have done for herself, such as fastening the white muslin corset cover with its trimming of hairpin lace and buttoning the two white petticoats in the back. Melinda let them do that, but when it came to combing her hair, she would have no help at all.

"I'll do that myself," she said. "Just the way I always wear it."

And she did, pinning the two dark braids across the top of her head, not even trying to make any curls.

Then it was time to get out the box with the wedding dress in it. Mama reached for it, took off the lid. She removed the dress, shook it out. A fine scent of dried rose leaves filled the room.

Melinda slipped into it, being very careful, for it was cobweb frail. Mama buttoned it down the back, and that took a long time, for there were dozens of tiny buttons. When she had finished, she stepped back and said,

"I wish Mother could see you, Melinda."

Katie knew why; Melinda did look exactly like Grandmother Tillery's picture.

"Call your father," Mama said.

She was speaking to Katie, but Carolyn, with the privileged attitude that came with being the baby, ran ahead.

"Papa, Papa!" she cried. "Come see Melinda in her wedding dress. She looks most gorgeous beautiful."

Papa came. He looked at Melinda with a strange expression on his face. He didn't say anything, just stood there looking.

"Papa—" Melinda said, coming swiftly toward

him. She looked as if she were going to cry. "Papa—"

"Katie," Annie broke in, "Carolyn—come on. We'd better get out there and see if everything is all right."

She got the two girls out of the room, leaving Mama and Papa and Melinda together. Katie went, a sick hurt in her heart. Annie didn't really think there was anything that needed to be looked after. She knew Papa and Mama wanted to be left alone with Melinda. This was something that shut out the others—Carolyn, Katie, even the twins. Mama and Papa and Melinda—they were the grown-ups now, bound together in an adult companionship into which the others could not enter. Katie was just a little sister, not greatly different from Carolyn.

"My goodness," Annie declared, "we better get dressed ourselves!"

Which was what they did, hurriedly, for Annie was right when she indicated there was much to do before the guests arrived. Katie and Carolyn had hung their dresses in the closet in Mama's room, and Annie's lay on the bed. It was really pretty. She had made it herself—a blue one with white lace around the yoke and on the edge of the flounces.

"Stuck my fingers a jillion times while I was making it," she said. "Just hope a seam don't give way right when I'm pouring out a glass of that punch-stuff. I'm no seamstress," she finished, showing no real regret. As a matter of fact, she knew she had done all right with that dress, just as she managed to make out on anything she had to do.

Katie slipped into her own dress. Annie buttoned it for her.

"My goodness, Katie!" she marveled. "You look like a valentine—a real pretty-lace-and-flowers one."

Katie flushed with pleasure. She ran the comb through her hair which, thank goodness, wasn't tangled this morning because Mama wouldn't have time to help her with it.

"Put on your dress, Carolyn," Katie said. "I'll do your buttons for you, and your hair."

Carolyn got into her yellow dress with the ruffles on the yoke. Katie brushed her hair, brought the ribbon around it and tied it in a bow on top of her head. Carolyn's fair, straight hair hung down almost to her waist in the back, making her look like the pictures of Alice in Wonderland.

"You look lovely, Carolyn," Katie told her.

"I know," Carolyn agreed calmly. Coming from anyone else, that would have sounded vain, but in Carolyn it didn't. She was different; sure of herself as Melinda was—and individual. Katie sighed a little. It must be wonderful to be confident and unafraid, she thought, and brave enough not to be always minding what people thought of you.

It was a good thing that Annie had urged them on, for already people were beginning to arrive. First to come were Dennis and his aunt and uncle. Mrs. Kennedy looked very smart in her blue silk foulard and stylish hat and gloves—and very pleased, too. She was glad that Dennis was marrying Melinda, and so was Mr. Kennedy.

"Well, well," he said when Katie met them at the door. "What a pretty little girl we have here!"

Katie smiled at him, knowing she must overcome

her shyness and greet the Kennedys properly. They were glad their nephew was marrying a homesteader girl, and Mama was to be thanked for that. Mama had seen to it that they knew how to do things right, even if they lived in a dugout—things like setting the table correctly and using napkins and greeting visitors who came. Remembering that, Katie managed to get along all right in her role as hostess.

"I look very nice, too," Carolyn told him, as usual sounding as if she were stating a fact instead of being vain.

"Of course you do," Dennis told her. "You look perfectly scrumbumptious!"

Dennis himself was looking mighty well—tall and handsome. He was a little nervous, maybe, for he stumbled over a chair rocker when Katie led the way to the living room. She remembered the first time the Pierce children had ever seen him, that time he had helped to find Carolyn when she was lost. To Katie, he had looked as big as a man then—one to be trusted. Now he was taller and more grown-up, but he still looked like a person to be trusted. And he still had that nice, polite way about him. At first the twins had held this against him, just as they had not liked it because he enjoyed reading so much. They had got over this feeling, however, when they discovered he could ride with the best of them and work cattle almost as well as a cowboy and handle a gun.

"Hello, Katie," Dennis said. "Where's the rest of the family?"

"Mama and Papa are in Melinda's room," she told him. "And the boys are dressing. They said for you to come back to their room when you got here—"

Dennis walked off toward the boys' room.

Katie turned back to face the door just in time to see a boy coming quickly toward her. He was a stranger to her, but that wasn't to be wondered at, for new people were taking up claims all the time now. This would probably be one of the new homesteader boys. He was maybe sixteen years old, and tall for his age. He had dark brown hair which was combed neatly. He was clean, too, and carried himself well. But he wasn't dressed up, like all the other guests were. Her first thought was that maybe he had got to the party by mistake. And then she could see that he was very much excited, or in trouble, or both. It was strange that she should notice him so carefully, she was thinking, before he even reached her.

"Hello," she said, remembering that she was acting as hostess.

He spoke, but his words were not in greeting.

"I was told," he said, "that a doctor would be here."

"Oh, yes—" Katie said. Of course there was! Dennis was here.

"A lady sent me—I was just passing by and she came out and stopped me. She said to get the doctor, and quick. She thinks she's dying."

Katie's eyes opened wide. A woman dying! She must tell Dennis, and quickly.

"Her name's Mrs. Lister," the boy explained. "She told me there would be a doctor here." He hesitated a moment, then went on doubtfully. "Looks like you are having a party here, or something—"

Katie didn't wait to explain. She called over her shoulder, "I'll get Dennis—I'll tell him right away."

She ran to the boys' room, pounded on the door, which was closed. Dick opened it. Dennis and Bert were standing there, not saying much of anything. Maybe they were all a little nervous, each in his different way.

"Dennis," she cried, "a boy just came to tell you Mrs. Lister is awful sick. Dying, maybe!"

Katie was not prepared for the new stillness that fell over the room. The twins were looking at her, disgust and disapproval in their eyes. Even Dennis was regarding her doubtfully.

"I—the boy said to tell you—" Katie trailed off weakly, hating herself because she seemed to have done something wrong when she meant to be helpful; hating herself still more because she was weakly trying to shift the blame for what she had done.

"Mrs. Lister—" Dennis said, as if he were struggling with a bad dream. And again, "Mrs. Lister—"

Then Katie had no doubts as to the nature of the thing she had done. Mrs. Lister was always saying she was sick, maybe even dying, but when she sent for a doctor, he had to go, and by the time the doctor got there, she would probably be out walking around in the yard. This was the news Katie had brought to Dennis, who was a doctor.

"Listen, Dennis," Bert said. "You know how she is. You don't have to go."

"We'll send someone riding for old Doc Ferguson," Dick offered.

Even as he spoke, they all knew that his suggestion

was no good. Dr. Ferguson was thirty miles away and sick himself. And here was Dennis, five miles away, at best, and young and strong. The only trouble was that he was supposed to be getting married in less than an hour!

Bert must have been thinking that, too, for he urged, "You don't have to miss your own wedding for a thing like that, Dennis. If she was really sick, it would be different. Gosh— she's probably as well as you are by now."

Dennis might not have heard, for all the answer he gave. Instead, he started out of the room, walking very fast.

"Where are you going?" Dick asked.

"To talk to Melinda," he answered.

He didn't say about what. He didn't have to. They all knew.

Dennis turned and took the few steps that separated him from the door of Melinda's room. He knocked quickly. Papa came to the door, with Mama close behind him.

"Why, Dennis," Mama said, uncertainty and disapproval in her voice. "What is it?"

"I must talk to Melinda."

"But you can't," Mama protested. "Not right before the wedding."

Dennis knew that as well as anyone. The groom didn't see the bride in her wedding dress until the moment when she came in on her father's arm, to meet him at the altar.

"Is something wrong?" Mama asked uncertainly.

"Yes—" Dennis said.

"What is it?"

It was Melinda who asked this, pushing Mama and Papa aside to stand before Dennis in her wedding dress. He looked at her quickly, caught his breath a little, then gazed straight into her eyes, as if he were trying not to see the dress that it was not yet right for him to look at—as if he were trying not to see anything much.

"Mrs. Lister—" Dennis began. "She sent word that she is very sick. She thinks she's dying."

"Oh, Dennis—"

Melinda's disappointment was in her voice. And perhaps a little exasperation, as well. Everyone knew about Mrs. Lister and her sick spells. "Maybe someone's just playing a joke on you. How did you find out?"

"Someone brought the news to Katie. She told me." He turned to face Katie, who had followed closely behind him, aghast at what she had started. "Who was it that told you?"

They all turned to face her—Mama, Papa and Melinda as well. It was as if on all their faces was the accusation that she felt in her own heart. She hadn't needed to tell Dennis that Mrs. Lister had sent for him. Now that she had, he couldn't ignore the summons. Even she could understand that.

"A—a boy—" she faltered. "I didn't know him. He's a stranger—"

A stranger! It might be a joke in that case. Nobody who knew Dennis would play such a trick on him. People liked him too well to do that to him.

They all stood there, bound by a stillness that was

louder than any noise could be. It was Melinda who spoke first. Her voice was resolute and clear.

"Go on, Dennis," she said.

He looked at her, relief flooding his face, but he made no move to leave.

"What about the wedding?" he asked.

"We'll have it when you get back," she said. "It's not far—it shouldn't take you long."

"Melinda—" Dennis began. And then he stopped. Right there, with Mama and Papa and Katie looking on, he reached out and swept Melinda into his arms, wedding dress and all. He kissed her quickly, and then he kissed her again. Then, without another word, he rushed from the house.

Katie sat, alone and miserable, in the little shed off the corral. In bad weather it was used to shelter the stock, but now, in June, it was empty—empty save for Katie, sitting on a bit of feed left over from last year's harvest.

She was conscious of the not unpleasant smell of the grain, dry and clean, as she sat on it, unmindful of her new dress.

Outside she could see the sun getting low in the sky, which meant it must be close to seven o'clock, for June days are long. And in her mind was the one thought—Dennis was not back yet.

Katie had stood things as long as she could. She just had to creep away here, by herself, to think about her innocent and unthoughtful part in ruining the wedding.

Outside, she could hear the sounds of many peo-

ple talking, of games going on. The men had set up
a game of horseshoes. She could hear the iron clink-
ing against the stake when a "ringer" was made; the
dull *ping* when the shoe hit the ground. That would
be followed by shouts of good-natured derision from
the other players, just as a hit would bring sounds of
approval.

She could hear, too, the cries of the children engaged in various games of their own. And inside the
house, she had left the women visiting. Among them
Melinda moved, wearing her wedding dress that no
one was supposed to see until she came out to marry
Dennis. But Melinda had come out of her room,
joining Mama and the contrite Katie in trying to put
people at their ease, trying to fill in the time until the
wedding could take place.

As soon as Dennis left, Mama had turned to Melinda. It was strange to see Mama so lost as to what
must come next.

"What are we going to do now?" she asked helplessly, as much to herself as to anyone standing there.

"We'll wait until he comes back," Melinda said.

She spoke with conviction, although her voice was
not quite as confident as it had been while Dennis was
there.

"I'll go out and explain what has happened," Mama
said. And then, "Oh, if it had only been a little later!
Just an hour later—"

An hour later, the ceremony would have been over
and Dennis and Melinda would have been on their
way to Amarillo.

"Of course," Papa said quietly, "there is always the

chance that she may be *really* sick."

"Now Richard," Mama turned to him quickly. "You know how she is—" It wasn't like Mama to be so quick and impatient.

"Yes—" Papa said.

"But we have to go out and explain now," Mama said. "Come on, Richard—you go outside and tell the men."

"They already know," Papa said. "Remember—they saw him leave. Somebody probably went with him."

"Well," Mama declared, "I have to go explain, anyway."

She started toward the door. Melinda stepped to her side.

"I'm going, too," she announced.

"Oh, Melinda—you can't!" Mama protested.

"It may be hours before he gets back," Melinda told her. "I can't stay cooped up in this room. Besides, think of all those people out there. You'll need me to help keep them entertained."

"She's right, Katherine," Papa said. And Katie, even as upset as she was, could see Papa was pleased that Melinda would decide to do this.

"Oh, all right," Mama said. She opened the door, and out stepped Mama and Papa and Melinda, to join the crowd that had come for the wedding. Katie trailed behind them, unnoticed. She was just little Katie Pierce who could be of no help in this crisis which she had unwittingly helped to bring about.

The hours that followed were a sort of nightmare to Katie. The afternoon dragged on, with everyone seeming to be having a good time, even though the wedding hadn't come off. Sure enough, Papa was right. Nick had gone with Dennis, who had ridden Herman's horse. Herman and the twins had kept busy, seeing that things went right outside. It was they who started the men playing horse shoes. Mrs. Kennedy, Annie, Mama and Melinda kept things going in the house, visiting among the women. Katie marveled at the ease and poise of Mama and Melinda. Late in the afternoon, she saw Mama beckon to Annie.

"Annie," Mama said, "these people have been here a long time. They must be hungry. I think we'll let them eat now."

"Yes, Mrs. Pierce," Annie agreed. "Our kids, they're getting restless. I know a lot of the others are like that, too."

"We'll serve the food," Mama said, "but we'll save the wedding cake and the punch." She didn't say "for the wedding." Maybe she was thinking that Dennis would never marry Melinda now. Never.

Annie started toward the kitchen. Katie knew what she was going to do. She was going to set out the ham and the chicken salad and all the other wonderful things Mama had made ready for the reception refreshments. They would have the food, even though there had been no wedding. Katie could not stand the prospect. She slipped out of the house and to the little shed, there to hide and give way to the tears she could no longer keep back.

"There, it won't do any good to cry," someone said, almost at her elbow.

She stood up quickly, startled enough to stop

crying. The boy who had brought the news stood before her.

"I know you feel badly," he said, "because I do, too."

He stood there before her, shifting his weight from one foot to the other.

"I brought the news, you know," he reminded her. "But how was I to know what she was like?"

Suddenly Katie's own humiliation was forgotten a little in seeing the real concern of this boy.

"Of course you couldn't help it," she said. "But I knew—I didn't have to run and tell Dennis right off."

The boy was silent a moment.

"I wouldn't say that," he finally told her thoughtfully. "I mean—when someone sends for the doctor, we sort of have to tell him, don't we? And then leave it up to him about going."

For a moment Katie thought about that. Some of the soreness left her heart. You *couldn't* keep a doctor from knowing he was needed. Maybe she had done wrong in running straight to Dennis. Maybe she should have told Papa and let him decide—but she couldn't have kept the news to herself, once she heard it.

"That's the same for you," she said. "I mean, when Mrs. Lister stopped you, you had to do what she asked. That's the way people do out here."

"Sure," he said. And then added earnestly, "I guess that's the way people do anywhere. Back in Illinois, where we came from, people helped each other, too."

"Oh, you're from Illinois?" Katie asked.

"Yes—we just moved in a couple of days ago. My

name's Bryan Cartwright."

"I'm Katie Pierce."

"Sure, I knew that."

She examined him more carefully. She liked the way he looked—calm, and nice-mannered, even though he was upset and concerned.

"It's a fine mess I got myself and everybody else into!" He grinned. "Barged right in on a wedding I hadn't been invited to."

"Oh, nobody waits for invitations to things out here," Katie told him.

"My mother still won't like it," he said. "I'll have a hard time explaining it to her. And when she finds I broke up the wedding—in these old clothes—" His voice trailed off.

Katie grinned back in sympathy. She was feeling better by the minute—not entirely reconciled to what had happened, but better.

"I would have gone long ago," he said, "but I wanted to see you and apologize. And," he hesitated a minute, "I wanted to tell you not to feel so badly. My goodness—I watched you and you looked like you had murdered somebody, or something—"

"I felt like it was all my fault," she told him shyly.

"Well, it wasn't, so why don't you go back in the house and make the best of things, the way your sister is doing? She's marrying a doctor, and she knows what that is like."

Katie stood up. She smoothed down her dress. She could feel the boy's eyes on her, see the approval. Maybe it was the dress he liked; maybe he was pleased because she had stopped crying and was going back into the house to face things.

Katie stepped out into the afternoon sunshine. She was conscious of a growing excitement among the people standing around. And then she knew the reason for it.

Dennis and Nick were riding into the yard. They stopped. Dennis swung off his horse, started toward the house on the run. He looked tired, but he also looked sort of triumphant—as if he wasn't too sorry about the way things had happened.

Katie started toward the house, as fast as she could go. But even as she did so, she was aware of Nick's voice. His words carried clearly to her, and they were full of awe and wonder.

"—really was having a heart attack—should have seen him working with her—Yep, she's better—"

Above even the happiness that thundered in her heart at the knowledge that Dennis was back was another wonderful thought—Dennis really *had* needed to go!

It was strange, as if time had stopped hours ago, and only now was it starting ahead again. Just as before, Dennis slipped back into the boys' room. Katie went to the front room. And then, as if nothing unusual had happened, Mama came in. She sat down, looking very composed, but Katie could see her eyes kept wandering nervously toward the door. A little hush fell over the room, that quiet vacuum which creeps in just before something is ready to start. Nick and Herman came in, looking very solemn and a little ill-at-ease. Katie supposed that came partly from being in the front room, watching the wedding, and partly from wearing their new store clothes, with shoes instead of boots.

Just then Annie Foster came to the door, nodded slightly. Mama took her place at the organ. The twins marched in, very quiet and grave looking, not at all like themselves. Carolyn went to them and Dick reached out and took her hand in a protective kind of gesture. Mama looked at Katie, who moved over to the organ, to stand beside her.

Mama struck a note. Katie cleared her throat nervously. For one awful moment she thought she wasn't going to be able to make a sound. Then she was conscious of Dick, looking straight at her. His face was encouraging—it was something to cling to, like an anchor. She opened her mouth, the words began to come.

"Believe me if all these endearing young charms—"

It was funny, but the moment she began to sing she wasn't frightened any more. The words flowed, smooth and easy, from her throat. Nothing mattered—not the faces of the people in the room, nor yet those looking in through the door and the windows—nothing save the singing. Almost before she knew it, she was finished. And again a stillness hung over the room.

It was broken almost immediately by Mama's swinging into the notes of the wedding march. Then they came in together—Papa, with Melinda on his arm.

Melinda was a little pale, but very beautiful. Papa looked grave. It was hard to read the expression on his face, for it was part solemnness, part happiness. A very strange, divided expression.

The two moved toward the altar Katie had improvised. The mirror gave back the image of the tall white yucca, the green cedar. It gave back the image of Dennis, standing there waiting for Melinda. In it Katie could see her sister, moving toward him, taking her place beside him. Then, as if it were in a dream, she saw herself going to Melinda, standing by her side.

The minister stepped forward, began to speak. Katie was scarcely conscious of what he said. Papa moved back, the minister said a few more words. There was a prayer, and then Katie was aware of the voices of Dennis and Melinda, low but very strong and clear. Then the preacher spoke.

"I pronounce you man and wife," he said.

She's not Melinda Pierce any more, Katie was thinking. She's Melinda Kennedy.

The people pushed toward the bride and groom—Mama first, and then Papa and the others.

"My goodness, Katie," Carolyn said severely, "don't look so frightening—it's all over—"

Everyone began to laugh. And the congratulations and the kissing followed.

Mama led the way out to the kitchen, which was also the dining room. But today it didn't look like a kitchen at all. The stove was covered with newspapers, and over them one of Mama's good white table cloths had been placed. On this there was a lovely arrangement of zinnias. The kitchen safe, too, was draped with material that hid it so well you'd never guess it was a safe. The table itself was covered with the best table cloth, and all the good dishes were out. At one end of the table stood Mrs. Kennedy, with the wedding cake—tall and white and beautiful—before her, and at the other end was Annie Foster, ready to serve the punch from the glass bowl. She looked very serious. It was wonderful when you thought about it—Annie Foster standing across from Mrs. Kennedy.

But that was not half the wonder of it. Looking at the table now, you'd never guess how things had been only a little while before. Someone—Annie most likely—had made the table and the room neat, so that there was no trace of all the food that had been consumed while the guests were waiting for the wedding to come off. The flowers were in the center, flanked by the tall white wedding cake at one end, the punch bowl at the other. Things looked exactly as they should. Mama was moving about with composure and ease. Dennis and Melinda were standing near Mrs. Kennedy—Melinda glowing, Dennis looking a little embarrassed and a little shy, but happy, too—awfully happy. It was just as if nothing at all had happened to put the wedding off a single minute.

"You must cut the first piece, Melinda," Mrs. Kennedy said. "And Dennis—you must help her—"

So Dennis and Melinda, both laughing, went to cut the wedding cake. And after that, everyone came up for his own piece.

The sun was gone now, and twilight was settling over the country. But before it could be really dark, a great yellow moon began crawling up in the sky. Katie watched it, fascinated.

Just then she heard Mama calling her.

"Katie," she said, "come here."

Katie went to her.

"They are getting ready to leave," Mama said softly. "I thought maybe you'd like to help Melinda change into her traveling dress."

Katie followed Mama into the little room. Melinda was already out of her wedding dress. Annie stood there, holding the blue silk which Melinda was going to wear when she rode to Amarillo in Dennis' new buggy with the good driving team hitched to it.

Melinda put the dress on now. Mama began to fasten the buttons in the back.

Katie picked up the little dark blue hat with the bird on it.

"Here's your hat," she said, handing it to Melinda.

The words were hard to bring out of her throat. She could scarcely get them past the ache that was lodged there.

Melinda set the hat on her head. She pushed the hat pins through, reached to pick up her gloves.

"My goodness," Annie said, "you do look stylish. Better than any of them Amarillo women will look!"

Melinda, knowing Annie's loyalty, only smiled.

"You do look nice," Mama told her.

Melinda turned to Mama. She hugged her, tight.

"Thank you for everything—" Melinda said, a little thickly.

"Now don't you cry," Mama warned her firmly. "What would Dennis say if you came out with your eyes all red and watery—"

She walked to the door. "All right, Richard," she called.

Papa and Carolyn came in together.

"You look very beautiful," Carolyn said.

"Ready, Melinda?" Papa asked. "Dennis has the buggy out front."

"Ready—" Melinda answered steadily.

She turned and kissed Papa and then Carolyn. She came to Katie, who raised great anxious eyes to her sister's face. She had to say this. She had to.

"I'm sorry, Melinda—I was the one who ran and told Dennis Mrs. Lister sent for him."

Melinda kissed her tenderly. "Little goose!" she exclaimed. "Why shouldn't you? I knew what I was getting into when I promised to marry a doctor."

She turned to Mama and clung to her for a long, quiet moment. And suddenly she wasn't Mrs. Dennis Kennedy at all, but Melinda Pierce, a little frightened at the great adventure that lay ahead of her. Mama hugged her tight, and neither said a word. Katie had the awful feeling that, for one brief instant, Melinda was thinking she didn't want to go away at all.

She kissed Mama again.

Mama wiped her eyes quickly.

"And anyway, you were right as always," Melinda said, grinning a little. "You said a wedding as big as mine ought to be in the evening. It was!"

She turned and walked out of the door, with the others following her.

The moon was higher now, and no longer gold. It had spread a silver wash all over the face of the prairie. It was so bright, you could see almost as well as if it were daylight. Melinda walked through the light of it to where Dennis stood, waiting for her to come. The twins were standing near him. Melinda stopped, kissed them both. Then Dennis took her arm, helped her into the buggy. He tucked a light robe around her knees to keep off the dust. Then he walked around to the other side, got in beside her. Nick handed him the lines.

"Goodby—" everyone called.

Dennis and Melinda turned to wave. Someone threw a handful of rice. It caught in Melinda's hat, quivering there like little sliding raindrops. Dennis touched the team lightly with the whip. It bounded off.

"Goodby—good luck—" people called.

The team trotted off, drawing the buggy after them. Off into the silver distance, Melinda and Dennis went. Everybody stood and watched them for a while and then they turned away.

But Katie did not turn. She stood there until the team and the buggy were not even a small speck on the horizon.

Chapter 3

KATIE HAD KNOWN she would miss Melinda, but even so, she had had no notion of how much. The whole house was an aching spread of loneliness, concentrating in the room which the sisters had shared. The calico curtain in the corner, which served as a closet for their clothes, seemed very bare now with only Melinda's oldest, outgrown dresses left hanging beside Katie's. The chest Papa and the boys had made for Melinda on her birthday was still pushed under the bed. Before she left, she had given it to Katie. But Katie had not yet been able to put anything into it. It seemed sort of impolite—as if she were grabbing Melinda's things when she was unable to protect her rights.

"Katie," Mama suggested, "now that Melinda's gone, how would you like to take her bed and let Carolyn come in with you and have yours?"

"Why of course, Mama," Katie agreed politely.

She was glad to move into Melinda's bed, but it did not seem quite right to have Carolyn sharing the room. Not so long ago she and Melinda had linked themselves together in a shrewd though kindly campaign to keep the child out of the room. She had a way of scattering things, upsetting treasures.

"Mama, she's such a nuisance!" Melinda had once flared up.

"Try to be patient with her," Mama had urged. "She's really just a baby."

"I'm not a baby," Carolyn had wailed. "I'm not! I'm very, very grown-up."

That was Carolyn—taking all the privileges and petting that came of being the baby, but always insisting that she was as big as the rest of them. And here Mama was wanting Carolyn to share Katie's room.

Then a strange thought came to Katie. Carolyn was now just about the age she had been when the Pierces moved to the Panhandle, when Papa had made these double deck beds for her and Melinda. The thought sobered her. She herself was the age that Melinda had been at that time. She didn't feel nearly so old or half so capable. Melinda had always been the strong one, the one to take the lead. Katie was content to follow, usually without question. She even sought guidance, like asking Melinda which dress to wear, and what hair ribbon to tie on her curls. Among strangers, even around the family, Melinda took the lead and Katie followed.

Now Melinda was gone and Katie was the older sister. Only, she could never be the leader, as Melinda had been. She wasn't that sort of person. And, even if she were, Carolyn was not the one to be led. She was more like Melinda, not asking anyone what to do, but going ahead and following her own wishes.

Carolyn was delighted with the idea of moving

in. Almost before Mama had finished making the suggestion, she was busy carrying it out. She started bringing in all her treasures, depositing them where she felt they best fitted.

"It is very nice to be in the room with you, Katie," she chattered importantly as she worked. "It makes me feel so—so *adulthood*."

Katie smiled, knowing that the twins would have howled with laughter and then corrected her. Carolyn would not have minded much. She rarely lost her temper; she never seemed embarrassed at being teased. Katie admired her for this; she herself always shrank from laughter at her own expense.

Now she wondered if she ought to tell Carolyn that the word was "adult," but decided against it. She could see this was a big moment for the child. Most of all she wanted to have her sister accept her as an equal. Maybe, for all her acting so sure about things, she was feeling a little uncertain; maybe she knew Katie was thinking she was nothing but a baby and would just as soon not have her.

And besides, it wasn't for long. Two months and Katie would be leaving for school. The thought of it made her feel wise and generous and kind.

"I'm glad to have you, Carolyn," Katie said.

She *was* glad. She couldn't explain it at all, but in some strange way the very act of welcoming Carolyn made her feel a little less lonely for Melinda.

With the wedding behind them, Mama was now ready to turn her thoughts toward getting Katie ready to go to school. Only, before she could get to the matter a crisis hit. Miss Frazier, the school teacher, took it into her head to resign.

When the Pierces first came to the Panhandle, Mama had taught the children herself because there was no school. She had done this for two years and then, since more and more families had moved in, the parents got together and decided they must have a school. One was built and a teacher hired. For two years the school had been running with the same teacher, an older woman who had come to live with her sister on a claim. Katie supposed she was all right, but certainly not as good as Mama had been. She talked in a funny, shrill voice and she sniffled a little all the time. But she was the best they could do, as everyone said, and at least she kept the school going. She had taken the school back for a third term, but now she had decided her sister needed her and she wouldn't teach any more.

"Well," Mama said, "we'll just have to get busy and find someone else. A really good one, Richard."

All the time Katie was in school, Mama kept right on coaching her at home, too. She had a good reason for doing this. She wanted to be sure that Katie would get along all right when she went back to the Young Ladies' Seminary at Lewisville. Katie never could understand how Melinda could have turned down her chance. Giving up a chance to have music lessons and art; a chance to be where there were trees and flowers—and no wind.

Oddly enough, Grandmother did understand. Two years ago, when Mama had taken the three girls back for a visit, the old lady, who had not seen them for four years, regarded them long and earnestly. Finally she spoke.

"Melinda turned out just the way we might have expected. It's the pioneer blood coming out in her. Good thing she gave up coming back here to school. Katie, now—"

She turned to look closely at Katie, sized her up from head to foot. Someway, it didn't bother Katie at all, although she was usually embarrassed at being watched. She looked right back at Grandmother, feeling the pink come into her cheeks, but not dropping her eyes. Strange, but she wasn't a bit afraid of the old lady; a little in awe, maybe, but not frightened. Katie had always loved her grandmother dearly, feeling sure the love was returned. One of the things she missed most after they went to the Panhandle was slipping over to her house. In the four years since Katie had last seen her she seemed to have changed very little. She still sat very straight in her rocking chair, and her hair was combed as neatly as always and her voice was as lovely as Katie had remembered it. She smelled sweet—the familiar and delightful mixture of dried rose leaves and geranium and lavender.

"Katie is our lady," Grandmother went on. "She has all the earmarks."

She turned to Mama.

"You've done well, Katherine," she told her. "I said you couldn't manage, but you have. You didn't let yourself go and you have three well-behaved daughters instead of the wild Indians I thought you'd bring back to me. Melinda was bound to turn out the way she has, whether you stayed here or went to the ends of the earth. Katie hasn't been hurt. By all means, when the time comes, send her back here to school."

"May I come, too, Grandmother?" Carolyn asked.

"We'll see," the old lady told her. "Wait till the time comes."

"I'm going to be a great lady," Carolyn assured her. "I will be the biggest lady of you all."

"Humph," Grandmother said, smiling at Carolyn, just as everyone did. "That, too, we'll wait and see."

So, actually, Mama wasn't too upset over losing Miss Frazier. It was just that she had kept the school going, and with her gone, they must get a teacher to take her place. And they discovered that the Pierces were not the only ones interested in the matter.

Mama and Katie were in the kitchen, doing the dishes. Papa and the boys had gone to the corral. Mama, looking out the window, saw a buckboard driving up, and Katie, following her gaze, saw that a man and woman and a little girl were in it.

"My goodness!" Mama cried, snatching off her apron. "Company—and people I've never seen before. You go meet them, Katie, and take them to the front room. I'll be there as soon as I get myself straightened up a little."

So Katie went to the door, feeling a little uneasy as to how she would handle the job that was hers.

When she opened the door to the knock, the man began to speak at once.

"Good afternoon," he said. "Are your mother and father in? We're the Cartwrights."

Cartwright? Where had she heard that name before? Oh yes—the boy who had brought the news the day of the wedding was named Cartwright. These must be his parents.

"Come in," she said, forgetting to be shy. She led the way to the front room, asked the visitors to be seated. They took chairs, and Katie had time to look at them. The woman was small and brisk, like a busy brown wren. The man was tall and kind looking, with laugh wrinkles webbed around his eyes. The little girl, who was just about Carolyn's size, had her hair braided into pigtails, very smooth and neat. She had black eyes, like her mother's. The father's eyes were blue. Like—Just then Mama bustled in.

"I'm so sorry to keep you waiting," she greeted her guests cordially, extending her hand. "I was at the back of the house, and couldn't get here at once."

"Oh," Mrs. Cartwright said, "this is not a good time to run in on you, but we were passing by. I'm Mrs. Cartwright, and this is my husband, and my little girl, Meg."

"Cartwright—" Mama said. She looked very fresh and pretty in her clean calico dress, with her hair all smooth and neat. Katie wished that Mrs. Cartwright knew Mama hadn't gone and changed—that all she had done was take off her apron and smooth her hair. "I wonder if your son could be the Cartwright who came to my daughter's wedding. Such a fine boy."

"Thank you," Mrs. Cartwright said, smooth and polite as Mama. "We all felt dreadful because he brought the news that delayed the wedding. But he had no way of knowing—"

"Of course not," Mama said. "And it's a good thing

he did, for poor Mrs. Lister was really sick. Your son was instrumental in saving her life."

"He didn't know there was a wedding going on," Mrs. Cartwright explained.

"I realized that," Mama assured her. "I wish you had come, too. I did not know you had moved in, or I would have come over especially to call on you and invite you."

"We have been here only a few weeks," the woman said. Both she and Mama understood that, regardless of the custom of the country, they were not the kind of women who either gave, or accepted, invitations until that all important first call had been made. "And I know how busy you were, with the wedding and all."

All this time Carolyn had been edging closer to the little girl.

"Carolyn," Mama suggested, "don't you want to take Meg to your room and show her your dolls?"

"Come on," Carolyn said, taking her hand. "They are most gorgeous beautiful."

Meg did not hesitate, even for an instant. She and Carolyn walked out of the room together.

"I think we have two of a kind there," Mrs. Cartwright remarked. "But now—we must tell you why we came to see you so unceremoniously—" In other words, why the Cartwrights had presumed to call on Mama before she had got around to calling on them. "Tell her, Joe." She turned to her husband.

So, urged on by his wife, Mr. Cartwright explained that it was because of the school situation. They had come from Illinois, buying this section of land because they were told there was a good school nearby. Now, they found there was no teacher.

"We have two children to go to school," Mrs. Cartwright broke in. "Meg, of course. And Bryan, too, if there is a teacher who will make it worth his while. He wants to go back to Illinois to college in a couple of years, and he ought to have help if he's to pass those entrance examinations."

"I don't blame you for being concerned," Mama agreed warmly. "We have been, too. My husband is one of the directors, you know."

"That's what we were told. So we came to him."

"He has some applications," Mama said. "He's down at the corral now, Mr. Cartwright. Would you like to go talk with him?"

Mr. Cartwright said he would, so Katie was sent to direct him.

By the time the Cartwrights were ready to leave, all the Pierces were completely delighted with them. Mama and Mrs. Cartwright exchanged recipes and Mama gave her visitor a pattern for a pinafore for Meg. And Papa had asked Mr. Cartwright to go to Amarillo with him the day after tomorrow, to have interviews with the prospects.

Monday, as had been planned, Papa and Mr. Cartwright rode to Amarillo to talk with the applicants. Because it was thirty miles away, and because they wanted to have plenty of time to question the prospective teachers, they planned to stay all night.

"Oh," Mama said quickly, "you can go to Melinda's."

"Yes," Papa said. "I had thought of that—"

It was late Wednesday when Papa got back. All the family, even the twins, rushed out to meet him.

"Did you get a teacher?" they asked. "Did you see Melinda?"

"I stayed all night at Melinda's," Papa told them, taking the most important thing first. "She's fine. She said they were coming out Saturday night."

Melinda and Dennis coming Saturday night! For a moment that dwarfed any other information Papa might give.

"Oh!" Mama cried. "That's fine—just fine—"

"Did you find a teacher, Papa?" Carolyn asked.

"Yes," Papa answered, "I did. She sounds good."

"Come on in and eat your supper," Mama suggested. "You can tell us about her while you eat."

So Papa went in and while he ate he talked about the new teacher. Her name was Mildred Jordan, and she could teach music and art; and she had good grades in arithmetic and history, too; and geography. Papa had seen them.

"What's she look like?" the twins asked, doubtless remembering Miss Frazier who had sniffled all the time and worn just two dresses, both of them awful looking.

"Pretty," Papa answered. "Neat and pretty."

"Not too pretty, I hope," Mama protested. "That kind always marry before the term is half over and leave us without a teacher."

"I asked her about that," Papa said. "It seems she's engaged to a man who's studying to be a lawyer, so she wants to teach two years, while he's in school, and get some money ahead. Sounds real sensible to me."

"Yes," Mama agreed. "She certainly does."

"Cartwright liked her, too. By the way, Katherine, he seems to be a mighty solid person. I'm glad they've moved here."

The Cartwrights and the Pierces were not the only ones pleased about the prospect of the new teacher. Annie Foster rode over as soon as she heard the news.

"I'm that happy," she declared. "I tell you, it was hard going, keeping the kids in school with that Miss Frazier sniffing like a rabbit on the trail of a carrot. I couldn't make 'Lonzo finish out the year. The rest of them I had to work on all the time."

"You learned while you helped them," Mama reminded her.

"Oh, sure—but they need music and art, too—like you taught your girls."

She had never ceased to be impressed because Melinda and Katie—and now Carolyn—were taught to play the organ and sing and draw.

"The new teacher can teach them those things, too," Mama assured her.

"Good!" Annie exulted. "It's a real load off my shoulders, and that's a fact. Say, how's Melinda?"

"She's fine," Mama said. "Her father tells me that she sent word she and Dennis would be home for a visit Saturday evening. You come for dinner Sunday, Annie—I know she'll want to see you."

Annie's face lighted up.

"Why thank you, Mrs. Pierce. Thanks a lot. I'd be proud—"

Mama started preparations for the visit on Wednesday.

"My gosh," Dick complained, "we just got through scrubbing up for the wedding and now we're at it again."

Which was true. They cleaned the house until there wasn't a speck left anywhere. Mama, with Katie's assistance, cooked all the things Melinda liked best. Even Carolyn did her part, shelling the black-eyed peas and running errands. Mama would stand by the kitchen table, thinking hard, and then she'd say, "Melinda likes this—or that—" Then she'd start preparing whatever the item was. And often she'd say, "I know Dennis always liked—" and she'd name something else.

"Lot of scrubbing and cooking going on in here," Papa said.

"It's an important occasion," Mama reminded him.

Papa looked at her, a long, thoughtful look. Then he grinned.

"Mrs. Pierce," he asked, "how are you going to like being a mother-in-law?"

"Fine," Mama assured him. "Fine—" She was silent a moment and then went on. "Maybe a little scared. It will be their first trip home—" Her voice trailed off.

"If you're wondering whether she's happy," Papa said, "the answer is 'yes.' I saw her and I know."

"Of course," Mama agreed. "Dennis is a fine boy."

"And Melinda is a fine girl," Papa reminded her quietly.

Katie looked at Papa quickly. It came to her that Papa missed Melinda, too. As much as Mama did; maybe almost as much as Katie did. They had always been very close, had been able to laugh and talk with each other in a way that Katie, much as she loved her father, had never been able to achieve. She didn't want to be jealous, and she wasn't. But she sometimes thought she'd give a great deal to be able be understand the things Papa and Melinda found so interesting—even to be able to laugh at some things they thought funny. For the life of her, she couldn't always see the point of jokes that sent them off into gales of laughter.

"It will be wonderful to have Melinda back," Carolyn said. "She will be a young matronly—the first one in the family."

"Whoops!" Dick yelped. "Listen to the infant. The word is *matron*."

"I heard Mama say herself that Mrs. Hadley was a nice, matronly person," Carolyn defended herself calmly. "And I asked her what the word meant, and she said, 'a married woman.'"

"Oh—" Dick said. That was the trouble with Carolyn. You couldn't always find the right answer to give her. "Well, that may all be true. But a person is a *matron*, not a *matronly*."

"Any person is?" Carolyn persisted. "Could Dennis be one?"

"Oh, gosh—" Dick raised his eyes to heaven, as if imploring help. "Somebody explain to the kid—"

"A matron *is* a married woman," Papa said, taking over the explanation. "Matronly describes her. Do you understand now?"

"Of course," Carolyn said loftily, as if she wondered why everyone had made such a fuss over the matter to begin with. "That's what I said, didn't I?"

And Katie, listening to the conversation, had her own thoughts about the matter. Whichever word they might use—be it matron or matronly—the Melinda who came back would be a different person from the one who had gone away. Katie felt she would be a little shy around this big sister who had gone off into a strange new world.

Whatever doubts and fears she might have had, however, were settled when Melinda and Dennis finally arrived. Dennis stopped the horses, and before he could get out to help her, Melinda was over the wheel, running toward the family, which was assembled out at the gate, waiting for her. They all started running toward her—well, the twins weren't exactly running, but they were moving mighty fast. Katie was ahead of all of them; she had come right to Melinda when the look on her sister's face made her stop. Melinda was looking beyond her, straight at Mama. So Katie slowed down, and it was Mama who came to Melinda first. She looked at her daughter—a long, searching look. For just a second it lasted, and then they were in each others arms and Mama was kissing her and she was kissing Mama. When Mama turned, her face was as bright as Melinda's. Papa came next, and then it was Katie's turn.

"Oh, Katie!" Melinda cried, giving her sister a tight squeeze. "Oh, Katie! It's good to see you. I've missed you so—"

And suddenly the sore spot left Katie's heart.

Forever, she hoped.

"Hello, folks," she heard Dennis say. "I can see I don't count around here."

He was grinning when he said it, and didn't in the least believe what he said. But at his words, everyone turned to him. Papa shook his hand, pumping it up and down. Mama exclaimed, "Why Dennis—what a way to talk!" And, as she hesitated, Dennis asked, "Well, aren't you going to kiss me, too?"

"Why of course I am," Mama told him, standing on tiptoe and kissing him warmly.

After that, they all went into the house.

"It looks good," Melinda said. "It looks lovely—" She went from room to room, inspecting everything, as if she had been gone for years, instead of just a few short weeks.

Supper was wonderful that night. They sat around the table after it was over and talked and talked. Mama kept insisting that everyone have second helpings of everything, from fried chicken to plum cobbler. It was late before they were finished and got the dishes washed. Then Mama went into the front room and let down the folding bed and fixed it for Dennis and Melinda, just as if it had been the preacher visiting.

Sunday started out the same, with more eating and more visiting.

"Mama," Melinda said, "you just must see the house. Five rooms, and just for Dennis and me."

"She a pretty good cook, Dennis?" Papa asked.

"She does fine," Dennis assured him, speaking quickly—almost too quickly.

"Now Dennis," Melinda said, "go ahead. Tell them about the biscuits I burned. And those awful cakes!"

They both began to laugh, as if they had a joke no one else in the world knew. Katie, watching them, felt the old loneliness come back for just a moment. Then she pushed it back from her. Melinda was happy. She liked living in that new house in Amarillo. She liked being there, with Dennis. Katie must remember that, instead of thinking Melinda was here just on a visit.

Annie Foster rode over shortly before noon. She was off her horse in a flash and running toward Melinda, who rushed out to meet her. They hugged and kissed each other as if they had been separated for years.

"You look grand," Annie told her friend, standing back to get a better view. "I bet you're the most stylish looking woman in Amarillo."

"Oh, Annie!" Melinda said fondly. "Hush talking like that."

They walked toward the house, arms around each other. Dennis met them at the door.

"Hello, Dennis," Annie said. She was always a little shy and formal around him—maybe she couldn't forget about his being a rancher while the Fosters were only nesters.

"Hello, Annie. My, you are looking fine."

"Oh, now—" Annie flushed in pride and delight. She did look nice—in a new blue print dress, and her hair combed all neat and pretty. She was wearing a hat and gloves, and could have made out all right in Amarillo or anywhere she chose to go.

She went into the kitchen where Mama was busy with dinner.

"Hello, Annie," Mama said. "I'm so glad you came."

"Say, Mrs. Pierce," Annie told her, scarcely returning the greeting, "I brought you a letter. Pa rode over for the mail yesterday, and since he knew I'd be coming here today, he brought yours, too. And here it is."

"Now that was thoughtful of you," Mama straightened up from the oven, where she had bent over to look after the roast. She took the letter.

"I saw the postmark," Annie said. "I guess it's from your mother."

"No—" Mama opened the letter with a puzzled look. "No—"

She began to read, and then her face grew tense and worried.

"Something wrong?" Papa asked.

"It's Mother—" Mama began. "Mrs. Bartlett— that's her next door neighbor—has written. Mother's had a fall."

"Is she hurt badly?" Papa asked.

"She's broken her hip," Mama answered slowly, as if she still did not quite believe what she had read.

"Broken her hip—" Dennis was first to collect his thoughts. Maybe that came of being a doctor and knowing how serious a thing of that kind could be for a woman as old as Grandmother.

"Yes—" Mama said. Her face was pale, her lips quivering a little. Papa moved to her side, put his arm around her shoulders.

"There, there—" he said.

At his touch, Mama seemed to pull herself together. She stood still for a moment, then moved restlessly
around the room. Everyone was very quiet, even Papa.
When Mama was like this, they all remained silent,
letting her think things through. Finally she turned
and faced them, and when she did, they knew she had
made up her mind.

"I must go to her," Mama announced.

"Of course," Papa agreed.

"But what will you and the children do?" Mama
asked. "How will you manage?"

"We'll get along," Papa assured her quietly.

"It's almost time to be laying the row crops by,"
Mama said. "You and the boys will have to work from
early morning until late at night. You can't do anything about the cooking or the house."

"We'll manage," Papa said.

Melinda had been quiet, listening. Where before
she had been all brightness and gaiety, now she was
very sober. But when she spoke, there was the old im-
pulsive rush, the quick and firm decision.

"Mama," she said, "you go on. I'll come out and
take care of the family while you're gone."

Katie glanced at her quickly. Suddenly she remembered the way Dennis and Melinda had laughed
together, and the way they had looked at each other.
Melinda didn't want to come back here and leave her
husband. Dennis didn't want her to come. They both
wanted to stay in that house in Amarillo and laugh
over burned cakes and bad biscuits. Melinda's place

was in the house in Amarillo, not here.

But if not Melinda, who?

Katie?

Plain as anything, Katie could see a picture rising before her. The white columns of the school at Lewisville, with the girls walking back and forth on the flower-enclosed paths. The girls playing the piano. And painting. And sitting together in class rooms where the teachers called you "Young Ladies" and did not sniffle and knew how to be gentle and lovely. And among them Katie Pierce moved, happy and at ease.

No, not now.

She felt herself struggling, as if she were running from some deep terror. As if she were struggling to wake from a bad dream. As if she were trying to push herself forward to some great feat of courage, something greater than she had ever thought of achieving before. She looked at Melinda. She looked back at Mama. She cleared her throat. And then she heard herself speaking, her voice coming from far off, the way it always did when she was scared.

"Melinda," she said, "you don't have to do that."

Melinda looked at her sister quickly.

"Mama," Katie went on, "I'll take care of Papa and Carolyn—" She hesitated, feeling presumptuous about the rest of what she had to say, but continuing bravely nevertheless, "—and the boys," she finished sturdily. "I'll look after things while you are gone."

The room was very quiet. Even Carolyn had nothing to say. The whole family turned toward Katie, acting as if, of one accord, they were weighing the import of her statement. Here was Katie Pierce, who in spite of all her willingness, could never quite get the hang of how to do things—cooking or anything else—offering to take over the family. Katie, scared of things and people alike, offering to step in and assume Mama's place.

"Why Katie," Melinda burst out, "you can't—you're going off to school. Had you forgotten that?"

Had she forgotten that? As if she could ever forget!

"No—" Katie said, almost in a whisper. And then, "I can go next year."

Mama looked at her, a long, long look. She turned to Papa. He was quiet, in a way he had of letting them work out things for themselves. Finally Mama spoke.

"Thank you, Katie," she said simply. "It will be a great load off my mind."

"I would have been glad to come," Melinda declared. But all the time Katie knew she was relieved not to be going away from the new house in Amarillo, and from Dennis. "I'll come out as often as I can."

"You don't have to, Melinda," Katie told her. "I mean—there's no use of your rushing out so much. I can get along."

She was trembling a little, thinking of the magnitude of what she had promised. She felt a little sick at her stomach, too.

Just then Papa spoke up, clear and strong and sure.

"Of course," he said. "Katie will manage fine. We'll all help her."

It was arranged as simply as that—the thing Katie, in even her wildest dreams, would never have thought possible.

Katie wasn't going away to school at all.

Mama was going away and leaving her in charge of the family.

The next few days were so busy no one had much time to think. Really, there were two sets of preparations to be made—one for the journey, the other for the needs of those who stayed at home.

"You know I may have to be gone for quite a while," Mama told Katie. "I may not be back when school starts. If that happens, you and Carolyn must go right on to school. You mustn't miss a day, unless you are sick. With this good teacher coming, I want you to take advantage of all she can teach you."

"Yes, Mama," Katie said.

"I am going to be a very good studious," Carolyn promised. "I know my nine tables, and Dennis says they are the most difficult of all."

"A good student," Mama corrected her absently. "Carolyn," she went on kindly, "the new teacher—well, she may not like for you to talk the way you do."

"Why not?" Carolyn asked.

"Because—" Mama hesitated, looked helplessly at Katie. Carolyn was spoiled. Even the twins, who laughed at her and teased her, sometimes without much mercy, really loved and humored her. They might make fun of her use of words beyond her knowledge, but secretly they were proud of her wish to learn. They were proud, too, that she was neither timid nor shy, and that she never knew what it was to remain a stranger. Would the new teacher understand about her, realizing she was just the baby of the family and not a little girl trying to show off.

Katie had nursed her own fears about the new teacher, who was supposed to be such a superior young woman. She had been fearful lest this paragon would expect her to get the answers to all her sums correctly, and at once. Would she expect that her students should be able to bound the states and get the names of the capitals right, something Katie could never do; or name the bones of the body, a feat which always sent her into a complete jelly-like state herself, as if she had no bones of her own; or remember dates, which, for her, was almost impossible, since she was always getting 1492 and 1620 and 1776 all jumbled in her mind so that none of them meant anything!

But now, with Mama's worried eyes meeting hers, she forgot for the moment her own fears and remembered only that the new teacher might not understand Carolyn.

"Don't worry, Mama," she said softly. "Carolyn will get along fine. I'll—" She hesitated, thinking it was a foolish promise for her to make. "I'll try to help her," she amended quietly.

"I know you will, Katie," Mama said. And she sounded as if she meant what she said.

Mama went on with the packing, the preparations and the advice. She washed and ironed. She cooked meat and bread and baked cookies and a cake.

"Papa will help you with breakfast, Katie," she said. "You ought to try to have as good a dinner as you can manage. Then at night, you can eat what is left over."

"Yes, Mama," Katie said, trying not to remember

that she had never cooked a meal by herself, that she had only helped Mama with peeling potatoes and beating eggs and that sort of thing. How did one set about getting "as good a dinner as you can manage?"

"Keep the house as neat and orderly as you can," Mama went on, "but don't worry about it. If you make the beds and keep things picked up off the floor and wash the dishes and cook—that's about all you can expect. Papa and the boys will see that the washing gets done. Do the best you can with the ironing."

"I will—" Katie promised, dizzy by now with the instructions Mama was giving her.

At last Mama had everything packed. She stood in the middle of the sitting room floor, wearing her second best dress, her hat and her gloves. Papa and the twins and Katie and Carolyn were there, too. It was a solemn moment.

"You ready?" Papa asked.

"Yes—" Mama told him.

She kissed Carolyn goodby. She kissed the twins. Then she turned to Katie.

"My big girl," she whispered. "I'm leaving things to you."

Katie wanted to cry. She wanted to tell her mother that she couldn't manage—not at all. She couldn't look after the house and the family by herself.

"You'll get along fine," Mama said. She must have known what Katie was thinking, but chose to ignore the fact. "Write me. All of you—write me."

"I shall correspond with you regularly," Carolyn promised.

At that, everyone laughed. Mama seemed glad of this; she chose that moment to walk toward the door.

Once she was at the buggy, she turned to kiss them all once more. Then Papa helped her in. He got in beside her, slapped the lines across the horses' backs. They drove off, with Mama turning to wave as long as she could see her children.

Katie watched them, a long, long time. They were no more than a speck in the sky when she turned back to the house. The twins had already gone off to the maize field, which needed cultivating.

She went to the house, walked inside. There was a great stillness hanging over the rooms. A vacant, awful lonesomeness—a terrible lack of sound. It was the way the prairie had seemed to Katie when they first came out here—a stillness which had been both terrifying and mysterious.

"Well, Katie," Carolyn spoke. She sounded important and purposeful. "I think I shall get busy now and make a cake. A great, big, huge, 'normous coconut cake."

"No, Carolyn," Katie said steadily, "first we must wash the dishes."

Carolyn looked at her quickly, protest in her eyes, in the very set of her shoulders. For one awful moment Katie thought that she was going to go right ahead with her original intention, ignore her sister's words entirely. Katie didn't say anything; she just stood there, hoping she looked as if she meant what she said. Then suddenly Carolyn's face cleared.

"All right, Katie," she said in a voice in which

meekness and wonder were equally divided.

In years to come, I must remember this time, Katie was thinking.

Her first decision had been made. She had not given up weakly to Carolyn. She had not run and thrown herself down on the bed and cried, as she had wanted to do. She had said, with resolution and firmness, "We must wash the dishes."

She had said that, and Carolyn had abided by her decision.

Chapter 4

"WE'RE GETTING ALONG fine, Katie, aren't we?" Carolyn said, picking up a glass and polishing it thoroughly.

"Yes," Katie agreed. "We are doing all right, I guess."

She scrubbed a plate carefully, being sure to get all the egg off before she scalded it and turned it over to Carolyn to wipe. She liked washing dishes—that was something she was sure about, having learned how to do it right when she was much smaller than she was now. Each morning, while she and Carolyn were washing the dishes, she felt relaxed and sure. Making beds was all right, too, for that Mama had taught her. Yes—she guessed Carolyn was right. In the three days since Mama had gone, no great emergency had come up.

"The cake is gone," Carolyn announced, making a side trip to the cake box on her way to put the glasses in the safe, "and the pies, too. Don't you think we better make that coconut cake today?"

"We don't have the coconut," Katie reminded her.

"Well, a vinegar pie would be nice," Carolyn suggested.

"I don't know how to make a vinegar pie," Katie admitted.

And all at once she felt discouraged and uncertain. Knowing how to wash the dishes and make the beds wasn't very much help right now.

As a matter of fact, Carolyn had expressed only part of the truth. The pies and cakes were gone, but that was not the real trouble. Mama had cooked a part of a ham and a couple of chickens, but with appetites like the twins had, these didn't last too long. And there were only two loaves of bread left. Papa had taken notice of this early in the morning, before he and the twins left to cultivate the maize.

"Things seem to be getting a bit low, Katie. I wish I could stay at home and help you today, but the maize needs working."

"Of course, Papa," Katie said.

It was important to get a good crop. Once or twice since they had come to the Panhandle, there had been no crop. That was a hard time for all of them. With the grain growing thick and green as it was this year, Papa had to do all he could to insure a good crop. Plowing would help and that's what he and the boys were doing now.

"I can manage," Katie said. She looked at Carolyn who, for once, was saying nothing. Suddenly she knew how the child felt. Just the way she used to when Melinda was taking over an assignment and she herself wished she could help, but was afraid she wouldn't be able to.

"Carolyn and I can manage," she finished.

"Of course," Carolyn said, quite herself once more.

"I'll help Katie. I am a luscious cook."

"Oh, no!" Bert moaned. "Not that—we won't have to eat Carolyn's cooking, will we?"

"You might do worse," Dick said, patting the child on the head.

Every once in awhile he surprised them all—and perhaps even himself—by being very gentle and kind to Carolyn.

"You do the best you can, Katie," Papa said. "There's enough left for noon. Then tonight I can help you cook up some things for the next few days."

Now Katie rinsed out the dish cloth, hung it up to dry. She was thinking that she should cook some things herself, and not wait for Papa to help her because he would have to work very late tonight and would be tired.

She went to the cupboard, looked thoughtfully at the contents of the shelves. A sack of beans caught her eye. Ah, that was it—the very thing. These pinto beans were standard diet out here. They grew well, and were filling and nourishing besides. Papa said they had to be good, because the Fosters lived on them. The Pierces ate them a lot, too. By all means, she would cook beans.

She took down the sack, which was quite heavy. Carolyn watched her with bright, interested eyes.

"Beans are extremely nourishing," she said wisely.

Katie stood still, regarding those beans. Mama had always said the excellent thing about beans was that they were so easy to cook. She wished now that she had learned the "so easy" way of cooking them.

"What do you do first?" Carolyn asked.

"I—I guess you wash them," Katie told her. That seemed sensible, so she poured some water into a pan. A big pan, because Papa and the boys would be awfully hungry. Besides, if she had some left, that would be all to the good. After washing the beans, she heaped them in the pan until it was half full. Then she poured in water. Next she went to the pantry and got a piece of the meat. She could recall very plainly that Mama had always done this. Then she shook in some salt. Not too much—she could always add more, but she certainly couldn't take any out. She was quite pleased with herself for thinking about this. Mama was right—beans were easy to cook. Already she was putting them on the stove.

She started to slide the lid on the pan, then regarded it uncertainly. That looked like a mighty few beans. They wouldn't last for more than one meal, the way Papa and the boys ate.

She went back to the sack, got out some more beans. She washed them, added them to the others. The pan was full to the top now and she felt better about the matter.

"We'll make the beds and get the house straight while they cook," she told Carolyn.

This was accomplished without any difficulty; Katie was proud of the way things looked. She decided she would go out and pick some zinnias. She did, taking the bright blobs of color into the sitting room with her. She planned happily as she worked at arranging them. She'd have flowers on the center of the dinner table; she would even put a bouquet of them in Papa's room and on the table in the sitting room, just like

Mama did when they were having company, or for birthdays or other special occasions.

It took her quite a long time to get the flowers exactly the way she wanted. She forgot all about the beans, until she went into the kitchen with the bouquet in her hand. Then she remembered, took one quick and frantic look at the stove. There was no steam coming up at all. The beans weren't even cooking.

She lifted the lid. There they lay in the water, hard little white pellets. They were still cool; the stove itself was only luke warm.

"What is the matter, Katie?" Carolyn asked at her elbow.

"The fire's gone out," Katie answered. "I forgot to put in wood."

Together they rushed out to the wood pile. Together they came back, all in a hurry, their arms loaded with wood. Katie fed it into the stove—little twigs first, then shavings, then larger sticks. The fire began to burn brightly. It started to roar; the stove got red.

"They should cook very fast now," Carolyn said.

"Yes—" Katie agreed. "They will—"

By the time noon came, the kitchen was so hot Katie could not bear to think of Papa and the boys having to eat there. She decided she would let them have a picnic by the windmill, with the cold meat, the fragments of cake, and pickles and the other leftovers.

The twins, and even Papa, took kindly to the idea.

"A picnic," Papa said. "How nice!"

The boys, too, were pleased. Katie glowed with pleasure, seeing how well things were going.

The twins and Papa went back to the maize field. Katie and Carolyn took the dishes back to the kitchen. When they went into the room they were greeted by a spattering sound.

"My gracious, Katie!" Carolyn cried. "It's your beans—look—"

Katie did not need her sister's shrill voice to warn her. She herself could see the beans, running over the top of the pan, on the stove. They were sticking to the hot stove lid—the smell was awful.

"Do something, Katie—" Carolyn ordered impatiently. "Stop them, Katie."

Katie ran to get another pan. She ladled beans out of the full one into the receptacle in her hand. She filled it half full—then she put both pans back on the stove, covered them again.

"What a lot of beans," Carolyn said, round-eyed. "My, Katie, that's a lot more than Mama ever cooks."

"Yes," Katie agreed. "Yes—I know."

Carolyn stood around a minute longer.

"That smell is something awful, Katie," she said firmly. "I am going back to my room and play with my dolls until it gets better in here."

She walked out.

Katie stood in the kitchen, alone with the smell and the bubbling beans. Smoke was rising from the top of the stove; beans still lay thick on the lids. The first thing, she supposed, was to scrape them off. She got a knife, began to get them off the lid. This was not easy—the stove was hot, the beans seemed to have burned fast, as if they had been glued on. Once or twice she wished she could have given up entirely, but

she persisted, while the perspiration streamed down
her face, her neck and arms.

Finally she had the stove clean. Then she turned
to the dishes. But before she had even started, she decided to let them wait while she made a cake. Maybe if
she had a good cake, the boys wouldn't laugh so much
at her for cooking all those beans.

She got Mama's recipe book, read the instructions for cakes carefully. Finally she came to one that
sounded simple enough. She mixed the sugar and
butter, painstakingly and with great care. It did not
go easily, the way Mama's cake making did. The sugar
and butter took a long time about mixing; the mess
stuck to the spoon and the side of the bowl. The eggs
refused to separate right; and when she tried beating
the whites, they only looked tired and limp—not at all
the stiff mound Mama always wanted—or that Katie
herself got, when she was helping. She was ready to
weep with vexation and humiliation when she heard a
sizzling noise from the direction of the stove. She did
not need to look in order to know its source.

The beans were boiling over again!

"Oh!" she wailed. "Oh—"

She grabbed two extra pans, ran to the stove with
them. She began to ladle out beans, fast as she could.

It was almost dark when Papa and the twins came
in. They fed the teams and milked, and then they
came to the back step and washed. Once they were
in the kitchen, the boys took a look at the table, with
its vase of flowers and the cloth and the dishes sitting
nice and straight.

"Flowers—" Dick said.

There was also a dish of pickles and some of Mama's good preserves. There was butter, too, and Mama's bread. And a pitcher of milk. And, of course, the beans in the pan on the stove, keeping warm.

Bert went to them, raised the lid. "Oh, beans—" he said. He lifted the lid of another pan. "Beans—too." In rapid succession, he lifted three lids.

"Golly!" he exclaimed in amazement. "Golly—if she hasn't gone and cooked three pans of beans!"

Katie stood, her head hanging down in shame and embarrassment. She thought she had never been quite this ashamed before. The first bit of cooking she had tried by herself, and it had turned out like this! She wanted to run back to her room and throw herself on the bed, there to wail out her disappointment and chagrin.

"Beans are very nourished," Carolyn broke in staunchly. "They are good for you."

"We'll be nourished, all right." Bert grinned. "We'll be nourished right up till Mama gets back, if we eat all these."

Katie couldn't stand it any longer. The tears began to slide down her cheeks. There was silence in the kitchen.

"There you've gone and done it," Dick finally said. "Don't cry, Katie. We were just teasing."

"She's worked all day," Carolyn reprimanded them. "She's baked a cake and fixed flowers—and, well everything. Now you had to go and hurt her feelings."

"I didn't mean to," Bert said uneasily. "But why did she cook all those beans!"

"Bert," Papa began quietly. Up until now he had taken no part in the conversation. "Bert—if you were cooking beans for us, how would you go about it?"

"Why I'd—" Bert hesitated uncertainly. "Well, I'd just fill one big pan, and that would be it."

"Yes," Papa said, "that's what you'd do. And that's what Katie did. You both would forget—if you ever knew—that pinto beans swell as they cook. There is a saying around here that the cook 'starts with a handful—comes out with a panful.' Now why don't we fill a bowl with them and sit down at this pretty table and eat supper. I'm hungry."

They sat down. Papa asked the blessing, and then he started the bowl of beans around. Just as Bert was ready to make some remark, the nature of which Katie could well guess, he said, "I like eating with flowers on the table—makes things taste better."

Carolyn picked up the pickle dish—green glass, with a leaf design on it. "Do have some pickles," she said, acting as polite as Mama did when special company had come.

"The beans are very good," Dick said.

"Yes—" Bert began, and then caught Papa's eye on him. He gulped a little and finished quickly, "yes, Katie—you cooked them fine."

"I am going to get the surprise," Carolyn trilled. "You didn't know it, but there is a surprise."

They were all too polite to tell her they knew about the surprise—she had already told them. When she came back with the cake, they registered the right amount of enthusiasm. It was a very good cake, even though one side was lower than the other. The boys ate a great deal of it, and even Papa took a second slice.

Katie had washed the supper dishes, with Carolyn helping, and the last one had been put away. She thought she had never been quite this tired in all her life. She was going to bed, and right away.

Papa came in as she was washing her flushed, contrite little face.

"You got along all right, Katie," he told her cheerfully.

She looked up, ready to weep again.

"Oh, Papa," she wailed, "all those beans! I hid two pans of them. Papa, would it be all right to feed them to the chickens and not tell the boys?"

Papa's lips twitched.

"Wait and see," he said. "Wait a day or so. Maybe you'll be glad to have something cooked ahead of time. The way the boys eat, they'll manage to finish those beans before too long."

She looked at him gratefully.

"You go to bed now," he said. "Tomorrow is another day."

Tomorrow was, indeed, another day. They got up very early, even before the sun rose. The world was all cool and fresh, bright and new as a shiny penny. Papa and the boys milked while Katie got breakfast. This wasn't hard at all. She knew how to make coffee, and frying bacon and eggs was no trick.

"I wish we had some help on that maize," Papa said as they got up from the table. "I declare, there's more work out there than we three can manage by ourselves."

"Maybe we could get one of the Foster boys," Dick suggested.

"No," Papa said, "they'd be busy laying their own crop by. We'll just have to do the best we can."

And off they went.

With Papa and the boys gone, Katie started the dishes. She had almost finished when Carolyn came in.

"I had a most excellent night's rest," she said, busy and important. "And now I am going to prepare my own breakfast."

Actually the "preparations" consisted of pouring herself a glass of milk (which she spilled generously over the table) and cutting herself a piece of bread (which scattered crumbs over everything). Katie said nothing. For some reason, she was remembering how she used to do this very thing; and, too, Mama's patience at such times came back to her.

Carolyn spread butter thickly over the bread, helped herself generously to wild grape jelly.

"It is a most delicious meal," she said.

"Is that all you want?" Katie asked her, mopping up the spilt milk and brushing off the crumbs.

"It's quite sufficiently," Carolyn said.

"Sufficient," Katie corrected her absently. And even as she did so, she thought with astonishment, "Why—I sounded just like Mama!"

That put her in an excellent humor.

As a matter of fact, she felt a little more confident this morning. She could look back on yesterday's mistakes and, while not exactly pleased with them, could at least feel the willingness to put them behind her and plan today without too much regret for what had already happened and could not be changed. She made the beds, put the house in order. This done, she went back to the kitchen to study the food situation.

There were beans. She tried not to wince at the thought. Papa was right—she was glad she had this much to start with. For meat she could have the piece of ham she had cooked with them. There was only a part of a loaf of bread left. She decided she'd better make corn bread, saving those slices for any emergency that could come up in the next few days. She got down the recipe book, thumbed through it until she came to the breads. She found it—cornbread.

She read the directions through carefully. Certainly it sounded simple enough. But yesterday's experience had thoroughly humbled her. She decided to go ahead and make the cornbread early, so, in case she failed, there would be time to cook another batch. Papa and the boys wouldn't mind—they liked cold cornbread almost as well as hot.

She measured the meal, the soda, the other ingredients. She stirred and mixed. Finally it was ready, and she poured it into a long black pan, slid it carefully into the oven. This time she knew about watching the fire so that the oven got neither too hot nor too cold. Once or twice she peeped in, and the sight was highly reassuring. That cornbread looked just lovely. She was sorry now that she hadn't waited so she could have brought it, hot and smoking, to the dinner table.

She was just taking the pan of bread out of the

oven when Carolyn came back to the kitchen.

"Katie," she said, halfway between a whisper and an ordinary tone of voice, "a covered wagon has just stopped at the front gate and a man got out. He's coming to the back door—"

Katie's first impulse was to be frightened—her second, to hide her fear from Carolyn. The man getting out of that covered wagon was certainly a stranger, for the people they knew did not go about traveling that way. He might be the wrong kind of person; once, when they had first moved to the Panhandle, some bad men had come and stayed the night when Mama and the children were in the dugout alone. She still remembered very vividly that night of terror.

Mama had protected them then. Melinda had sat up with her, all night long. Someway, for Katie, that marked the real difference between herself and her sister. Melinda was grown-up and sat with Mama; Katie was still a child and went to bed with Carolyn. Neither Mama nor Melinda was here now; Katie must take the lead in this situation.

"What are we going to do?" Carolyn asked, just as the man came around the corner of the house.

Katie's first impulse was to say that they would go into the front room, lock the door, and refuse to answer the knock. But even as she thought of that she rejected the idea as being not only cowardly, but silly as well. The man had seen them by now. If he meant to make trouble, he would follow them to the living room. While she was thinking this, she heard his knock at the kitchen door.

She walked toward the door, trying not to show

her nervousness and fright. Carolyn followed, her little face pale, her eyes wide.

"Good morning," the man said when Katie got to the door.

He was a man of about medium height, thin and rather tired looking. There was an expression on his face that Katie could not quite understand—sort of ashamed, though why a grown man should look like that she couldn't understand. It was the way she knew she herself looked at those times when Mama was making her do something she didn't want to do but which had to be done anyway.

"Good morning," Katie said, forgetting to be quite so shy in wondering about the man.

"Is your mother at home?"

Katie's first thought was to say yes—that Mama was in the house. Maybe lying down, and couldn't talk to anyone. Maybe busy in the next room—too busy to come to the door. Anything, just so he wouldn't discover that she and Carolyn were alone in the house. She tried to say this, but the words wouldn't come.

"She's—she's not here," she said, almost in a whisper.

"When will she be back?" The man suddenly seemed even more tired and worn.

"Not for a long time," Carolyn broke in wisely. Apparently she had lost all fear by now. "She's gone to take care of Grandmother who had a tremendously bad accident. Katie and I are keeping house."

The man smiled, and now Katie was no longer afraid. The smile was a little lopsided, but it was very kind and understanding, and it lighted up his thin face which was not quite so ashamed looking now.

"In that case," he said, "maybe you two housekeepers could use a little help. You see—" He hesitated again, then went on bravely, "I have my two little children in the wagon and they are—" He hesitated again, and now his face looked all pained and hurt. "They are hungry," he finished simply. "And I thought if you had some work for me, I would gladly pay for their meal by working for you."

Katie was no longer afraid. She was only awfully sorry for two children who were hungry.

"Oh, go get them," she cried impulsively, her words coming out all in a rush. "Get them right away. I have just baked some cornbread and there is milk and—oh, go get them."

"And beans—" Carolyn added.

Katie looked at her quickly, realized she wasn't meaning to be funny.

Yes, thank goodness. Papa was right. The emergency had come, and she was glad she had the beans.

"Yes, beans—" she said. But the man probably did not hear her, for he had started, almost running, toward the wagon.

In practically no time at all he was back, carrying a little girl, leading a boy. Both children looked as if they had been crying recently, but they were neat and clean. Their clothes, while unironed, were tidy. Their hair was combed—parted all zigzag, but still combed.

"This is Billy," the man said. "And this is Sue."

"I'm six," Billy said, "and Sue is four." He seemed not at all shy, but Sue turned to her father, buried her face against his shoulder.

"Hello Billy," Katie said. "Hello, Sue."

"Say hello," the man admonished Sue. And then, to Katie, "She's a little shy."

Katie's heart went out to the little girl.

"Honey," she said, "you come right in here. I'll have some good breakfast for you right away. You'd like that, wouldn't you?"

Sue turned to look at her. Something in Katie's voice must have won her.

"Yes—" she said, and smiled.

"I'm hungry—" Billy said. The man's face flushed up to the roots of his hair.

"You are going to have some breakfast right away," Katie told him. "Mr.—" She hesitated, suddenly realizing she didn't even know the man's name.

"I'm Bill Palmer," he told her.

"Sit down at the table, Mr. Palmer," she said. "I'll have something for you in just a minute."

Katie moved very fast. She hadn't thought she could manage so smoothly and well. Almost before she knew it there were three plates on the table, with the silver and the napkins. Carolyn got out glasses, chattering like a magpie. She took the glass of plum preserves and set it on the table; she got the butter.

Katie took the lid off a pan of beans. They were hot; she dished some up. She cut the cornbread. For the two children she poured glasses of milk; for Mr. Palmer she filled a cup with coffee that had been left from breakfast. She broke eggs into the skillet, pushed it up where they would cook in a hurry.

When things were ready, Katie said, "Now you eat all you want." She looked at Mr. Palmer shyly. "I hope you don't mind beans," she said. "They aren't quite the thing for breakfast, but I had them already cooked."

"I like beans," Mr. Palmer told her.

"Eat lots of them," Carolyn urged generously. "We have ever so many. Katie cooked a 'normous big lot yesterday. About a jillion pans full."

Mr. Palmer looked a little startled. Then he smiled again.

"In that case," he said, "I like them a great deal."

Suddenly Katie wasn't one bit ashamed of all those beans.

Mr. Palmer helped fill the children's plates first. Then he served himself. He looked at the food as if he couldn't wait to begin eating, and still when he did, he had nice manners. Billy fell on his beans almost at once. He grabbed the glass of milk, began to gulp it.

"Careful, Billy," Mr. Palmer admonished him quietly. He had stopped eating to feed Sue who, torn between shyness and hunger, was just sitting there looking at her plate.

"Let me feed her," Katie said.

She sat down beside the child. She put a bite of egg into her mouth. Sue smiled, with her face tucked down—a shy, baby smile.

"You're sweet," Katie said warmly. "Here, honey— take a drink of milk."

The child drank, obediently and greedily, as if she could not get enough.

Katie had not thought it possible for people to eat as much as Mr. Palmer and the children did. They kept helping themselves, and each time they did, Mr.

Palmer looked at her with apology on his face.

"They were very hungry," he said. And then he added honestly, "So was I."

Finally they were finished.

"And now," he said, "what was it you had for me to do?"

"But I don't have anything—" Katie started to say. But then something told her she could not do this. Mr. Palmer wasn't a beggar. He would be embarrassed, terribly humiliated, if she fed him and refused to let him work it out. He was not from the Panhandle. She could tell this by the way he talked—a crisp, clear way of speaking that had nothing of the Texas pattern in it. But even more than that, she could tell by his ignorance of the customs of the country. Here you fed anyone who came to your door, just as you ate with neighbors whenever you happened in at mealtime.

And then she understood. It wasn't lack of knowledge of the custom of the country which made Mr. Palmer feel humiliated; he would have taken food gladly enough if he hadn't needed it so badly, or if he had money with which to pay. She didn't know how she knew this; certainly it was not information she could have had a chance to learn. Maybe she had— maybe being a homesteader in a land of ranches had taught her to feel the hurts of others in her heart.

"I wish you would dig some potatoes," she told him. "Papa and the boys are so busy they haven't had a chance to do this for several days now—and I am afraid I'll ruin the vines if I try."

"I'll be glad to," he said, looking proud once more. "Tell me where I can get a bucket and a digging fork."

Katie got him the necessary articles. He started off, looked uncertainly at Sue, who began to follow him.

"Why don't you stay with Carolyn and me, Sue?" Katie asked wheedlingly.

The man hesitated.

"I can take care of babies awfully good," Carolyn told him gravely. "I am expert at it."

Mr. Palmer gave her a startled look, as if he wanted to laugh, but was too polite.

"All right," he said, "Stay if you want to, Sue."

"Want to," Sue said, smiling up at Katie, who felt her heart do a quick flip of happiness.

Carolyn came into the kitchen with some dolls and blocks. She and Sue sat down on the floor to play while Katie put things back in order. The pan of cornbread was almost gone—she would make another. Now that she knew how, it seemed no trick at all. She mixed it quickly, slapped the pan in the stove just as Mr. Palmer came to the door with the potatoes. He had washed them carefully at the windmill, and let them drain so there was no mess about them.

"Here they are," he said. "Anything else you want done?"

"No—" Katie told him, wishing she did have something. He seemed so anxious to help, worked so quickly and well. And then something came to her. Papa needed help. He had said so at the breakfast table. She opened her mouth to say as much to Mr. Palmer, and then it occurred to her that she couldn't speak for Papa.

"I don't have anything," she said, "but Papa might

need some help. If you'll wait until he comes in to dinner, you can talk to him about it."

This much she could report with a clear conscience.

Mr. Palmer looked at her with light dawning on his face.

"I'll go back to the wagon and wait until he comes," he said. "That is, if you are sure you have no job for me."

"I'm sure," she said.

She hoped with all her heart that Papa did need him.

Of course, the wagon was the first thing Papa saw when he came in for dinner. There it stood out front, with the boney horses still hitched to it. By this time, Mr. Palmer had taken Billy and Sue out to the wagon to make them rest awhile.

"Well, Katie," Papa asked, "you have company?"

Katie told him, all in a rush.

"And I fed them, Papa, and they were ever so hungry."

"Huh," Carolyn said, "you just should have seen them eating those beans!"

Papa smiled at that.

"And he wanted to work for the food, and I let him dig potatoes. And I told him to wait—maybe you might want him to help. I didn't say you really *would*, Papa," she finished quickly.

"That was right, Katie," Papa told her, approval in his voice. "You did exactly right, honey. Let's call him in to dinner, and I'll talk to him. If he knows anything about farm work, I can surely use him."

"Yes—keep him," Bert said. He and Dick had just walked into the kitchen in time to hear what Papa was saying. "He'll be somebody to help eat up those beans!"

A wonderful thing happened to Katie then. She joined in the laugh that followed his speech. She laughed as much as any of them, and forgot all about feeling embarrassed.

Chapter 5

IT TURNED OUT that Mr. Palmer knew a little about farm work, so Papa immediately asked him to stay on.

"You can help us," he said. "You can do the chores, and that way we can work later and get into the fields earlier in the morning. Maybe you could lend a hand to Katie now and then. And of course, there is always the field work. Would you like to stay?"

"Very much," Mr. Palmer said. "But then—there are the children—"

Papa was silent. He's waiting for me to speak, Katie thought. He's waiting for me to offer.

Could she do it? Could she look after two children in addition to the other responsibilities she had taken on? The cooking had grown a little easier now, it was true. For that very reason, wasn't it better for her to leave things as they were? She looked at Papa, her face uncertain. He looked back at her with kindness and understanding, but no advice one way or the other. He's waiting for me to decide, Katie thought. Oh, dear—it would be easier if he just *told* me what to do.

Sue was playing on the floor with the old battered

doll Carolyn had given her. Now she got up, walked over to Katie.

"See," she said. "My pretty doll."

She leaned against Katie's knee, lifted the doll for her to see. The child's eyes were shining; her curls jumbled up all over her head. When she smiled, a dimple came out just at the corner of her mouth.

That did it. Katie reached out, put her arm around Sue. She turned to Mr. Palmer.

"I—" she began, and then she caught Carolyn's eyes on her, large and solemn and waiting. "Carolyn and I will look after the children," she finished firmly.

She was conscious of Papa looking at her with a great deal of pride on his face. She was also conscious of Mr. Palmer looking as if he had been given the world and everything that was in it.

"Thank you," he said. And then, "But Katie—you are taking on quite a job, looking after two small children."

"I'll manage," she said stoutly.

"I'll help you," he promised. "I'll help all I can. I'll look after them evenings, and let them sleep in the wagon with me."

"I could let down the folding bed for them," Katie offered. Ordinarily that was kept for special company, like the preacher and Dennis and Melinda. But she knew Mama would understand and approve of this new offer.

"No," Mr. Palmer told her. "Thank you, but I think it would be better for me to keep them with me nights. We'll sleep in the wagon."

And that's the way they worked things.

Mr. Palmer turned out to be a very good helper indeed. He took over the milking and all the other chores. He helped in the fields. At night he was never too tired to offer his assistance to Katie—wiping dishes, digging potatoes, killing and dressing chickens so she could cook them for dinner the next day, carrying in buckets of water. And when he was at the house, he had the two children with him much of the time.

Katie managed three meals a day, and that was about all she got done. The beans disappeared in no time. She cooked more, and now she knew how to go about it. It seemed to her that she was always going in a run, getting three meals on the table, washing dishes, keeping an eye on the children. Carolyn was good about playing with them, but even so, there were emergencies that Katie had to take over. By night she crawled into bed, so weary she was asleep almost before she straightened out. It seemed only a few minutes until she would hear Papa calling her, "Katie—time to get up."

And another day had started.

Mama had been gone a little over a week. One letter had come from her. Grandmother was doing as well as they could expect, considering her age and the nature of the injury. But even so, it would not be possible for her to come home for a long time. They must be good, and write her often, and remember she loved them and missed them.

Now, on Sunday, Papa and the boys were at home all day so Papa said they must all write to Mama.

Katie had a difficult time knowing what to say. At

first she thought that, of course, she'd tell about Mr. Palmer and the children. She mentioned the matter to Papa. He looked at her gravely and said, "Do you suppose it would worry your mother, knowing you had three extras to look after?"

Of course it would. She hadn't thought of that. She couldn't make Mama understand that she liked having those two children, that Mr. Palmer helped ever so much. Oh dear, letters were simply awful. Just sitting down to write to Mama made Katie feel all the more lonesome for her.

She thought a long time. Then she began writing, asking Papa about the spelling of a word now and then. She said she had learned to make cornbread and had baked a cake that was "not too bad." She said Papa and the boys were busy. She said she missed her, but she was getting along fine.

"Tell her you've learned to cook beans," Bert teased her.

"You tell her," she said, smiling at him. And she was very pleased with herself. She hadn't even blushed. Maybe she was learning—just a little—how to take the boys' teasing.

Since it was Sunday, and Mr. Palmer was not working either, he took over the care of the children. That afternoon, while they were asleep, he got to talking about himself. Not much—just enough to explain why he was here.

He and his wife and three small children had come from Illinois, thinking they'd be able to stake out a claim in Texas. She wasn't very well—they hoped the climate would help her. But once they got to Texas, she grew worse rapidly, and finally she and the baby both died. He didn't know what to do, left with Bill and Sue. So he decided he'd take them back to Illinois, where his mother would look after them and he'd get a job.

They didn't have much money, because his wife's illness had been expensive. He thought he'd do odd jobs on the way back to Illinois, making money for the trip as he went. But it was hard to find work he could do and still look after the children.

"I guess I didn't know how to manage right," he said.

"I think you managed fine," Papa told him.

"Oh, no— I had to sell the cow. I was at my wit's end when I got here. You can't imagine how much it means for you to have taken us in the way you did."

"We were as glad to see you as you were to see us," Papa told him.

"I sort of hate to go back to Illinois," Mr. Palmer went on. "I feel this country is full of promise. But I think I can get a job back there, and as soon as I save a little money for the trip, I guess I'd better go."

He looked really sad at having to leave, Katie thought. She wondered why he didn't try to stake out a claim and stay. And then she remembered that Papa had said he was willing enough, but not much good at farming. She wondered what his job had been—he hadn't said. Whatever it was, she guessed he didn't see any chance of going into it here.

One morning, two or three days later, Annie Foster

came riding over. She brought two loaves of bread, a pot of black-eyed peas still hot, and a big square of gingerbread, also warm from the oven.

"I would have come sooner," she said, "but we've been awfully busy around our place. Laying the crops by, and that means Pa and the boys are as hungry as bay wolves. Looks like I've been chained to a stove."

Katie had never heard of a bay wolf and she didn't know why that brand would be hungrier than any other, but she let it pass.

Just then Carolyn came in, followed by Sue and Bill.

"Who are they?" Annie asked.

"Sue and Billy Palmer," Carolyn said, acting as if she were a grown lady introducing people at a reception. "Sue, may I present Annie Foster. Billy—"

Sue hung her head, lifted her eyes to Annie's face and smiled shyly. She looked adorable. "Hi," Bill said. "Come on, Katie—you said you'd get us some bread with butter'n sugar."

"Hello, kids," Annie said warmly. She had a way with children. And then to Katie, "What are they doing here? Kin?"

"Oh, no—" Katie explained what had happened.

"So that's their wagon out front," Annie said. "I saw it and wondered if you were fixing to move away."

Katie only smiled at that. Annie knew the Pierces weren't going to leave this country.

"It is all right to give Sue and Bill some butter-sugar bread, isn't it Katie?" Carolyn asked.

"Of course," Katie told her absently.

Carolyn went out of the room, followed by the

two children. When they were gone, Annie turned to Katie.

"Now Katie, you handle these children just real good. But isn't it too much of a job for you to have them on your hands, with all the rest you have to do?"

"Oh, no," Katie said quickly. "They help me. Mr. Palmer. Papa. The twins." She hesitated a moment, and then she added something else, something which loyalty as well as truth bade her say. "And Carolyn is a lot of help. My goodness, Annie—she looks after the children all day long."

"You have to do the cooking," Annie reminded her. "But goodness—I got so interested in these kids, I haven't told you a real fine piece of news."

It seemed that 'Lonzo had ridden into Amarillo to get a replacement for a broken piece of the cultivator, and he had seen Melinda.

"Oh," Katie asked, "how is she?"

"Fine," Annie told her. "Just fine. Anyway, she sent word she was coming out to spend a few days. Dennis has to drive over to the Ranch to see his aunt, who isn't feeling very well. He's going to bring Melinda on his way over."

Now that was news of the most wonderful kind. Katie's face glowed to hear it.

"When will they be here?" she asked.

"This evening," Annie said. "I reckon about supper time. I just thought you'd like to know. Want me to stay and help you get ready for them?"

"Oh, no thank you, Annie," Katie told her. "Not with all that cooking you have to do at home.

I'll manage."

Once Annie had gone, Katie took a quick look around the house. It was really straight enough, with things pretty well in place. Of course the floors weren't shining, like Mama always wanted them to be for company, and there were marks on the windows which she would have insisted must be washed off. But all in all, it looked pretty good.

Fortunately, too, the food Annie had brought would make up the bulk of the noon meal and Katie could devote her attention to getting a good supper for Dennis and Melinda. She took another look around, and felt quite pleased with herself. Maybe even a little complacent. Melinda was coming home, and she could see that her sister was managing just all right by herself. Katie let her mind dwell happily on the compliments Melinda would give her and the thoughts of them were sweet to her, even before they had happened.

She thought it would be nice to have flowers in the house; Melinda would enjoy that. She went out to the windmill to cut the zinnias blooming there.

"What's going to happen, Katie?" Carolyn asked from her place at the base of the tower where she and the children were making mud pies.

"What's gonna happen?" Sue asked, imitating Carolyn so exactly that Katie almost laughed in her face. My goodness, Sue's little, Katie thought. Like a doll. No bigger, really, than Nealie Foster, who was just past two.

"Melinda and Dennis are coming," she told Carolyn.

"Oh, goody!" Carolyn cried. "When?"

"Tonight—in time for supper—"

Carolyn got up, turned to the children.

"You will have to stay out here by yourselves," she explained gravely. "I must go inside and assist Katie with the preparing." She started toward the house.

"Oh, no—" Katie told her quickly. "I can manage. You had better stay here and watch Sue and Bill."

"I don't see why," Carolyn protested. It was the first time she had really rebelled against one of Katie's decisions.

"Because—" Katie started to say that it was better for Carolyn to keep the children out of the house, but she hesitated, knowing in her heart that this wasn't the real reason. She wanted to get ready for Melinda all by herself, and that was the truth. She wanted to surprise her by having things as nice as possible, and she wanted no help from anyone in doing this.

"If you want to, you set the table for dinner," she said. "Annie brought almost enough food."

Carolyn settled down a little reluctantly.

"Well, all right," she said. "But that will be for Papa and the twins, not for Melinda, and I know she would expect me to assist you."

"You'll be doing that by staying out here and watching the children," Katie told her, realizing as soon as the words were out that they weren't very kind.

By the time she had the flowers arranged in vases, it was almost noon. As usual, she lost herself in the job, trying new arrangements, stepping back to get a better look, going to them once more and changing a few flowers, a bit of green leaves. But finally they suited her and she took them to the living room and bedrooms, and to the kitchen. Later, when she had the table set, she would put a bouquet in the middle. She was going to do things exactly right.

Just as she set the last vase in place, Carolyn came in, followed by the children.

"My gracious, Katie," she said importantly, "here come Papa and the boys and I hadn't remembered my job!"

She started taking the dishes out of the safe.

"Wash your hands first," Katie reminded her. She sounded bossy, she knew, and didn't like herself for it. What had got into her today, anyway?

Carolyn looked at her, a little hurt. But she washed her hands obediently and started setting the table. Katie put some meat in a pan, pushed it to the hot place on the stove. The fire had gone down—she seized wood and built it up. Thank goodness for Annie's contributions! With meat and canned tomatoes and coffee, that would be a fair enough meal. But even as she worked, she was awkward and inept. The fact was, she hadn't started dinner early enough, and now was bungling things in her haste to make up for lost time.

Before things were ready, the men came in.

"Melinda's coming," Carolyn told them importantly.

"Oh, she is—" Papa said.

Katie gave him the details, turning meat with a fork as she talked.

"Now that's fine," Papa said. He looked keenly at Katie, her face flushed, standing by the stove.

"Think you can manage to get ready for them by yourself?" he asked.

For the first time in her life, Katie felt anger—real anger—at Papa.

"Of course I can," she said. And the way she spoke, her voice sounded even worse than it had when she snapped at Carolyn.

Even so, the twins and Mr. Palmer had given her some help before they went back to the fields. The boys dug potatoes and washed them very clean at the windmill. Mr. Palmer killed two chickens and dressed them, quick as lightning.

"You just stick them in the oven," he told Katie, not even asking if she already knew. "Or put them in a pan to stew on top. You can forget about them until they are done."

Papa and Carolyn helped with the dishes, so that they were done in short order. Then the men went back to the fields.

Left alone, Katie stood regarding the chickens. Even while Mr. Palmer had been talking to her about the ways to cook them, she had known what she would do. She'd stew them, because she was going to need the oven for something else. She had had this in her mind from the very minute that Annie had told her Melinda was coming.

She was going to make a vinegar pie.

That was the way Mama always celebrated special events. Almost Katie could see one of those pies right now, as if it were sitting there before her—amber, quivering, with the little beads of syrup on the meringue, and a spicy, aromatic odor filling the air. Yes, Katie was going to have one for Melinda, who would know and appreciate the real significance of the dish.

She got down Mama's recipe book—by now she had almost worn it out. Pies—custard, apple, berry. She passed them up, came finally to vinegar. She read it through carefully, and with deep concentration. Directions were never easy for her to follow—she got lost in the labyrinth of them, forgetting to check what she had put in against the list of what was necessary.

But this one sounded simple. First you made a crust, and baked it in the oven. When it was cool, you put in the filling, which you had cooked on top of the stove. Then you beat the egg white and added sugar for the meringue. That was usually Katie's job when Mama baked—beating the egg whites. She suddenly felt very confident and sure. These pies were going to be good.

She decided she had better make three, adding quickly in her head the number of people who would be there. The boys always wanted second helpings, too. She began measuring the flour for the crust, multiplying the recipe by three.

"Oh, dear!" she thought. "I guess Miss Frazier was right when she said we need arithmetic for just about everything!"

Finally she had the dough mixed, however, and started rolling it out. She was sure that crust must be possessed of an evil spirit! It stuck to the board; it balled up on the rolling pin; it broke when she tried fitting it into the pie plates. By the time the three crusts were in the oven, she was worn out.

She turned to the mixing of the filling. Sugar, flour, eggs, vinegar, flavoring, butter—she mixed with care and concentration. This went better. Once more, a sense of pleased complacency came to her, increasing as she came to the end of the mixing, set the pan on the stove to begin cooking the contents. She could almost hear Melinda saying, "Vinegar pie—oh, Katie, how wonderful! And you made it all by yourself!"

She knew Mama stirred the filling as it cooked, a job Mama sometimes entrusted to Katie. So, she stirred conscientiously. Round and round the spoon went. Round and round—

Suddenly she was aware of the smell of smoke. She sniffed. Surely Carolyn hadn't decided to build a campfire for the children. That was dangerous. Besides, right now they were supposed to be in the wagon, taking their naps. An unpleasant thought came to her. Maybe Carolyn, hurt by Katie's crossness, had made the fire just to show she could. She sniffed again.

This time she located it. It came from the oven.

She flung open the oven door. A cloud of smoke rolled out. And there sat the source of it—three pie crusts, black as pieces of coal!

"Oh, dear," she thought again. "Whatever will I do?"

Pies had to have crusts. There was really no question of what to do. She must make some more. She turned to get out the ingredients, and as she did so was conscious of a *spat—spat*—on the stove. She ran quickly, knowing what was wrong.

The pie filling was boiling over. Probably by now it

was also burnt; if not, it was certainly all lumps. Katie grabbed the pan off the stove, hoping to repair the damage as soon as possible.

The pan was much too full; she should have used a larger one. Or better still, she should have been less ambitious and made only two pies.

She didn't know exactly how it happened, but the handle twisted. She was conscious of a scalding hot sensation on her hand. She heard, as if it were none of her own, the piercing scream that came from her lips, filling the kitchen, reaching out to the yard.

"Katie—Katie—what happened?"

Carolyn was beside her. Her little face was very pale, her eyes frightened. "Oh, Katie!" she cried.

Above her pain, Katie was aware that Carolyn was not alone.

"Say, what's going on in here?" someone asked.

It was Bryan Cartwright.

For a moment, Katie forgot the burning in her hand. She remembered only that the kitchen was a mess, with broken egg shells on the table, even on the floor; with the smoke of the burned crust still filling the air; with the pie filling running over the sides of the pan, on the stove. And she must look awful—her dress soiled and wrinkled, her hair untidy. She and the room both looked as if a cyclone had struck. And besides, she was crying like a big baby, tears brought on partly by pain and partly by humiliation and disappointment.

"Are you hurt?" Bryan asked again.

"I—I burned my hand," Katie whimpered. But she managed to stop crying and was proud of herself for that.

"Where's the soda?" he asked. "Here—"

He found it quickly in the cupboard, began mixing a paste with water. This done, he spread it over Katie's hand, which was very red and inflamed looking now. The mixture felt cool and wonderful. The pain stopped a little.

"Feel better?" he asked.

"Oh, yes—" Katie told him. She wanted to cry again, but this time it was from relief.

He took out a clean handkerchief and bound up the injured hand. Katie watched him, forgetting to feel embarrassed in seeing how quickly and deftly he managed it. When he had finished, he stepped back.

"How'd it happen?" he asked.

"I was trying to make a pie," she told him, her voice very low.

"I had offered to assist you," Carolyn said reproachfully.

"I know," Katie admitted humbly. "But I thought I could manage. Only, I burned the crust."

"I can see that," Bryan said, grinning at her. "And I can smell it!"

Carolyn picked up a spoon. She took a taste of the filling.

"It is very excellent," she said. "It tastes like Mama's."

Katie flushed, both pleased and humbled by the praise.

Bill and Sue had been watching all the time without so much as saying a word. Now, their fears were overcome by Carolyn's action.

"Give me a bite, Carolyn," Bill demanded.

"Me, too," Sue said.

Carolyn gave each of them a taste.

"*Uhm-m-m!*" Sue exclaimed. "Good."

"In that case," Bryan said, "we can't let it go to waste. You'd better make some more crusts to put it in, Katie."

"I can't," Katie told him. "I mean—with this bandage, and the soda spilling into the crust—"

"I can mix," Carolyn volunteered. "I have watched Mama—"

"It isn't much different from those mud pies you were making out there at the windmill when I came up," Bryan told her. "Why don't you and I—with Katie here to tell us how— have a try at making pie crusts!"

"Fine," Carolyn said. "Let's start right this minute!"

And that's how it happened that Bryan Cartwright and Carolyn, with Katie giving directions, made three very acceptable pie crusts and got them out of the oven without burning them. Katie almost forgot about the throbbing in her hand in helping them and being helped by them. As they worked, she went about the kitchen, trying to put things to rights with one hand. When the pie crusts were out of the way, Bryan took over the beating of the eggs for the meringue.

Katie couldn't get over wondering what sort of a person this strange boy was. He was big and strong— as big as the twins. They yelled at having to do any bit of house work, but here he was, offering to help out and doing well at it. He managed Carolyn with a joking good humor that won the child over completely.

"No you don't," he said when she was all for plunging into mixing immediately. "First you wash those mud pies off your hands." She obeyed quickly, grinning at him happily.

He beat those egg whites as if it was no job at all; Katie noticed how brown and strong his arms were. He must work hard, as hard as the twins. And yet, he would stop to help her out of this mess. She raised her eyes to him, feeling both wonder and timidity.

"Thank you," she said. "You've been awfully good. I mean, about bandaging my hand and helping and all—"

"Oh," he told her airily, "I think this is fun!"

He reached out, picked up the hat he had taken off when he came into the kitchen.

"Well, I'd better be drifting along," he said. "But here—I almost forgot what I came for. My father sent me over to see if maybe he could get the man who's helping your father—of course, only when your father doesn't need him any more. We have more work piled up over at our house than Pa and I can do, working all the time the way we are."

"I'll tell him," Katie promised, pleased that here was a chance for Mr. Palmer to have more work.

"Well, thank you," he said. "And goodby."

"Goodby," Katie said. "And thank you for helping me."

She was thinking that always after this he would remember her the way she had been when he came in—an untidy, silly little thing who had let the kitchen get all in a mess and had burned the pie crusts and herself. More than anything else in the world she would have liked to appear well in his eyes. Why couldn't he have come one of the days when she had everything going fine, for she did have such days.

"I'm sorry things were in such a mess," she told him.

"Oh, it wasn't so bad." He looked around curiously, and then back at her. "I hear you're taking over while your mother's away," he told her. "I think you're just real smart to do it."

In spite of the pain in her hand, Katie was conscious of a great happiness. It was a wave that swept over her, and she knew she had never felt quite like this before. "Thank you," she said shyly. And then she saw he was grinning at her, a crooked, merry sort of a grin. And suddenly she wanted to grin back, and she did.

"I certainly manage to burn pies," she said, knowing delight that she could toss the sentence off so lightly. "I manage that fine."

"Oh, anybody can have an accident," he reminded her casually, walking toward the door. "Now you tell your father to let us know about the help."

"I will—" Katie promised.

"Goodby—"

"Goodby—"

And he was gone.

By the time Melinda and Dennis arrived, things were in order. With Carolyn's help, Katie had the table set, the vase of flowers in the center, the dishes and silver on correctly. Carolyn had loved helping, acting as grownup as if she were at least twice Katie's age, even bossing her a little.

"Here, Katie, you must not do that. It will hurt your hand all over. I will put the plates around correctly."

And she did.

The pies, only a little lopsided, were sitting on the window sill to cool. They were brown and lovely, with globs of syrup clinging to the meringue which, while not as tall as Mama's, still looked passable.

It was late—almost time for Papa and the boys to come in from work when the two girls heard the sound of a buggy driving up into the yard.

"Here they are now," Carolyn cried and ran out the door, forgetting completely her role of grownup assistant. Katie was not far behind her.

Together they escorted Melinda and Dennis into the house. By this time, Sue and Bill were trailing along, too.

"Company?" Melinda asked wonderingly.

"No—" Katie explained the situation.

"My goodness, Katie!" Melinda exclaimed. "Two children and an extra grown person for you to feed, with all the other things you have to do."

"It hasn't been so bad," Katie said, feeling humble now. "They helped—Carolyn helped a lot."

Now that she had said it, she felt better all over. Even her hand seemed to hurt less.

"What's wrong with your hand, Katie?" Dennis asked.

"I—I burned it," she answered.

"Come on in the house—let me see—"

Once inside, Dennis unwrapped the bandage. He saw the soda. "You did just right," he said. "I'm going to put an ointment on it now, and it should be well in no time."

Melinda was looking around.

"Katie," she remarked, "how nice you have things. Flowers everywhere. It looks wonderful."

"And there's a surprise," Carolyn said. "A lovely, lovely surprise."

"She'll tell," Katie thought. "She'll also tell how careless and stupid I was in getting that surprise ready."

"A surprise—" Melinda acted just as eager as Carolyn could have wished. "What is it?"

"Guess—"

"Well, if Mama were here, I'd say vinegar pie. But now I don't know."

"It is—oh, Melinda—it is—"

She led the way to the kitchen, and there they sat—the three vinegar pies, cooling on the window sill.

"Why, Katie!" Melinda exclaimed, honestly impressed. "I don't see how you did it. I haven't even tried one yet, and only last week Dennis was asking me to."

Carolyn was standing there silently, not saying a word. And then Katie felt words coming to her lips—good words, words that made her happy as she said them.

"I didn't do it by myself," she heard herself saying. "I tried to and made an awful mess. That's how I burned my hand. Then Carolyn and—and a neighbor helped me, and we got along fine."

Suddenly Carolyn's face was bright with pride and happiness.

"I helped," she said. "And Bryan helped. It was fun."

"Who's Bryan?" Melinda asked.

"Bryan Cartwright. He came to your wedding," Katie explained.

"Now that I wouldn't remember," Melinda said, and she smiled at Dennis—that just-between-us smile.

Carolyn seemed to have something else on her mind.

"But Melinda," she went on, "Katie did the most important thing about the pies. She made the filling, and that's the part that tastes best."

"Oh, I wouldn't say that," Melinda told her. "It seems to me they depend on each other, the filling and the crust."

Depend on each other. The words stuck in Katie's mind. Papa had said that about the people out here, when they first moved out and had to borrow water from the Kennedy Ranch. What was it he had said? Oh, she remembered now.

"It's harder for us to ask than for them to give," he had said.

She hadn't wanted to ask for help. It hadn't been easy to accept it, as necessary as it had been. Even now she was feeling embarrassed and ashamed that she had needed it.

Papa had said that helping each other was the law of the land out here. Maybe it was anywhere. And then something else came to her.

Carolyn and Bryan had been pleased at a chance to help. They had had fun doing it. People who needed help shouldn't feel embarrassed at the asking, because helping others was one of the real adventures in life.

"I couldn't have managed without Carolyn today, or any of the days since Mama has been gone," Katie told Melinda. "She's been a big help."

"Oh, thank you, Katie," Carolyn said primly. But her little face was one picture of delight.

Maybe, Katie thought as she watched her little sister, maybe giving praise is the nicest kind of help anyone could think of.

Chapter 6

MELINDA'S VISIT had been pure delight. She and all the family laughed and talked with each other, teasing, joking. There was a vitality about Melinda, a radiance which had increased since her marriage. Katie kept wishing for Mama; it would do her good to see how happy Melinda was.

"I wish Mama was here," Melinda said soberly, and that was the wish of all of them, for every one said, almost at the same time, "Me, too."

"I know she'd like to be here, too," Papa said. "But she can't, and that's the way it is."

Dennis fitted in fine—just like one of the family. Katie remembered she had said that to Melinda, before her sister was married, and she had been right. Dennis laughed and talked as much as anyone, and got in on the teasing and the jokes. The meal was a gay one, that first evening. Even Mr. Palmer joined in the fun. In fact, he told more about himself than he had ever volunteered before.

He and Dennis began talking about far off things—Mr. McKinley, and what was going on in Washington, and about the Spanish American War.

Papa joined in, and occasionally the twins; even Melinda had something to say. Katie listened, utterly fascinated. The conversation was bouncing around like a bright balloon, with everyone trying to give it a toss when it got to him. And it seemed that Mr. Palmer was doing the best of all.

"You certainly do keep up with things," Dennis told him, admiration in his voice. "You talk like a history teacher I had at State."

"Well," Mr. Palmer said with quiet pride, "that's what I did, before I came to Texas. Not in a university, but an academy."

Suddenly he seemed taller, somehow, and he certainly held his head higher.

"How'd you happen to come to Texas?" Dennis asked.

The old weariness and the old pain came back to the man's face. "For my wife's health," he said. "But it was too late."

"I'm sorry," Dennis told him gently.

"Thank you," Mr. Palmer said. And then he seemed to shake himself, as if freeing himself of an old hurt.

"You going back?" Dennis asked.

"I suppose so," he said. "I believe you said you were through with me, Mr. Pierce?"

And then Katie remembered what mission had brought Bryan over. In the excitement of Melinda's coming, she had forgotten until now.

"Oh, Papa," she cried, "Mr. Cartwright sent word he wanted Mr. Palmer to help, if you were through with him, and you are—" It seemed wonderful to be the bearer of good news.

"All right, Katie," Papa said. "Tell us now—slowly, so we can understand—"

She did, and Mr. Palmer said that was fine—he'd be glad to go. Only, he wondered if Mrs. Cartwright would mind having the children.

"Oh, leave them here," Katie urged. "We'd love to have them."

"I don't want them to be too much trouble," Mr. Palmer said. "You have such a lot to do, anyway. I don't see how you do it all."

"Oh, I'm getting along fine," Katie told him, flushing with pleasure. Someway, the words meant all the more because Melinda and the others were listening.

Actually, he was right. At times she wondered how she would get things done. At night she was almost too tired to undress. But even so, she had a good feeling. She had seen a day through, had done most of the things she had to do—maybe not as well as she should have, but after a fashion. She didn't keep the house as neat and tidy as Mama did, and the things she cooked didn't always turn out right, but they got eaten. Even having the children wasn't really hard. It gave her a feeling of responsibility, of being grown-up.

"You're sure you won't mind? It isn't too easy, looking after a couple of small children. I'll come home nights, but it is sure to be late—"

"I—" Katie began. Across the room she caught Carolyn's eyes on her. There was something almost shy in her gaze, and ordinarily that was a trait Carolyn never exhibited. She looks at me exactly the way I used to look at Melinda, hoping she would think I was doing things right, Katie thought. Maybe that's a little the way Carolyn feels about me.

"Oh," she said, "I'll have Carolyn to help me. If it weren't for her, I couldn't do it."

"Oh, Katie," Carolyn said, smoothing down her skirts, like a grown woman. Her face was bright with pleasure. "Oh, Katie, I do thank you. It is fine to have you so appreciatively."

"Wow—" Bert yelped. "That's a good one—"

The family was acting quite like itself.

Katie was busy in the kitchen. Melinda was gone now; the whole place seemed an aching wash of loneliness without her. She had offered to stay longer, but Dennis came driving up for her and Katie knew, just by the way they looked at each other, that they wanted to be back in Amarillo, together in that bright new house. So she said, "Now you go on home with Dennis, Melinda. I'll get along fine."

She liked the way she spoke, very sure, when all the time she was wanting to say, "Stay, Melinda—stay a while longer."

Mr. Palmer helped finish up the work Papa had for him, and then he went to the Cartwrights. He came home nights, quite late, but he always put the children to bed himself. He said the Cartwrights were fine people, and Mrs. Cartwright had said he should bring the children right over there with him, but he was glad to leave them here. The poor little things had moved around so much in the last year that he was glad to let them stay in one place for a while. It was good of Katie to keep them. His gratitude was very real.

The remembrance of it was with her as she

worked—and also a pleasant awareness of how much easier it was for her now. Things which had seemed almost impossible to accomplish, when she first took over the household, now gave her little worry. She laughed a bit to herself, remembering how she had worried about the first cornbread she ever made, and those pans and pans of beans she had cooked. Now she knew instinctively how many beans to put into the pan, and she could whip up cornbread easy as anything.

She was getting along fine. Well, she corrected herself quickly, she and Carolyn were getting along fine. She realized that, without Carolyn to help, they could never have taken over the added responsibility of Billy and Sue. Carolyn played with them and looked after them all day. That kept her from being much help to Katie in the housework, but it was the greatest help in watching after the two children.

Sue was sleeping late this morning. Ordinarily she was up and running around as early as any of them. Mr. Palmer, when he ate breakfast, said she had been restless during the night; Katie supposed that was why she was still asleep. Even as she was thinking this, Carolyn trailed in with Sue and Billy at her heels.

"Want your breakfast, honey?" Katie asked Sue.

"Uh-huh—" the child answered listlessly, not showing much interest one way or another.

"I'll eat hers and mine, too," Billy bragged. "I'm ever so hungry. I'm getting big—see—" He flexed his little arm, proudly displaying what he thought was muscle.

Katie spread two slices of bread with butter and

jelly; she poured two glasses of milk. Billy began gobbling his immediately; Sue only pecked at hers. From somewhere in the back of her mind Katie remembered Mama saying, "It's just as well not to eat too much when you're sick."

So she didn't push the child. Sue ate a few more bites, then she followed Carolyn outside.

"We'll play with our dolls out by the windmill. Want to do that, honey?" Carolyn asked.

"Yes—" Sue answered apathetically.

"I'll be a cowboy," Billy said. "I'll ride up and see you while you're playing with your children. Like Nick and Herman."

Already the little boy had grown to idolize the two cowboys, just as the Pierce children had done when they first came to the Panhandle. They didn't stop by so often now, because their headquarters had been moved. But when they came, they still were about the most welcome visitors the family had.

The three children went outside. Katie could see them through the window, settling down by the windmill to play in the shade of the vines that crawled up over it. Billy had found a long stick and was galloping around on it, kicking up his heels and beating it with a switch, as if to make a mettlesome steed yet more frisky.

"Gid-ap!" he cried. "Here, Jingo, gid-dap!"

And he galloped around the windmill again.

Katie went back to her preparations for dinner. She had a good mind to try to make biscuits, the first ones she had had the courage to attempt. But this morning she felt wise and capable. It would be as good a time as any.

She was just getting down the recipe book when she looked around to see Carolyn at the door, carrying Sue in her arms. The child looked no more than an over-sized doll.

"Katie," Carolyn said, "I—there's something wrong with Sue. She's sick—"

One look at the baby's face, and Katie knew Carolyn was right. Sue was sick—very sick. Her face was flushed and she was tossing her head from side to side. She was most certainly in great discomfort, if not actual pain.

Katie dropped the recipe book, unheeded, to the table. She turned around quickly, brushing a cup off with her elbow. She heard the tinkle of the pieces rolling across the floor, but she didn't even wonder what Mama would say about her breaking a good cup. Sue was too sick for her to think of anything else. She ran across to Carolyn, who was still holding the little girl.

"Here—" she said, "give her to me."

She took the child in her arms. Her face and hands felt hot—so hot they almost scorched you. "She's burning up with fever," Katie thought.

Suddenly Sue stiffened in Katie's arms. Then she began to make convulsive movements—threshing about, throwing her little arms and legs back and forth.

"Oh, Katie!" Carolyn cried. "What's the matter with her!" No grown-up talk out of Carolyn now. She was just a little girl herself, and a very frightened one.

"Sue—Sue—" Billy began to scream. He had trailed the two into the house, still riding his stick horse. But it was a quiet, inactive nag now. No cavorting whatsoever. "Sue's sick—" he wailed at the top of his lungs, letting the stick drop to the floor.

Sue gave another twist in Katie's arms, almost falling out of them. One little arm brushed across Katie's face—the heat of the skin was like a fire. And Katie, feeling it, knew terror—real terror. All those other times in her life when she had been frightened seemed stupid and foolish now—things not even to be given a second thought. What were snakes and water dogs, storms and even people, beside this awful thing that faced her.

And then it was as if the very magnitude of the terror she felt burned away the hesitation, the uncertainty.

"Carolyn," she said, surprised to find she could speak with coherence and decision, "run fast—get me a quilt out of Mama's room. Spread it here on the floor!"

Carolyn needed no second command. Almost before the words were finished, she had flashed out of the kitchen, was back with the quilt. She spread it on the floor.

"I brought a pillow, too," she said, putting it on the quilt. Then she turned to face Katie, her face very white.

"What'll you do now?" she asked.

And again, from Katie's childhood came the memory of Mama, bending over her to sponge her with cool water when the fever was high. The comfort of it was with her, even now.

"Get me a pan of cool water," she said. "And a wash cloth."

Carolyn ran for the pan and the cloth. She filled the pan from the water bucket on the cabinet, spilling a great deal of it in her haste and terror. But she got to Katie with a pan partially full.

Katie stripped off the little girl's dress, took the cloth out of the water, began to sponge off the feverish body.

"I could get her some medicine," Carolyn offered.

Medicine? What did Mama give? All Katie could remember was paregoric. It was for pain. Surely Sue must be in great pain, or she would not be twisting around the way she was.

Katie herself got up and ran to the shelf where the medicine was kept. She found the paregoric bottle, jerked up a spoon. She measured out some of the medicine with shaking fingers—how much? She poured back a little, then, with what was left in the spoon, ran back to Sue. She put her arm around the child's shoulders, lifted her. She put the spoon into her mouth.

Sue twisted her face away quickly, as if she did not mean to swallow the medicine at all. Then suddenly she relaxed and swallowed the portion Katie had measured for her.

For a moment, Katie knew a great relief. But only for a moment. Then another terror, greater even than the first one she had known, rushed over her.

What if she had given too much of the medicine? She could always remember how carefully Mama had measured out the dosage, on those rare occasions when she administered it. What if she had—? She pushed the awful thought from her. She bent over, listened for the sound of the child's breathing. It seemed two life-times before she heard the sound of breathing—just a little. Very slow, but breathing.

"Oh, Katie!" Carolyn sobbed, frightened by the sight of Katie's fright. "Oh, she's awful sick! What are we going to do?"

"Sue's sick—" Billy began to wail anew.

Katie straightened up.

"Carolyn, Billy," she said, "stop crying and listen to me." Even as she spoke she was wondering if maybe Melinda had not sometimes acted from fear as she was doing now, rather than from courage and certainty. Maybe that was what Melinda had done, those times when her little sister had turned to her in crises.

"Carolyn, you go to the field where Papa's working. He's close today—not more than a quarter of a mile. See—you can look out the door and see where he is."

"All right," Carolyn said, once more steadied by Katie's command.

"You tell him to come home—right away."

And then something else came to Katie. Once when Manilla Foster was very sick, Dennis had come riding for Mama. Mama went—that was the way people did out here in time of sickness or trouble.

"And tell him to have one of the boys ride for An-nie Foster," she finished, feeling as she did so that she was calling for the very core of strength and sureness.

"I'll go with you," Billy said, his face still wet and streaked from crying.

Katie's first impulse was to say no, but then she realized he would be better off running with Caro-lyn than milling around here. So off the two of them went, terror lending wings to their feet.

Papa couldn't have been long in arriving, and yet the time seemed years to Katie, sitting there on the floor by the pallet on which Sue lay, watching the little chest rising, falling, rising, falling. Papa came in with a great rush, and Katie lifted her finger to warn him.

"She's asleep," Katie whispered.

Papa knelt beside the child. He touched her face gently. He saw the empty spoon, the pan of water.

"I sponged her off," Katie explained. "She was so hot—just burning up." She hesitated. "I gave her paregoric, too—like Mama used to."

"That was exactly right," Papa said. "I expect you should bathe her again before long. The cool water will help to lower the temperature. The medicine will make her sleep."

"Is there anything else we ought to do?" Katie asked.

"We'll wait until Annie gets here and ask her," Papa said. "With all the children the Fosters have, she can probably tell us whether it's just some childish upset or a matter we should send for Dennis about."

"Papa," Katie asked hesistantly, feeling the words come from her with difficulty, "how much paregoric should I have given?"

"How much did you give?" he asked her gravely.

She picked up the spoon, dipped it into the pan of water and brought up the size of the dose.

It seemed to her that all her life hung on what Papa was going to say.

"Oh," he said, "that's all right. A little more than necessary, but not enough to hurt her. It's helping her to sleep now, and that, in itself, is a fine medicine."

A gladness, a great relief flooded Katie's entire being. She raised her eyes to Papa's face. Her great happiness was mirrored in her eyes—and humility, too, for so easily she could have done the wrong thing.

"Katie," Papa told her warmly, "you did fine. You did fine in every way. I couldn't have managed any better had I been here."

The glow was still with Katie when Annie Foster came into the room.

She came quickly, but without any sense of bustling—just sure, fluid movements, bringing courage and hope with her. She knelt by Sue, still sleeping on the quilt. She put her hand on the child's forehead.

"My—" she said. "High fever—"

"It's gone down a little," Katie told her, not knowing exactly how she knew, but confident just the same.

"That's because you sponged her off," Annie said.

That was Annie again—she saw the pan and wasted no time in questions, drew her own conclusions.

"She gave her a dose of paregoric," Papa filled in details.

"That was good."

"Do you think we ought to send for Dennis?" Papa asked.

"I think we'll wait until morning," Annie decided. "Know what? I think this kid maybe is taking measles. Have you had them?"

"Yes," Katie told her. "Every single one of us."

How well she remembered that awful period, with the five Pierces getting sick one at a time, except, of course, the twins, who had it together, as they did everything else. It took most of the winter to get rid of the sickness in the house.

"Oh, sure—I remember," Annie laughed. "Four years ago—and we caught them from Dennis, who had caught them from you. If you thought you had it hard, how do you reckon we managed."

They all laughed at the thought of the nine Fosters taking the measles one by one, or even two by two.

Annie stooped down, lifted Sue in her arms.

"I'm going to make up the folding bed and put her in it," she said. "Tonight I'll sleep with her. By morning I can tell whether or not we ought to have Dennis. And by the way—as soon as Bert came, I sent him on for Sue's father. He ought to be here any minute now."

Annie placed Sue on the quilt once more while she let down the folding bed and put on the fresh sheets and pillow cases Katie brought her. This done, she lifted the child and laid her gently on the newly made bed.

Isn't it strange, Katie was thinking, that never before have I realized Annie is pretty. I've thought she was nice looking—after she learned how to keep clean and neat. And I've thought she was solid and comforting—but never pretty. Now, bending over the bed to lower Sue to the comfort of its cool softness, Annie looked more than pretty—almost beautiful, actually. There was a softness about her face, a kind of glow. Something that went beyond beauty—like Melinda's face, a little, but in a different way.

And even as Katie was thinking this, she heard a

sound at the door. She looked up, and there was Mr.
Palmer. His face was as white as the sheet on which
Sue lay, and it had a look of frozen terror on it, as if
he would not even let himself think until he found out
what the real situation was.

"How—is she?" he asked, almost in a whisper.

Annie looked at him, the softness still on her face.
It was a look Katie could understand in her heart, for
Annie was going to give him good news about his
child, and it was a wonderful privilege to be able to
tell someone a happy thing. Mr. Palmer must have felt
her answer before she gave it, for his face grew calm.

"She's better—" Annie said.

"I'm her father," the man said.

"Yes, I know—" Annie told him. "I'm Annie Foster, a neighbor. Katie sent for me."

Katie stood there, feeling very young and foolish.
At least, she might have remembered to introduce the
two. Mama would be very disappointed at her lack of
manners.

"Thank you for coming," he said.

"Oh," Annie told him, "I haven't done anything.
Katie—now she is the one who had things all in hand
before ever I got here."

Mr. Palmer turned to Katie. She thought that
always she would remember that look on his face—
mingled gratitude and happiness and joy.

"Why, Katie," he said, and he sounded close to
tears. Imagine that—a grown man, ready to cry! "Katie—I don't know how to thank you. I'll never forget
this. Never."

"Oh," Katie answered, a little embarrassed at his

words, "that's all right."

She was going to add, "I didn't do anything." But fortunately she stopped the words before she got them said. By the way Mr. Palmer was looking at Sue, sleeping there in the folding bed, he showed very plainly that anyone who did something for his child had done a great deal for him.

"I guess that's the way Papa would feel if something happened to Carolyn—or to Melinda—or to me," she thought.

And felt wise and grave and adult at the idea.

Annie Foster was everywhere at once.

"Katie," she said, "you look just about worn out. Why don't you go back to your room and take a nap?"

Katie did, indeed, feel weak and washed out. The worry, the excitement, the terrible time she had gone through had all put their mark on her. But even so, she didn't feel she ought to give up now. Here it was, past noon, and nobody had had a bite to eat.

She hesitated, "I ought to fix some dinner."

"Tell you what," Annie said, "it's late now, so why don't we all just drink milk and eat some bread and fried eggs and such stuff we can get in a hurry. Then I'll send you off to bed and I'll get up a first rate supper."

That was what they did. Katie found that she was suddenly very weary, now when the need for her to take the lead was past. She went, without much protest, to her room. It seemed she had no more than straightened out in her bed than she was sound asleep.

It was late when she awoke. She could tell it by the way the shadows slanted against the window of her room. She stretched lazily. From the kitchen came smells of food cooking, delicious smells. For one lovely moment she thought Mama was out there and soon she'd call them all to supper. Then remembrance came to her, and she jumped out of bed quickly. That was Annie, not Mama, out there in the kitchen, and Katie shouldn't be leaving everything to her.

"Oh, Annie," she cried, rushing into the kitchen, "I'm so sorry—I just slept and slept—"

"And well you might," Annie told her cheerfully. "You've had a hard time of it—not just today, but ever since your mama left."

Katie regarded Annie thoughtfully.

"Not so hard, Annie," she finally said. "It's just that I had such a lot of things to learn."

"My goodness!" Annie exclaimed. "I know how you feel. Just think of all the things *I* had to learn. You Pierce kids had such a head start on me, I couldn't catch up with you if I worked at it all the rest of my life. Say, I got supper about ready. You want to call the men in?"

Katie looked around the kitchen. There was a pan of biscuits, all puffy and white, ready to be flipped into the oven. There was a platter of fried chicken, golden brown and luscious looking. The table was set, neatly and right, with dishes of pickles and grape jelly and a pat of butter in the exact center. A pan of beans was bubbling on the back of the stove. The whole room had a fine, home-like look about it.

"What a grand supper you've cooked, Annie," Katie told her. "You shouldn't have worked so hard. And me sleeping like a lazy bones." Then she remembered. "How's Sue?" she asked quickly.

"She's sleeping. I sponged her off again."

Annie had found time for that, too.

"I plan to stay and watch her real close for a few days," Annie said. "I think she's going to get along fine. Some kids act like that when they get a high temperature. Now Manilla used to act almost that bad when she got even a little upset stomach."

"Why Annie," Katie protested, "you can't stay here. I mean, won't they need you at home?"

"I'd like to know why I can't," Annie retorted calmly. And then she exclaimed. "My goodness, Katie, look out that kitchen door and see if you see what I do!"

Katie looked, and evidently she was seeing the same thing—Dennis and Melinda, stopping their team out at the hitch rack!

It was like a happy dream, eating supper that evening. Dennis and Melinda were sitting with the other Pierces around the table. Annie and Mr. Palmer and Billy were there, too. Ten people altogether, eating Annie's good meal. There seemed no end to the biscuits she pressed upon them, and the fried chicken and the beans. For dessert there was a cake, still warm.

"I think this is positively the most luscious food I've ever eaten," Carolyn said, helping herself to another piece of cake.

"You keep on eating, and you'll have a *luscious* stomach ache," Bert told her.

"I never tasted a better meal, and that's a fact," Melinda said, coming in hastily to cover up the laughter. "Just like Mama's."

"Oh, Melinda," Annie cried, flushing with pleasure and gratitude, "what a way for you to talk!"

She was horrified that Melinda would even imply such a thing.

Annie had always been like that, Katie was thinking. Nothing she could ever do would, in her own mind, come up to the accomplishments of the Pierces. Art and music and reading books—those things always made her regard Melinda and Katie with the greatest awe and admiration. Beside them, whatever she might do seemed nothing at all.

Katie looked at all the people sitting around the table, relaxed and at ease. Annie had prepared their delicious meal. But before she had let anyone eat a bite, she had sent Dennis in to have a look at Sue. He came back to report that Annie's diagnosis was in all likelihood correct. Sue did seem to be coming down with the measles, and the treatment had been correct, too. The patient would be all right in a few days. He'd leave some medicine.

Katie was aware of Mr. Palmer's looks of gratitude in Annie's direction. She remembered her own deep sense of comfort at the sight of Annie when she had first arrived this afternoon. And, remembering all these things, Katie wondered if maybe Annie didn't have a gift of her own—the gift of making people happy.

Perhaps that was the finest gift of them all.

"Well," Papa said finally, "not that I'm not glad to see you and all, but what brings you two out here? Your aunt worse, Dennis?"

"No," Dennis told him, "she's getting along pretty well. I did want to check on her and thought I might as well stop on our way over."

Melinda looked at him, a level, straight look.

"All right," Papa said. "What else. You heard something from Mama you don't want to tell us?"

"Oh, no!" Melinda exclaimed. "I guess she writes us the same news she does you. Grandmother's getting along as well as we can expect, at her age. But Mama can't leave her, yet."

"That's what she tells us. Now—what is it?"

"You tell him," Dennis turned to Melinda.

"It's the new teacher," Melinda said.

"What about her?" Papa asked. "Now don't tell me she's not as good as her recommendations let on."

"No," Melinda answered, "from all I hear, she's even better. But the fact is, it won't do you any good. She's not going to teach here."

Papa looked up stupidly, as if he couldn't believe what he heard.

"Not going to teach—" he echoed. And then he went on quickly. "What's wrong? She want more money? Because if that's it, I might be able to persuade the directors to offer a little more. Not much, but a little."

"That's not it," Melinda said. "It's like this—"

And then Melinda went on to explain. The young woman had heard that Melinda was Papa's daughter and so had come to break the news to her. She was going to leave right away and marry the young man she was engaged to.

"Marry—" Papa repeated, as if he'd never heard the word. "And she was all for waiting until he finished school."

"I know," Melinda said, "but she had a chance to get a school right there in Austin, and she's going to teach while he goes to school."

"She can't!" Katie burst out. She recalled this wonderful young woman, with all the virtues that were hers—painting, music, knowledge of history and mathematics and all the other subjects which terrified Katie, even to contemplate. A woman as smart as that couldn't go back on her word. It did something to Katie, just to know she would even think of such a thing. Surely she didn't mean it!

"Well, she's going to," Melinda said cheerfully.

"But she promised," Katie insisted stubbornly. Usually she didn't stand up to Melinda like this, but the magnitude of the act had made her cast aside her own uncertainties. "It's not right."

"Well, I expect she promised that young man she'd marry him," Melinda told her gently.

"In a way you're right, Katie," Papa said soberly. He looked worried—very worried.

"My goodness, Mr. Pierce," Annie cried, "whatever are we going to do? I had built up so many hopes on that school teacher for our kids. 'Lonzo, now—he's the smart one of us. He could make something out of himself, if we had a good teacher. And then all the others coming on. It's so late now—how will we get another teacher?"

"I don't know—" Papa was thoughtful. "We'll just have to try. But as you say, it's late."

"I don't want that Miss Frazier coming back—sniffling away like she did," Annie said.

Papa laughed, in spite of his worry.

"Oh, she wouldn't come back," Papa said. "I know that."

They were all silent, thinking about the matter. It was awful—not just for the Fosters, as Annie had said, but for all of them. Katie had felt bad about having to go to school here, instead of to Lewisville. What if she had to miss all this year of school? She'd not only lose out on what she was to learn, but she would forget what she already knew. And she remembered something else.

Bryan Cartwright. His parents had driven over especially to check on the teacher. It meant a lot to them. Bryan wanted to go off to school, too. She remembered the merry blue eyes and the way he had helped when her hand was burned. Suddenly she felt she just couldn't stand it if there was no school this year.

And then the idea came to her. She didn't know exactly how, or why. Yes she did—it came from seeing Mr. Palmer, sitting there quietly, not entering into the conversation at all, but having a strange look on his face, as if maybe he ought to speak up and then, again, he thought maybe he had better not.

"Papa!" Katie cried. "Oh, Papa—Mr. Palmer is a teacher. Couldn't he—"

She stopped, abashed at her own daring.

For one moment, the room was very still. Katie knew she had made a great mistake. She should have gone to Papa privately and made the suggestion.

Papa turned to face her. "Katie," he said, "you've made a most excellent suggestion. How about it, Bill?"

Mr. Palmer cleared his throat. "Why, I don't know—" he began uncertainly.

"Do you have your certificate?" Papa asked.

"Yes—it's in the wagon. But I taught history in an academy. This would be all subjects in all the grades. Do you think I ought even to try?"

"You taught, and that's enough," Annie told him. There was warmth and certainty in her voice, and it seemed to communicate itself to every one in the room, even Mr. Palmer—perhaps to him, most of all. "The way I look at it, if you're a teacher, you can teach anything you set your mind to."

"Not anything, Miss Annie," Mr. Palmer said, smiling at her. His face was bright and happy— younger looking, some way. He hesitated a moment, then turned to Papa.

"Yes?" Papa's voice nudged him encouragingly.

"If you think I can," Mr. Palmer said, "I'd—I'd be pleased and proud."

Papa stood up. He shook hands solemnly with Mr. Palmer, as if they were making a bargain.

"If the other directors are willing," Papa said, "and I see no reason why they shouldn't be, you have yourself a job teaching our school this coming year, Bill."

"It's a stupendously fortunate thing to happen," Carolyn said firmly.

"Right you are," Bert agreed. "First thing you better do, Mr. Palmer, is start studying the dictionary. You'll need it, with our little Carolyn around."

Chapter 7

KATIE AND CAROLYN were washing the breakfast dishes while Sue played on the floor with her doll. Billy was building houses out of dominoes—putting them up, knocking them down. Both were utterly content, entirely happy.

"We should be getting a letter from Mama soon," Carolyn said, polishing off a glass. She held it in her bare hand. Mama always insisted that the dish must rest on the towel while you wiped it. Melinda and Katie both knew this. But Carolyn, being the baby, hadn't done many chores before Mama left. Now here she was, learning things the wrong way. Katie wondered if she ought to let the child continue in her mistake, or if she ought to correct her. She tried to remember how Mama taught her daughters, and couldn't.

I guess Mama just knew in her bones the right way to go at the matter, Katie thought. And then she had another thought, a truly amazing one. Maybe Mama hadn't always been so sure, either. Maybe she had to think things through the way Katie did. Maybe—and Katie was appalled at the very idea—maybe she even sometimes made mistakes and had to start all over again. Someway this new thought gave Katie a feeling of strength and courage.

"Carolyn," she began, as tactfully as she could, "if you'll just hold the glass in the dish towel, instead of in your bare hand, it would be easier for you. That way, you wouldn't get any finger prints on it," she finished hastily.

"Thank you, Katie," Carolyn answered politely, "but it is easier for me the way I'm doing it."

Well, Katie sighed to herself, I tried, anyway.

"As I was saying," Carolyn went on, "we should be hearing from Mama again soon. She has been a very faithful correspondence."

The twins would have taken care of that one in a hurry, but Katie let it pass.

"Yes—" she agreed.

Carolyn was right in the spirit of her announcement, at any rate. Mama had written once a week, ever since she had been gone. She had reported on Grandmother, who was getting along fairly well, but still too sick for Mama to leave her. She always had an individual message for each member of the family. Katie cherished hers. "It is fine to know you are getting along so well with managing things, Katie." Carolyn fairly glowed over hers. "Carolyn, I am glad you are being such good help."

"I don't imagine Mama will be home for a long time," Carolyn said. "Maybe several decades."

"Oh, no—" Katie burst out quickly. "You don't mean decades. A decade is ten years!"

"I mean she'll be gone a long time," Carolyn said, in slightly injured tones. "I was only exaggerated,

Katie."

"Oh, I know—" Katie said, speaking more calmly.

As a matter of fact, Carolyn's statement had given Katie a terrible shock. Ten years without Mama! The child's words, even though she knew they came from nothing more than a desire to appear grown up, had jolted Katie out of any wish she might have had to be tactful.

The whole truth was that Katie wanted Mama. Here it was the last of August, and Mama had been gone over a month. Next week school would start. If Mama didn't come home before that time—and she had said nothing about doing so—Katie would have to take over the responsibility of getting herself and Carolyn ready for school. That meant she would have to iron her own dresses as well as Carolyn's. She would have to see that both of them were very neat and clean every morning, for Mama was most particular about this.

And then there was the relatively simple matter of combing their hair. Katie was embarrassed that even now, with her fifteen years old, her curly hair got so tangled that Mama had to comb it for her. Katie got along all right when she was staying around home, but for an important occasion like school, she needed help.

She sighed a little, thinking that she could turn to Papa for aid here, although she hated to have to ask. Maybe Papa would realize her difficulty and offer to help. He usually seemed to know just the moment when things were getting too much for her, but never humiliated her by taking over at such times as she was getting along all right. It seemed to her that he had been more sure of her ability to manage since Sue's illness. Indeed, even the twins had treated her with more respect since then. And they were really pleased and impressed by the fact that she was the one who had first thought of asking Mr. Palmer to take the school.

This idea served to bring on a fresh sense of responsibility. She had Billy and Sue to look after, as well as Carolyn. When the matter of what could be done with the children had come up—as it did while Mr. Palmer was considering how to go about this new job—he had announced that, of course, Billy would go to school, as he was six. He thought a moment, and then said he could take Sue, too. She was too young, of course, but it would be a place for her to go.

And that was the way they left it, although Katie didn't like the idea very much. It would be hard for Sue, cooped up all day in the school room with nothing much to do. She needed to rest every afternoon, especially now that she had no more than finished recovering from the measles. And it might not be as easy for Mr. Palmer to teach with a small child underfoot. But there seemed no other way to do it. Mr. Palmer had decided to move his wagon right up in the school yard, and camp there until the weather got too cold. By that time, maybe some other way would open.

Katie was thinking about these things when she heard someone say, "Hello, there." She looked up. Annie Foster was at the door.

"Hello," Sue cried, running to Annie and holding up her arms. Ever since her illness, when Annie had taken such good care of her, Sue had clung to her.

"Hello, honey," Annie said, picking her up and hugging her. "How's my sweet baby today?"

"I'm no baby," Sue said with dignity. "I'm a big girl—"

"Sure—sure you're a big girl," Annie agreed. She sat down, and Sue crawled into her lap and cuddled against her exactly like the baby she had just denied being.

At that moment, Mr. Palmer came into the room. He had been working in the garden, a chore he had taken over, now that the field work was finished.

"Oh, hello, Miss Annie," he said. "And how are you today?"

"I'm fine," Annie said, speaking with dignity. She was always a little shy around him. Annie would never get over being a little in awe of anyone she felt knew more than she did. And to her, teachers knew more than anybody.

"I stopped at Cartwrights on the way over," she said.

Katie felt herself flush a little, although she didn't know why she should. Bryan Cartwright was nothing to her. He hadn't been near the place since the day he bandaged her hand. She guessed he didn't want to come back to a house which held as silly a person as she had been. He probably couldn't forget that awful kitchen, with the smell of burned piecrust and all the mess. She had hoped—oh, she had never admitted it, even to herself, but she had wished—that sometime he would come back to see the twins. After all, he wasn't a great deal younger than they were, and homesteader boys did gather at each others' homes on Sunday afternoons. Of course, this had been a busy time, and nobody was doing much visiting. But all the same—

"Yes," Annie continued, "they are just real pleased to have you for a teacher, Mr. Palmer."

"They may feel different about it, once I start," he said. "After all, I can't even pretend to come up to that paragon I'm replacing."

"Paragon or not," Annie sniffed, "she didn't see fit to show up. At least you plan to keep your word. Anyway," she added sensibly, "seems to me a man teacher is better than a woman. I hear some real cautions have been settling in the district this summer."

Mr. Palmer looked a little dismayed—as if maybe he wouldn't quite know what to do with "cautions," even though he was a man.

"What do you plan to do with Sue?" Annie asked.

"I'll take her to school with me," Mr. Palmer told her.

"Nonsense!" Annie said crisply, forgetting her awe of Mr. Palmer in expressing the kindness in her heart. "She's too young. What will she do about her nap?"

"Well, I'm going to move the wagon up to the school yard—Mr. Pierce says it will be all right—and I'll put her there for a rest each afternoon."

"You planning to live in the wagon?" Annie was scandalized at the thought.

"There's no place else," he said. And, as Katie started to protest, "Of course, the Pierces have generously offered to let me stay here, but I've taken enough help from them."

"You don't have to do either one," Annie told him. "I know the very thing. There's an empty dugout not

far from us. People who built it just decided to give
up their claim and they're leaving. It's close to school,
too. I know you could move in there, if you wanted to.
Nobody would care."

Katie thought she'd never forget the way Mr.
Palmer looked at Annie—as if he had been given a
priceless gift.

"Why, Miss Annie," he exclaimed, "that is kind of
you."

"And besides that," she said, "you can bring Sue
over every morning and I'll look after her while you're
teaching."

"Oh—that would be too much for you," he protested, even while Katie could see he wanted to say
yes.

"It's not much to do," Annie said, "seeing that you
are going to teach my brothers and sisters. No price is
too high to pay for someone who will do that. Besides,
I love Sue. It would be fun to take care of her."

Mr. Palmer looked at Annie strangely. Finally he
spoke, softly and with wonder in his voice.

"There's nobody like you, Annie," he said. "Thank
you—and bless you for offering. I'll do it—"

The house seemed very strange and lonely with
Mr. Palmer and the children gone. Annie had helped
them to get settled and had come back to report that
things were going to be all right—just fine. Katie,
knowing how Annie handled anything she took over,
had no doubts at all.

And now, here it was Sunday, with tomorrow the
day school was to open. The Pierce family had just

finished writing their letter to Mama and were talking about the great event. At first they had thought they would conceal from her the fact that the fine teacher had gone back on them, but finally Papa had agreed that she should be told, adding that they had a good one in her place. It was Carolyn, as much as anyone, who had influenced him in this decision.

"I think we better," she said wisely, "for Mama will know *distinctively* that something is wrong."

Even the twins had to think that one through. Then Papa said, kindly, "I think you mean *instinctively*. But I also think you are right. We'd better tell her."

So they did.

"It is very bad that we don't have music and art," Carolyn had said, "so I think we had better not tell her that."

Her tone, as much as her words, implied that the loss was almost too great to be borne.

"Without them, we will probably grow up to be uncivilizationed," she finished sadly.

"Oh, I wouldn't worry about that," Dick told her. "Mr. Palmer can use that extra time drilling you in using the dictionary."

Katie was as dismayed at the prospect of a lack of music and art as was Carolyn, but for a different reason.

Those were the two subjects in which she could do well. Try as she would, she couldn't always get her sums right. Last year had been awful, with Mama or Papa helping her every night. And all those dates—she sometimes thought that if someone had asked her to tell, right quick, when her birthday was, she probably would have fumbled the answer.

And then a thought came to her—really it was more a wish. Maybe this year would be different, because she was a little different. Last year she had been just little Katie Pierce, Melinda's younger sister, afraid of everything. Now she had taken care of the family for almost two months. She had conquered a lot of fears. Maybe this year she would get along just fine.

Monday morning Katie awoke, very early, with a tingling sense of excitement. For a moment, she couldn't remember just what the reason for it was, but then, as she stretched herself awake, it came to her.

School started today!

She jumped out of bed, dressed and hurried to the kitchen, where she found Papa already starting preparations for breakfast.

"Thought I'd just help out this morning," he said, "since this is your first day."

Once breakfast was over, Katie packed a lunch box for herself and Carolyn. She took out her best print dress in honor of the day, and had Carolyn get hers. She combed her hair very carefully—thank goodness it didn't tangle. She helped Carolyn with hers, plaiting it in two pigtails, tying a ribbon on the end of each.

"I will look most beautiful," Carolyn said complacently.

Katie wondered if she ought to tell Carolyn that people didn't go around saying they were beautiful. Carolyn was lovely—her hair was getting darker all the time. She had big, dark blue eyes and long black lashes. Her skin was very white and fair. It stayed that

way no matter how much she played out in the sun
and wind. Katie got red if the sun shone on her even a
little bit. As for Melinda—she was brunette and never
gave the matter a thought.

Katie always wore a bonnet; Melinda hated them.

"Let Katie wear one and stay pink-and-white,"
Melinda would say with a laugh when Mama urged
her to protect her skin. "She's our lady. I couldn't be
one if I tried."

"It's a good thing we have *one* in the family," Mama
would retort crisply.

Katie always knew Mama was referring to her. She
didn't like being called "a lady." She always associated
the word, someway, with her timidity and fears, her
shyness. Carolyn, now, was a fine combination. She
had a certain grave dignity about her, a sureness and
confidence. She wasn't afraid of things, the way Katie
was, nor did she show herself to be the tomboy Melinda was. And she was going to be the prettiest of
them all. Actually, she looked a lot like Grandmother,
who, even as an old woman, was still beautiful. Katie
thought of that now, and decided she wouldn't repri-
mand Carolyn for saying what was so obviously true.
She'd have sense enough not to mention it outside her
own house.

When Katie and Carolyn rode up to the school
hitch rack on Cleveland—the horse who had been at
the claim when the children and Mama got there, six
years ago, and who was very fat and lazy by now—
there were already a number of children playing in the
school yard. Katie, who was riding in front because

she was the oldest, guided the horse over to the rack. Actually she didn't much like riding, even a horse as gentle as Cleveland. But she did it, sitting on Mama's side saddle with Carolyn riding behind, holding on with her arms around Katie's waist.

Even before they dismounted, Manilla Foster made her way to them.

"Hello," she said.

She had a neat, scrubbed look. Her hair was still a little damp, which came of Annie's having dipped the brush in water before she fixed her sister's hair.

"Hello," Carolyn and Katie said together.

Carolyn slid off the horse. "Let's go inside," she said to Manilla.

Manilla was a couple of years older than Carolyn, but she was very little taller, being small for her age and rather delicate. Carolyn's wise, grown-up ways made her seem the older of the two. Actually, they got along fine together because Manilla usually let Carolyn take the lead, an arrangement highly satisfactory to both.

But, for once, Manilla would not agree.

"No—" she said, her face concerned and earnest. "No—"

"Why not?" Carolyn asked, more surprised than disappointed. She was not accustomed to rebellion from this quarter.

"Because—because Mr. Palmer is in there. He's thinking. Annie says we ain't—we are not—to bother him if he's thinking," Manilla finished desperately. As Annie had described the process, it took on great importance.

At least, Katie told herself, I know of six children who will give no trouble—the Fosters, beginning with 'Lonzo and going right on down through Babe, who was just beginning. No, eight, she corrected her thoughts. There will be Carolyn and me. And then, she quickly thought of Bryan Cartwright, flushing a little as she did so. He and Meg wouldn't bother either—that was ten. It made her feel happy and excited a little, just thinking about him.

She brushed the thought quickly from her. Maybe he wouldn't even come to school, for all his mother had been so anxious for him to. After all, he was past sixteen, and a big boy. Anyway, even if he did come, he probably would never know she was in school. She flushed again, remembering how she had looked, how the kitchen had looked, that day when he came by.

She tied Cleveland's reins to the hitch rack, although, old and lazy as he was, there was little danger of his going off. This done, she started to walk toward the school.

"*Yippeee!*" she heard a voice yelling close to her. Almost before she could turn around, a boy ran by her, snatching at her bonnet as he passed. The force of the gesture brought her bonnet strings up under her chin so hard that she reeled a little, partly from pain and partly from surprise. Before she had recovered from the shock, he ran ahead of her several paces and then turned back, headed in her direction once more.

"*Yipp—eee—e!*" he yelled again, swerving close, but not touching her.

This time Katie could see what he looked like. He was a big, loose-jointed boy wearing a pair of overalls, ragged and not at all clean. His hair hung down over his forehead in a dark forelock, making him look like a colt that has been out on pasture all winter. She shrank back from him. Aside from the fact that her throat still smarted from the yank of the strings against it, she didn't like the way he looked and didn't want him touching her.

This he seemed to know, for he reached out to give the strings another pull.

"Hey, stop that," someone said. "Hey, Hank—quit."

Hank stopped quickly, like a horse trying to buck off a rider. He didn't say anything at first, just stopped. For a minute he looked as if he had no intention of obeying.

"Come on," and it was Bryan Cartwright speaking. "Let's go play ante-over."

"Oh—all right," Hank finally agreed. And walked off.

"Hello, Katie," Bryan said carelessly over his shoulder as he walked away.

"Hello—" Katie said.

She stood still, watching the two walk off. She was pleased at her deliverance from her tormentor, surprised that the boy named Hank should have obeyed so quickly and easily. Just then she saw some-one throw the ball over the school house roof. From where she was standing, she saw Bryan jump up, grab it. Before the other side knew what was happening, he had flashed around the corner, touched several oppos-ing players with the ball, immediately putting them on "his side." He threw the ball, hit another boy—the best player of all.

And Katie realized why Hank had obeyed. Already he knew Bryan could beat him throwing a ball and running—and maybe even in other things as well.

Just at that moment Mr. Palmer came to the door and rang the bell. The children began to crowd into the schoolroom. Katie and Manilla and Carolyn, who were closest to the door, went in first. Carolyn walked unhesitatingly over to a seat.

"I am going to sit here," she announced calmly. "Manilla, will you sit with me?"

Even though Manilla was older, they were in the same grade, so this arrangement was excellent. Katie chose a seat just behind them. At that moment another girl came in, breathlessly, and looked straight at Katie. She was tall, but very wiry. Her hair was a mousy sort of brown, braided in two plaits—very tight, so it looked as if it was lifting the skin on her forehead. She had on a faded blue dress—mended, but squeaky clean. She looked straight at Katie, and there was a sort of entreaty in her eyes—anxious, a little timid. And suddenly Katie was able to read the message in those eyes.

"Would you like to sit with me?" she asked.

The girl slid into the seat so quickly it seemed as if she wanted to get established before Katie changed her mind.

"My, your curls are pretty," she said, bringing her words out all in a rush. "I ain't never had them. I've tried every way, but my hair won't curl no more than a board would."

Katie scarcely knew how to answer this.

"My name's Reilly Adams. What's yours?"

"Katie Pierce," she said.

At that moment, Mr. Palmer tapped on his desk for order, and the buzz in the schoolroom died down slowly, like distant thunder fading out.

Mr. Palmer stood up behind his desk. Standing there, he looked slender and not too strong. And, Katie thought, scared—scared as she would be. Sensing this, her heart went out to him, hoping he could get hold of himself.

"Good morning," he said. He had a very nice voice, pleasant and friendly. Miss Frazier had talked shrill as a piece of chalk scraping against the blackboard; it had made Katie nervous just to be in the same room with her. "Good morning," he said again. "I'm glad to see you here. I don't know your names yet, but I'm going to learn them. My name is William Palmer."

He turned and wrote it on the board in a nice, firm even hand.

"I know your name," someone called from the back of the room. Katie, along with all the others, turned to see who it was. She had not needed to—even before she turned she was sure it would be the one named Hank—the one who had yanked at her bonnet. Now he looked even more untidy than he had done while he was outside. And, someway, bigger, too. Much bigger than Mr. Palmer, even.

"I know you," the boy repeated. "You don't know the first thing about teaching. Pa said so."

A slight flush rose to Mr. Palmer's face.

"You have the advantage of me," he said, quietly enough. "You know my name but I don't know yours."

"Hank Adams."

Katie looked quickly at her seatmate.

"He's my brother," the girl said in a stage whisper. In the stillness of the room, her voice sounded very loud. Somebody giggled. Reilly's face got red. She looked unhappy, as if she would give a lot to be able to stop that big brother of hers from whatever he meant to do.

"Well, Hank," Mr. Palmer went on, calmly enough, "maybe your father is right. But I plan to try."

Another giggle sounded. Perhaps, had it not been for this, Hank might have been willing to settle down. But he knew this fresh burst of mirth was *at* him, not *with* him, as the first had been. So, of course he had to continue.

"And I got a brother," he said. He looked around. "Cy," he commanded, "get up and say hello to the teacher."

At that, a smaller boy popped up, like a jack-in-the-box when the lid is opened.

"Hello—teacher—" he said, hesitating before the word with deliberate malice.

For just one moment Mr. Palmer looked upset. Then his back stiffened as if he meant to let them know he wasn't going to give up—not without a struggle, he wasn't.

"Now that we've met two of the students," he said to the roomful of pupils, who had grown very quiet, "I think it would be an excellent idea for *everyone* to introduce himself." He was acting as if Hank's idea had been a very good one. Hank, unprepared for this turn in events, looked somewhat disconcerted. He's stupid, Katie was thinking—he's not only a bully, but he's dull and slow.

"We'll begin with you," Mr. Palmer said, pointing at Bryan Cartwright.

Oh, that was smart, Mr. Palmer, Katie thought. You know you can depend on him. You know the others will fall into line, once he sets the example. She felt very proud of Mr. Palmer.

Bryan stood. "My name is Bryan Cartwright," he said, politely and nicely, just the way he should talk. Katie looked at him admiringly. He was clean and neat, and his hair was combed. What a contrast he was to Hank, who was dirty, untidy, rude. "I'm past sixteen, and I moved here from Illinois just this spring."

He sat down. Katie knew a great pride in him. My, she hoped when her time came she could give the information as easy and natural as that.

The other children did, as Katie had anticipated, fall quickly into line.

"I am Carolyn Pierce," Carolyn rose to announce. "I am practical nine years old."

A hoarse burst of laughter came from the back seat. Hank, again.

"Oh, dear!" Reilly exclaimed, moving restlessly in her seat.

Carolyn turned to face the disturber.

"It is not polite to laugh at people," she said severely, fixing him with her loftiest gaze.

And, wonder of wonders, Hank Adams subsided.

The name giving was finally finished, having gone as well as anyone could have hoped for.

"Get your books out," Mr. Palmer said. "I am going to listen to you read now, one at a time, and try to divide you off into classes."

Everybody began to take out books. Katie chose a reader—one that Melinda had used before her. It had Melinda's name in it. "Melinda Pierce: Her Book." Katie took her pencil and just below Melinda's name she wrote "Katie Pierce: *Her* Book." It made her feel grown up and important, doing this.

"Hey," Hank's hoarse voice broke in again, "you forgot something."

"What?" Mr. Palmer asked, honestly puzzled.

"You didn't have us sing. Pa said it ain't school if you don't start with singing. Back in Arkansaw, where he went to school, teacher had 'em all singing first thing every morning. Anyway, we had a teacher hired that could sing, and you ought to do it, too."

Mr. Palmer stood there, looking helpless and uncertain. Hank nudged his brother, as if to say, "He's not going to wiggle out of this like he did the first time."

And indeed, he wasn't. Katie knew this. One of the reasons why Mr. Palmer had hesitated to take the school was because he couldn't sing a note.

"I'm tone deaf," he had explained to Papa. "Those children are expecting a teacher who knows music."

"They can do without music for one year," Papa said. "You know the important subjects, like arithmetic and history."

And now here was Hank, hitting upon Mr. Palmer's weakness before he had a chance to show how much he knew about the important things like history and arithmetic and geography.

Katie couldn't stand it a minute longer. She didn't know arithmetic, but music she knew. Another time she would have been scared to death to offer. She would have done anything to keep from walking up to the front of the room and, once there, facing those awful Adams boys, and even the Fosters, whose faces would blur together as she looked at them in her terror, and Bryan Cartwright, who would think her forward for offering to do what the teacher himself could not do. But the look on Mr. Palmer's face decided her.

"Mr. Palmer," she said, feeling her voice shake a little. "If you want me to—I mean, I'll try to lead a song."

She knew he would be glad, but she was not prepared for the look of intense gratitude that flashed across his face.

"Thank you, Katie," he said simply. "Will you come to the front of the room?"

Katie started to the front, her knees shaking, a sick feeling in the pit of her stomach. Once there, she turned to face the pupils. A stillness hung over the room. Even the Adams boys had nothing to say. She stood there, rooted to the floor, not knowing what to do, now that she was in a position of leadership, feeling that, even if she opened her mouth and tried, nothing but a rusty squeak would come forth.

Mr. Palmer must have sensed this. And, even as she had come to his rescue, now he came to hers.

"Hank," he said smoothly, "wouldn't you like to choose the song, since it's your suggestion?"

Hank drew back a little. Obviously he had never

expected events to take this turn. He gulped once or twice, seemed to be thinking hard. Then he blurted out, "Don't know any." He hesitated a moment, then brightened. "'Cept *Darlin' Clementine!*" he finished, regaining his composure.

Katie shrank back a little, thinking of what he would do with those lines about "Her shoes were number nine." He'd come out on them, hard and long, and send the whole school back into laughter and disorder.

Suddenly Bryan spoke up—smooth and cool and easy.

"Why don't we sing *America?*" he asked.

Katie flashed him a grateful look. If he suggested it, she might as well start off right now. The Adamses would fall in line fast enough.

She cleared her throat. She hummed a note or two, feeling the song flow through her. Now, as always when she was really starting to sing, confidence and poise came to her.

"You must sing with me," she told them, smiling shyly.

She threw back her head, let the words begin to come.

"My country, 'tis of thee," she sang.

The others began to join in. She could hear Carolyn, singing a little tonelessly, but getting the words right. The Fosters joined in, with more force than melody. Bryan was singing in a really good voice. Last of all to join were the Adams boys—Reilly was with Katie from the first note.

Katie led them through three stanzas. Then she

said, "Thank you for helping me," and walked back to her seat. Just as she sat down, she was conscious of Bryan's eyes on her. Admiration was there, and respect.

She thought—maybe this will make him forget just a little bit about that other time. She thought, too, that she was awfully happy, and maybe even a little glad the woman teacher hadn't come. This way, Katie had a chance to sing right away.

"Get your books out now," Mr. Palmer said. He sounded very sure of himself. "I'll bring you up here to my desk, one at a time, so choose a piece you'd like to read to me."

Katie opened her book. She was glad for the singing, but she thought maybe she was even happier in remembering something else.

She, Katie Pierce, who had always been scared of everything, had been the one to help Mr. Palmer this first hard day at school. Someway, that seemed more important, more satisfying, than that she herself do well.

Chapter 8

SCHOOL WENT BETTER after that, although anybody could see that Hank and his brother weren't really reformed at all. They were just waiting for a good chance to start something. The first one that came, they'd be off and away into whatever mischief offered itself. Katie knew Mr. Palmer was aware of this, that he was constantly braced for what might happen.

Afternoons were the difficult times. The little ones were restless by now, finding it hard to stay quiet in their seats. They all tried to be good, but it was not easy.

One day Meg went to sleep, her head on her desk. Babe Foster and Billy, seeing her, began to nudge each other and giggle a bit. Mr. Palmer looked at them in a puzzled, baffled way, as if he knew he should do something, but just what was beyond him. Finally he seemed to have an idea.

He came back to Katie's desk and leaned over to say, "Katie, I wonder if you'd like to take the first graders outside for a little while. They get so tired in here."

Katie was delighted with the idea. The afternoon was beautiful—the Panhandle at its best. The sky was as blue as it had been in June, the clouds as white, the air as soft. She herself had cast an occasional wishful look outside, and she was not one to crave being outdoors. She got up, ready to carry out Mr. Palmer's suggestion. As she did so, she saw Reilly watching her, a terrible longing on her face. Reilly had heard what Mr. Palmer said, and she wanted to go, too. It was as plain as if she had spoken the words.

"Mr. Palmer," Katie asked softly, "would you mind if Reilly went with me?"

"Not at all," he said smoothly. "In fact, I was about to suggest it myself."

So Katie and Reilly went out of the school room, trailed by the six youngest children.

"Say," Reilly told Katie, once they were outside, "now that was just real nice of you, asking Mr. Palmer to let me come with you. You and me are the two big girls in school— I like to help you."

The two big girls in school! The very thought gave Katie a shock. Nobody for them to look up to; nobody for them to follow. She and Reilly Adams, the two oldest girls in school, the leaders!

"Oh, that's all right," Katie said, a little shaken by the idea which had come to her. And then she had another thought, a wiser, kinder one.

"I like to have you," she said. "And besides, I need you."

Reilly flushed happily.

"Katie Pierce," she declared, "you're just—just *real* nice!"

As a matter of fact, Katie had spoken the truth. She did need Reilly. Six small children, playing outside while others were trying to study, could be a real problem. They might well cause more disturbance inside the school than if they had stayed there. Katie, with Reilly helping, led them to the farthest corner of the yard. Even here, it wasn't a good idea for them to yell or play any active game. Katie knew—and she was sure Reilly was also aware—that any confusion here would be picked up by the Adams boys inside the schoolroom.

She lined the little children up for quiet games— drop the handkerchief, follow-the-leader. This was all right for a while, then Billy wanted to play ante-over.

"No!" Katie ruled that out quickly.

"Why, Katie—" For weeks now, he had been accustomed to getting his way around her, so he could see no reason for refusal at this time.

"Because that would disturb the children working inside. You don't want to upset your papa, do you?"

"No—" Billy said, but indicating that he didn't much care.

"We had ought to have brought their books outside," Reilly said, a little disconcerted at the turn things had taken.

"I tell you what," Katie suggested. "Want me to tell you a story?"

That was it. She remembered how Mama used to do when the weather had been bad for a long time and they were all restless from staying inside. She had read to them, or told them stories.

"Oh yes!" Meg cried. She settled down at Kate's

side, instantly quiet. All the others followed suit, and Katie cleared her throat, trying to think of some story to begin with.

A fairy story. That was it. One from the book Grandmother had sent her when she was a little girl. It was childish of her she knew, but even now she liked to go back and read it sometimes. The tales she especially liked were about princesses in distress and the princes who came riding to the rescue. The cover of the book had the picture of a prince on it. He was riding a white horse and his head was thrown back a little, as if he were listening to some sweet voice calling to him to come and kill the dragon—as if he were seeing a vision, maybe.

When she was small, Katie had believed it was a picture of a real person. Nobody could have told her anything different. As she grew older, a funny thing happened. She ceased believing that the prince was real; but she did think that, somewhere, she was going to meet someone who looked like him. This was very silly of her, for things just didn't happen that way. People in books didn't come to life and ride up to you and say hello. But all the same, way back in her mind was the child-like assurance that some day *this* one would, and when he did, she'd know him at once, with no difficulty.

Well, at any rate, he was coming to her rescue now, for the story came to her—the one to tell.

"All right," she said, "I'll tell you about Cinderella."

And she began, with Reilly listening as avidly as any of the children. So enthralled were they that it seemed only a minute before Mr. Palmer came to the door to beckon them in.

"Thank you, girls," he said simply.

After that, each afternoon, Katie and Reilly herded the youngest pupils outside. First they had a game or two, to stretch their muscles, and then story telling. Katie went back to the fairy tale book, just to refresh her mind. And each time she did, it seemed to her that the prince on the cover was looking at her with approval in his eyes.

This approval, real or fancied, meant much to her.

September, which had been so lovely, decided to leave the world with rain. It started soon after school began in the morning and filled the sky with grayness, shutting off light. The school room was close and stuffy, but if they opened the windows, in sloshed the rain. There was a smell of wet clothing, of the lunches left over in boxes out in the hall. Above and beyond this, there was a sense of restlessness, even of trouble brewing. Out of the corner of her eye, Katie could see Hank Adams fashioning a miniature bean shooter out of a rubber band, a bent pin and some paper wads. Cy was watching him, admiration and complete delight on his face. Hank wouldn't be so bad if Cy didn't approve of all his meannesses with such utter abandon.

For the sixth time since noon—no more than an hour ago—Babe Foster raised her hand to ask permission to get a drink. Each time it had been given, and she had tiptoed to the back of the room, then out to the cloak hall where the water bucket was kept. Because the day was cool, she was wearing shoes for the first time this fall. They were new, and they squeaked, playing a tune for her to walk by, as a band plays for marching soldiers. Each time she squeaked back to her seat, Hank Adams grew a little more tickled. He was too big to do that, Katie was thinking. He ought to see that Babe was just a baby, and not let her squeaking shoes disturb him.

Oh, dear, Katie thought, why doesn't she just *stay* out there in the hall with the water bucket?

And then an idea came to her—swift and sudden and altogether perfect. She raised her hand, and when Mr. Palmer nodded permission to her, she slipped up to his desk.

"It's too bad to go outside," she told him, eager to rush quickly on to her fine idea, "but if you wanted us to, Reilly and I could take the children to the cloakroom and—and tell stories, or something."

Now that she had put the idea into words, it didn't sound so good. The sound of her voice telling stories could be plainly heard through the door, even if it were closed. But Mr. Palmer was ready to grasp at anything.

"That's a fine idea, Katie," he said. "Go ahead."

She went back to her place and communicated the idea to Reilly. Even as she talked, she was aware of the Adams boys watching her. Maybe they'll behave, she was thinking, if they know Reilly is helping out. Mischievous as they were—sometimes downright impossible—they still seemed to be fond of their sister.

Reilly got up to follow Katie. Together they passed on the idea to the six little ones, who immediately fell in line behind them. Once they were all in the cloakroom, Katie took the dinner pails off the long bench which held them and had the children sit down.

"Tell us a story, Katie," Meg pleaded. "Or let's sing."

Katie hesitated. Neither of these activities would do. Her voice could be heard inside, and that would be as bad as the restlessness of the children. What had Mama done, at such times, besides read to the family? Ah, she had it! Mama had given them paper and crayons and let them draw pictures to their hearts' content.

"Wait a minute—" she told the children.

She slipped into the school room, to her desk. In a minute she was back with her tablet and her package of colored crayons. She handed each child a piece of paper and let him choose a crayon.

"All right," she said, "draw a picture."

"What kind of a picture?" Babe asked.

"Oh, anything you like. A dog. Flowers. A house—"

They started, drawing a few wavering lines. The color on the paper evidently inspired them to greater efforts, for soon they set about the business in earnest. Billy got off the bench, stretched full length on the floor. Katie let him, not reminding him to keep his clothes clean.

"Take your time," she told the children, "and—" here inspiration came to her—"if some of them are good, I'll ask Mr. Palmer to hang them on the wall."

At that, the artists really went to work.

Katie watched them, torn between her pleasure in what they were doing and her fear that she had made a foolish promise. Maybe those pictures would look something awful, giving the Adams boys just another chance for a big laugh. Maybe Mr. Palmer would think she was taking too much on herself, asking such a thing. Oh dear, why had she ever said anything like that in the first place?

"Katie," Reilly broke out, speaking in a stage whisper, ever mindful of the others in the school room, "look—ain't that picture Meg is doing the prettiest thing?"

"It is," Katie said. Six faces were raised to hers, each wanting his own bit of praise. "They're all fine," she said quickly. As indeed they were. She'd have to ask Mr. Palmer now—there was no way out of it.

She thought quickly. If Meg's is good, Bryan won't *let* them laugh at the pictures. Goodness, how she did depend on him! Now all she had to do was to mention her idea to Mr. Palmer. It was as if he read her thoughts, for at that moment he appeared in the doorway.

"All right—" he began, and then, seeing what was going on, he stopped. "Why these are fine!" he exclaimed enthusiastically. "We'll have to hang them up for the others to see."

Katie flashed him a grateful look. Maybe he had heard her promising, the door being so thin and all. Maybe not. But anyway, he had saved her the embarrassment of having to ask, and she was grateful to him.

The pictures were the wonder of the school. Manilla, seeing them, was very wistful and said she wished she could make some, too. So did Cissy. Even 'Lonzo was interested. Annie had evidently persuaded her family that art was a wonderful thing, and all the Fosters were craving to have a try at it. Reilly was delighted, too. One day she picked up a piece of paper and drew a few lines, and then decided to put in a sunset. By the time she was finished, it was a fearful and wonderful thing to behold! Mr. Palmer, with considerable wisdom, put it up on the wall. After that, the Adams boys at least had, if not praise, no belittling remarks to make about the project. Bryan was pleased, too, on account of Meg.

"I say, Katie," he said in the off-hand way in which he always spoke to her, "it's good of you to help Meg. I've told my mother. She's real pleased."

Katie said "Thank you," breathlessly, but before she had even finished, he was off to play a game of ball with the other boys in the school yard. She sighed a little, and then she told herself he wouldn't be nearly so nice if he didn't want to be with the boys his own age. But all the same, his approval was a warm and glowing memory in her heart.

The art period for the small ones had been going on for a little more than a week when Mr. Palmer approached Katie privately.

"Katie," he said, "I wonder if you'd be willing to—" He hesitated a moment, as if he were searching for a better word than the one which had first occurred to him. "I wonder if you'd be willing to help a group with drawing, here at school?"

Katie hesitated, torn between a great pride and a great timidity. He hadn't said *who* wanted to be helped. Maybe it was the Adams boys, doing this only to torment her.

"It would be only those who really wanted to," Mr. Palmer assured her, evidently sensing her thoughts. "You see—some of the mothers and Miss Annie have come to me to say what a fine thing it would be for the boys and girls to have art."

Annie would. But Katie wondered who the other mothers were. Mrs. Adams? Surely not.

"Mrs. Cartwright was especially anxious," Mr. Palmer went on. "She says Meg is fascinated—wants to draw all the time when she is at home."

Mr. Palmer looked very young and shy, standing there trying to explain the need to Katie—almost as shy as Katie herself. And very anxious to have her say yes. For a minute Katie let herself remember how she herself had hoped the new teacher would be able to teach art and music. Maybe Mr. Palmer knew this. Perhaps he was thinking about all the children who had counted on having art and he was feeling sad because he couldn't help them. Now he was doing the next best thing—trying to find someone who could. Katie pushed aside the thought of the Adams boys making things difficult for her—and ran straight into another prospect which was even worse! What if Bryan decided he'd like to come into the class? She did not know which idea was the more terrifying.

"Will you, Katie?" Mr. Palmer persisted.

She couldn't say no—much as she wanted to, she couldn't.

"I'll try, Mr. Palmer," she said, scarcely above a whisper. And then an idea came to her—she wasn't sure whether it was because she thought it might help to take care of Cy and Hank too, or whether it was because she really felt the need.

"I'd like to have Reilly to help me," she said.

The minute the words were uttered, she knew. She really wanted Reilly's help. She wanted it very much. More than that—Reilly was her friend. She wanted her to have a share in this new venture.

Mr. Palmer looked at Katie quickly, a smile quirking up the corners of his mouth. He looked like Papa did when he was planning some harmless trick with one of his children. Seeing this look on Mr. Palmer's face, Katie felt suddenly adult and quite pleased with herself—and happy. She would make out fine. She and Reilly would. It wouldn't be a real art class, but someway, they'd make out.

"Thank you, Katie," Mr. Palmer said. "I'll make the announcement this afternoon."

The art class was started the following Monday, with Reilly and Katie in charge. Reilly was entirely overcome with the honor bestowed upon her, so much so that her contribution as helper was almost worthless. She bumbled around, humbly wanting to assist, but only succeeding in getting in everyone's way. For the most part, the big boys left the class alone, choosing rather to read their own school books during that period. Katie was devoutly thankful for this. Bryan did stroll up occasionally, look at Meg's work and tell her she was doing fine. Then he went back to bury himself in his reader. The Adamses gave no trouble at all. They pretended not to notice what was going on, and that was just all right with Katie.

As for herself, she was completely delighted with her new role. It seemed as though she had no more than told the children to get their paper and crayons out than it was time to stop. She brought all her old crayons from home and let the children use them. Even so, they were going down at an alarming rate. Finally she had to resort to lead pencils, and the young artists didn't like this a bit.

"I do not think black pictures are at all attractive," Carolyn said firmly.

"Use your colored ones," Katie said softly.

It was a little embarrassing, trying to teach your own sister, with everyone looking on. But Carolyn observed the most thorough and strict code, always courteous, even to the point of formality. Now when Katie suggested that she use her own colored crayons, she signaled her older sister, who promptly bent closer over her desk.

"It doesn't seem very generous to use my crayons when the others don't have theirs," Carolyn said in what was meant to be a whisper, but actually was heard all over the room. Mr. Palmer heard it—he looked at her quickly. Katie could see an idea was coming to him; what she did not know.

The idea may have been Mr. Palmer's, but Katie felt pretty sure it was Annie Foster who suggested the plan for carrying it out.

Annie came by the Pierces one day, just to thank Katie for the art lessons.

"I can't get over being thankful to you, Katie," she said earnestly, as if the very foundations of the world itself rested on those lessons.

"Now Annie," Katie protested, embarrassed by the girl's gratitude, entirely out of proportion to the importance of the achievement, "we're not doing so much—I just sort of get them started and then they work by themselves."

"You got them started," Annie agreed, "and that's the big thing. Why I tell you, that Manilla is just drawing all over everything. The minute she gets home, she's at it. Some day she may be almost as good as you are, Katie."

"She wouldn't be too good at that," Katie said. "I wish we had some real drawing paper for her to use and some better paints. I wish they all had some."

"Maybe we could manage to buy some," Annie said.

But even as she spoke she and Katie both knew that money for such things didn't come easily for homesteaders.

"I tell you what," Annie said thoughtfully, "this neighborhood needs to get better acquainted anyway. We ought to have something—a pie supper would be good. That way we could get together and make some money for the school besides."

"What's a pie supper?" Carolyn asked curiously.

"The girls bring pies and the men buy them, and the money goes to the school," Annie explained.

"*All* the girls?" Carolyn asked, preening herself a little.

"All the big ones," Annie told her.

"I am very mature," Carolyn said. "Papa says I am growing very rapidly."

"Of course you are," Annie agreed warmly. "You must take a pie. You and Manilla, too."

"Of course I will take a pie," Carolyn said. "If I didn't, I wouldn't be recuperating."

"*Co-operating*," Katie started to say, but she didn't. She was too busy thinking that, if all the girls took pies, she would take one, too. And if the boys bought them—Oh, well, she'd just wait and see what happened.

So of course, when Mr. Palmer announced about the pie supper, Katie wasn't at all surprised. She thought it was a lovely idea, and that the week before it was to take place was the longest one she had ever known. To add to the excitement, Melinda had written that she and Dennis were coming. Annie, who was assuming a great deal of responsibility for the affair, had suggested that Dennis act as auctioneer for the pies, and he had thought it would be fun. Melinda had said Katie wasn't to worry about making the pies—she'd take care of them when she got there.

But Katie wasn't going to leave that for Melinda. This time she would manage to make the pies with no accidents. Didn't she have a whole summer's cooking experience back of her? So she started very early Saturday morning, and in due time there were three pies sitting on the window sill to cool—vinegar pies, for certainly this was a special occasion. That done, she set about decorating boxes to carry them in.

She became so absorbed in this that she did not realize how time was slipping by. When Papa and the boys came in for dinner, she hadn't done the first thing toward getting it ready. But there were three boxes decorated—a pink one for Melinda, a blue one for Katie, and a yellow one for Carolyn. They looked perfectly lovely.

"Well," Dick said, "I guess we're just supposed to eat the boxes instead of dinner."

"No," Bert told him, "those pies in the window—they're for us."

And he went over to them, pretending he was going to eat every one of them.

Katie just laughed at the twins. By now she was learning to take their teasing casually.

"You can just eat whatever we happen to have around the house," she said. "Bread and jelly, or anything. I'm waiting to cook a good meal tonight for Melinda and Dennis."

When the Pierces, with Dennis and Melinda, drove up to the school house that evening, a number of wagons and buckboards and riding horses were already there. Katie, seeing them, felt excitement brimming up in her heart. She smoothed down her dress with a secret delight, a real joy.

Before Melinda came, Katie had thought she'd wear the flowered dress which she had worn at Melinda's wedding. Of course, it was really a summer dress, but still, it was her best one. With Mama gone, there hadn't been any new dresses this fall. She slipped it on, and Melinda looked at her quickly.

"My goodness, Katie," she said, "you can't wear that. It's way too short—you must have grown a couple of inches since June."

Her words sent Katie into a happy glow. Her delight was, however, followed by despair. If she couldn't wear this dress, what would she do?

"There's no time to let out the hem," Melinda decided. "I tell you what—you can just wear the blue one I brought for extra. It ought to fit you pretty well."

"Oh, Melinda," Katie burst out. "Not your new blue dress!"

"The very one—" Melinda told her. "Here, let's try it!"

Katie slipped it on. It fell softly around her hips, came almost to the floor. The color was the blue of the Panhandle skies, neither dark nor pale, just a lovely lacquered blue. Above it, Katie saw her eyes shining, a little bluer than the dress, her cheeks pink with excitement. Even her hair seemed more curly, now that she had the dress on.

"It will do fine," Melinda said. "I'll just have to shorten it a little, but I can run that hem up in no time."

She didn't explain why it would be easier to take this hem up than it would be to let down the bridesmaid dress.

And now here they were at the schoolhouse, with Katie wearing Melinda's dress, her hair looped up in a grown-up fashion which Melinda had helped her with.

"Tell me again," Papa said as they all walked toward the building, "which is Carolyn's box, which is Katie's?"

"The yellow one is mine," Carolyn told him. "That has always been my color."

"Blue for Katie, yellow for Carolyn," Papa repeated, as if he were memorizing the multiplication tables.

Katie saw that Annie Foster was already there, taking the pies from the girls and putting them up on the teacher's desk and on a table, so that they would be ready for Dennis to reach for them when the auctioning started. Several big boys were outside, peeping in at the open windows, looking as if they'd like to come in but were scared to do so. The twins and Papa were in the back of the room. And my goodness, there were Nick and Herman, back again!

"Hello," they called.

"Hello," Katie answered shyly. She wondered if they were noticing how she was changed into practically a young lady. She wondered if everybody was noticing. If the cowboys did, they had no time to say so.

"Hello Nick. Hello Herman," Carolyn said easily. "My pie is in the yellow box. Papa is going to buy it."

"Well that's just real nice of him," Nick said. "But maybe I'll beat him to it."

"Oh no you must not," she told him easily. "It would be most ungracious of you."

The cowboys laughed, not in a way to hurt Carolyn's feelings, but just enough to make her feel happy.

Katie and Melinda and Carolyn made their way up to the front of the room where women and children occupied the seats. The place was full, with more people coming all the time.

"It looks as if we will have a vast crowd," Carolyn said. "My goodness—I'm excited!"

Just at that moment Reilly Adams came in, pushing her way through the crowd to Katie's side. Her hair was pulled tighter than usual, a feat which Katie would not have thought it possible to achieve. She had on a bright red dress—quite the reddest Katie had ever seen. Green silk bows were sewed on it at intervals.

"Ain't it pretty?" Reilly said proudly, catching Katie's eyes on her. "It's an old dress of Ma's. It was kind of faded, so she dyed it. And we thought it needed some trimming, so she got out this green silk. Used to be on a hat."

The effect was like a Christmas tree in reverse, but this Katie certainly could not tell Reilly, who was so pleased with herself. She said yes, it was lovely.

"And look what I found—" Reilly went on. She lifted one hand, to show a yellow glove, faded by time and many washings.

"We looked everywhere, but couldn't dig up the other one. Ma says she doubts if we ever had it. But I put this one on because gloves are so—so—"

She paused, searching for the word.

"So elegant," Carolyn put in helpfully. "It is better to have two, but I suppose one is better than none."

Katie and Melinda looked at each other, knowing they were both restraining their wish to giggle.

Mr. Palmer came around now, speaking to people. He wasn't pushing, just sort of nice and quiet and easy mannered. Then he and Dennis went to the front of the room. Mr. Palmer called the group to order, said he was glad to see everyone there, and then announced that the pie selling would start with "Dr. Dennis Kennedy in charge." Katie felt proud. And she could tell by looking at Melinda that she was, too.

Dennis was very good for this sort of assignment.

He was so easy and natural, saying things to make everyone laugh. People knew him and liked him—there couldn't have been a better choice for an auctioneer. He started with the little girls' pies first. Mr. Foster bought Manilla's and Papa bought Carolyn's. She sat very straight, looking as grown-up and important as if she were at least Mama's age. Mr. Cartwright bought Meg's, and she called out while he was bidding, "That's mine, Papa! It's apple." Everybody laughed at that.

A pie was put up for sale. Someone whispered that it belonged to a homesteader girl and there was a rush of bidding. Nick bought it. Then Herman bought another. Mr. Palmer bought a pie, too, although Katie didn't know whose it was. The next one up Katie recognized—her own! Her heart stopped beating. She felt as though everyone must know it was hers because she caught herself blushing in that silly way she had.

"Now here's a good looking one," Dennis said easily. "You can feast your eyes on the decorations, if you can't eat the pie. What am I bid?"

"Quarter—" Katie heard Papa say.

"Thirty cents—" someone else called. She looked around quickly and saw Hank Adams, looking very mischievous, very pleased with himself.

Oh no, Katie was thinking. Not Hank Adams! I won't—I can't sit there and eat with him. I'd run to Papa and hide before I'd do it. I'd cry. I'd go home.

Papa must have known how she felt.

"Thirty-five—" he said.

"Forty—" Hank said.

Forty cents was a lot of money for a homesteader boy to pay for a pie. The Adamses didn't have much money. Hank had probably made it helping somebody, or maybe trapping. Maybe he didn't have the money at all. That was it. He was just being mean, knowing Papa wouldn't let him have Katie's pie with her showing so plainly how she felt.

Katie turned around a little to look at him. Yes, he was just trying to tease her—and maybe even upset Papa. A lock of hair fell across his forehead; he was wearing overalls and a blue shirt and a coat much too small for him. Catching her eye on him, he grinned impishly.

Papa was silent, evidently uncertain as to just what to do. He couldn't go on forever, bidding on his own daughter's pie against a boy who seemed to be determined to have it. And yet, sensing Katie's agonized appeal, he seemed to think he should go on. He was just ready to bid again when another voice sounded. "Fifty—"

It was Bryan Cartwright.

Katie felt the blood rush to her face. There was a drumming in her ears. She had hoped—no, she hadn't even let herself hope. Just a fleeting thought, that was all. Wouldn't it be nice if Bryan—She hadn't even let herself finish. But the little half-thought was there, all the while she was baking the pie. This time he could see she had learned how. This time she hadn't burned her hand.

Hank was evidently silenced for a moment, but not for good. He saw now a chance to torment someone who usually had the upper hand of him.

"Sixty—" he said.

"Seventy-five—" Bryan flashed back, quick as

anything.

Anyone could see that Hank was getting ready to bid again. This was a fine game to play—he could go on bidding it up, certain that Bryan didn't mean to stop.

Hank hesitated just a moment, but everyone could tell he was going on. He had been acting like a cat with a mouse—waiting just long enough to scare Katie, and then going ahead. It was evidently a game Mr. Palmer had no notion of allowing to continue. He said a quick word to Dennis, and Dennis in turn spoke just as quickly, ignoring Hank, who even at the moment was opening his mouth to make another bid.

"Sold, to Bryan Cartwright for seventy-five cents."

Hank looked angry. He glared at Mr. Palmer, and at Dennis—but mostly at Mr. Palmer, for he knew as well as anyone else that the teacher was the one responsible. Mr. Palmer knew Katie would rather eat with Bryan; he knew Hank was only trying to torment everyone concerned. He probably didn't have more than a couple of dimes in his pocket. And even if he had plenty of money, Mr. Palmer wasn't going to stand by and see Katie embarrassed by having to eat with him when all the time she could eat with Bryan Cartwright.

The selling was over at last. The men and boys went up to claim their pies and pay for them, with Papa acting as cashier. He was very polite and nice, smiling at Bryan when he came to pay for his. Katie watched Dennis go back to Melinda, carrying her pie.

Then there was Mr. Palmer, finding Annie. So that was the pie he had bought! And then there was Bryan at Katie's side, carrying the blue box.

"Well, Katie, why don't we find some place to sit down and eat this?" he said easily, not acting a bit embarrassed.

"All right—" she agreed shyly. She had never been to a pie supper before and didn't know exactly how to act.

"Here's a seat," he said. "This all right?"

"Oh, yes—" she assured him.

They sat down and he put the box on the desk in front of them. "If the pie's as good as the box is pretty," he said, "it ought to be something."

Katie smiled at him, grateful because he was being so easy and natural about it all. She was conscious of Hank watching them, and she was grateful, again, because Bryan had saved her from having to eat with him. She started to tell him so, and then stopped, realizing it wasn't a very polite thing to say. Besides, she was caught in an even greater dilemma. Was she the one to suggest that they start eating? Oh, my—if only she had thought to ask Melinda beforehand! Out of the corner of her eye she saw her sister opening her box. Katie took courage; she began to untie the string of hers. She took off the lid, and there it was. The vinegar pie.

"Say, that looks good!" Bryan exclaimed.

"I made it myself," she told him. "It's vinegar. That's what we always have for special, at home."

"Vinegar pie—" he repeated after her. "That's my favorite."

Again she smiled at him, feeling a little less shy. She took a knife from the box, made a clean swift cut across the middle of the pie. She made another, across in the other direction. There was the pie, in four equal pieces. She was quite proud of herself. She took two small china plates from the box, and two forks. She handed her partner one of each.

"Which piece do you want?" she asked politely.

"Oh, you take yours first."

"But I cut it," she started to say. Then she stopped, for something came to her. That was the way Mama had always made them do—the one who divided chose last. That was the way children did—but she wasn't a child. She looked down at the blue folds of Melinda's dress; she was aware of the way her curls were looped up on her head. A delicious excitement flowed through her veins; it had brought a flush to her cheeks, had made her eyes seem even more blue.

Bryan was aware of this change in her, too. She could tell it by the way he looked at her—with a dawning curiosity, as if maybe he was meeting her for the first time.

"Say," he said, "you sure do look nice tonight. Sort of—well, older maybe."

Katie didn't know exactly what to say. She probably couldn't have said it anyway, for she was suddenly so happy words wouldn't come. Instead, she reached out quickly and helped herself to a piece of pie. This done, she put another piece on his plate and handed it to him.

He took a bite.

"Say, this is good—" he said.

Words came to Katie now. She didn't feel shy at all. She looked up at him through her lashes. She smiled a little—easy and natural, like a grown-up lady.

"Thank you, Bryan," she said. "I'm glad you like it."

She was also glad he did not mention that awful time when her pie making hadn't turned out so well.

"Your brothers are having a good time," he said, nodding slightly toward Dick and Bert who had bought the pies of a couple of homesteader girls, newcomers to the community. They were pretty girls, laughing and gay. The boys seemed awfully pleased with the world—and themselves.

"Yes," she said. "But how did you know them?"

"Oh, have you forgotten? I saw them the day of the wedding. My mother didn't much like my coming to that without being asked. She has been telling me I ought to apologize to your mother, or something."

"Oh," Katie told him, honestly surprised, "everybody comes to everything out here."

"That's what I told her. It wasn't like that back in Illinois, where we came from."

Katie's daring carried over.

"You must come back some time," she said. "The boys would love to have you." Then she added politely, "We all would."

She felt as grown-up as Mama being mannerly to Mrs. Kennedy.

"I'll sure do it," he told her. And then, "I *told* Ma you people wanted me at that wedding."

They were driving home—Papa and the twins,

Carolyn and Katie, Melinda and Dennis. The moon was bright; Katie thought she had never seen it so bright.

"It went fine," Dennis was saying. "They bought those pies better than I thought they would."

"Yes," Papa agreed, "Mr. Palmer and I checked. We made a nice little sum."

"That pie—it was delicious," Melinda was saying.

A quicksilver happiness flowed through Katie.

"That Bryan fellow—the one who got your pie," Bert broke in, sounding a little puzzled and curious, "he sure did spend the money on you."

He was surprised, and yet he couldn't figure out why.

"He go to school?" Dick asked.

"Yes—" Katie answered briefly.

"He is a very smart boy," Carolyn explained. "He is the most intelligence of all the boys in school."

"Intelligent," Bert corrected her automatically. "Better stay with your own size, Carolyn."

"Isn't he a bit big to be going to school?" Dick asked.

"He's just a little past sixteen," Katie said.

"Well—" from the vantage of their almost-eighteen years, the twins looked disdainfully down on such a tender age.

"He says he wants to come to see you some Sunday," Katie said hesitantly. What if the twins thought he was too young for them. What if they teased him, the way they did her. Oh dear—she wished he wouldn't even try to come.

"Oh, he wants to see us," Bert said.

"*Us*—" Dick repeated with knowing emphasis.

"Tell him to come, Katie," Papa said quietly. When he spoke in that tone of voice the boys always settled down, and quickly.

"Say, Katie," Dennis broke in, "you looked mighty pretty this evening. You're getting to be quite a young lady."

"That pie was mighty good," Papa told her. "Just about as good as Mama's."

Katie felt herself surrounded by happiness, and a sweetness. The twins hadn't teased her, much. Bryan had bought her pie, and she hadn't been shy with him, much. She had worn Melinda's dress, and looped her curls up. She knew no night had ever been this lovely and golden before, no air so soft, no sky so deeply blue.

The land stretched away from them—big, level, mysterious. It went on and on, until it and the sky were one. The sky itself was a wide blue bowl, cupping down over them.

For the first time since she had come to the Panhandle, Katie felt really drawn by it. It was her home now, her land. Maybe she didn't feel the way Melinda did about it; maybe she never would. But she at least had known this moment where it was all beauty, all happiness.

Whatever happened to her, she would remember this. All her life she would remember.

Chapter 9

"I AM SO EXCITED I can scarcely endure it, Katie," Carolyn said.

They were riding Cleveland, who was plodding along even more slowly than usual, apparently overcome by the weather. It was warm as spring, not at all like November. Katie and Carolyn wore print dresses, and even then had taken off their light wraps, letting them fall down around their hips as they sat on Cleveland's fat back.

"It is going to be most enjoyable," Carolyn went on, "staying a whole weekend with Manilla. We can play outside, it is so nice and warm."

"Yes—" Katie agreed. Actually she wasn't as pleased with the prospect of playing with Manilla as she was with seeing Annie. Annie always seemed next best to having Melinda. Katie guessed that was because the two of them had been such close friends—still were, as far as that went. Annie knew a lot of the escapades the Pierce children had managed to get into, had been in some of them herself. Then there was something else. Since Katie herself had been trying to hold the family together while Mama was gone, she seemed to understand even more the tremendous job which Annie had accomplished in changing the Foster family so that now they were just about like anybody else.

It was going to be fun, spending the weekend with Annie. Papa and the twins had gone to Amarillo for supplies. They had waited longer than usual to take the trip, thinking that Mama would be back to make out the list of necessary items. But she had written that she couldn't leave Grandmother yet, and that Papa had better go to Amarillo for supplies before winter set in. She had sent a list of suggestions, and Papa and Katie had checked it against the supplies on hand. Katie felt very important doing this. She would look at the boxes and cans in the cupboard, regarding them with a frown of concentration between her eyes, and then make a suggestion to Papa, who would write it down.

"Beans—" she said.

"We probably needed them the first week after Mama left," Dick commented slyly.

Of course Katie knew he was referring to the time she cooked those pans and pans of pinto beans, right after Mama left. How far away that seemed. She smiled a little now, thinking that it was fine she didn't mind Dick's teasing—not very much, anyway.

"The way you ate them, it's a wonder I had enough to last a day," she said, feeling very proud that she could even come back at the twins occasionally.

When they had finished, Papa read the list to her, just as he always did to Mama. Flour, sugar, coffee. Molasses, matches, salt. They went over it carefully. When you lived thirty miles from town, you took great care not to run out of supplies. You went only twice a year, and it took careful planning to buy enough to last a family six months. Actually, Katie wasn't much help on the amounts. She left that to Papa, who always helped Mama and now was able to make the major decisions.

At first Carolyn and Katie were all for going to Amarillo with Papa and the boys.

"You can't very well do it," Papa reminded them. "We'll have to go Friday, shop Saturday, and drive back Sunday. You'd have to miss school. I'll ask Annie to stay with you. Nick will come and tend the stock Saturday."

That settled it. No missing school. So they reluctantly gave up the idea.

But about that time Bub Foster rode over to see the twins. When he found out what was going on, he said he and Pa and 'Lonzo had been planning a trip, and why didn't they all throw in together? Papa said that was a fine idea.

"I had planned to ask Annie to come stay with the girls," he said. "Could she leave, with all the men in the family gone?"

"No reason why Katie and Carolyn couldn't go spend the weekend at our place," Bub suggested.

Which was the way they planned it.

The Cartwrights, who by that time had grown to be good neighbors (privately Katie took credit for this, for just after the pie supper, Bryan had started coming over to see the twins), found out what was going on, so Mr. Cartwright and Bryan said they would make the trip at the same time. Meg, who heard about the plans at school, begged to stay with the Fosters, too, and Annie sent word to her mother that she might as well. Mrs. Cartwright protested only a little, finally saying she'd be really pleased, for she wanted to go to Amarillo and do some shopping herself.

Early that morning the wagons had set off—the Pierces and the Fosters in one, with the Cartwrights following in a buckboard. They'd stay all night in a wagon yard in Amarillo—that is, all except Papa and the twins. They would go to Melinda's. She was anxious to have them, for Dennis was making another quick trip out to the Ranch to see his aunt.

"It is going to be a real party," Carolyn said now, still discussing the anticipated joys of the visit. "Aren't you just tremendously thrilled, Katie?"

"Yes—" Katie said. Maybe not as thrilled as Carolyn, but pleased.

When they rode up into the school yard, they saw that the rickety spring wagon in which the Fosters rode to school was already there. Where usually there were six Fosters crowded into it, today there were only three, 'Lonzo and Jack having gone with the group to Amarillo. Boy, who was twelve, had rebelled at going to school in a wagon filled only with "girls and babies," so at the last minute Annie had said he might stay at home and help her take care of things. That left Manilla to drive the fat and lazy horse attached to the spring wagon, a job which gave her great stature in the eyes of Cissy and Babe, her only passengers. She was waiting when Carolyn and Katie rode up to the school yard.

"Oh, Carolyn," she cried, almost breathless with

happiness, "ain't it just wonderful?"

"Yes—" Carolyn agreed, and slid down to stand beside her friend. Katie dismounted more slowly, tied Cleveland to the post inside the shed provided for the horses, and walked to the school house.

It seemed very lonesome today. Katie didn't want to admit it, but that was partly because Bryan wasn't there. With him away, she thought the whole room seemed vacant.

The Adamses were there, though. They grinned impishly at Katie when she came in, almost as if they knew what she was thinking. She felt herself flush a little. She quickly averted her gaze from them, but even as she did so she thought they seemed even dirtier than ever, and more bent on mischief.

Ever since the pie supper, three weeks ago, things had been bad. Hank seemed always to be trying to make trouble—so slyly it was almost impossible to know what he was doing, yet openly enough so that it was almost impossible to ignore him. Mr. Palmer was aware of this, but even with his awareness there was an uncertainty as to what was best to do—overlook his actions, or try to punish him. Even Katie could see it would be silly to punish a boy for something you couldn't quite prove existed.

She sighed. In a way, she felt responsible for Hank's actions. For a while she wasn't able to figure things out, but finally it dawned on her that he was mad at Mr. Palmer because he knew the teacher had seen he was ready to bid on Katie's pie again and had blocked this by telling Dennis to hurry and announce that it was sold to Bryan.

"Hank didn't really want my pie," she thought. "He just wanted to torment me by bidding on it. He knows I'm afraid of him. He knows he can embarrass me. It makes him feel important, being able to do this."

What she couldn't understand was why he didn't resent Bryan, for he didn't; not at all. Maybe he was afraid of Bryan. Maybe he respected him. Whatever the reason, he showed no anger with the boy, choosing rather to center his dislike on Mr. Palmer. He took this out in many ways, one of which was making life miserable for Billy. He did this especially when they were out on the playground.

This made things really difficult. Mr. Palmer couldn't very well interfere unless the situation got really out of hand, and Hank was too clever to go that far. He was also careful when Bryan was around. But there were countless times, and countless ways, in which he could torment Billy without Bryan's knowledge or Mr. Palmer being able to do anything about it. Looking at the Adams boys now, Katie knew this was going to be a hard day for Billy, and, naturally, for Mr. Palmer.

Once she was seated, her eyes flew to the spot back of Mr. Palmer's desk. What she saw there gave her a feeling of greatest satisfaction. The material for today's art lesson.

Last week the art supplies had come, the ones bought with the pie supper money—drawing paper, pencils, crayons, water colors.

"All right, Katie," Mr. Palmer had said. "They are yours. You can get busy with them at art period this afternoon."

"Oh, dear!" Katie had exclaimed, breathless with excitement, with pleasure—even with fear, lest she fail in this new phase of her undertaking.

So far, the art classes had gone very well. She was so interested in what she was doing that she had almost forgotten to be shy about conducting the period. In fact, one of the happy things about today was the fact that, at its end, it would bring the art class.

Lessons went haltingly that morning. Hank and Cy seemed possessed of all the imps of Satan.

"Hank, what is the capital of Illinois?"

"I dunno."

"But you held up your hand."

That was a mistake—Mr. Palmer knew it as soon as the words were out.

"I was jest scratching my head. Fellow's got to scratch when he itches, don't he?"

Cy laughed uproariously at his brother's wit, so loudly, in fact, that it took a little time to bring the room back to order.

The morning went on with Hank answering questions not at all, or if he did, answering them in such a way that it would have been better had he remained silent. By this time Mr. Palmer had wisely decided to ignore him, a decision which disappointed Hank, who would have liked nothing better than an open scene.

By noon Katie was so nervous with the strain of it that she wasn't hungry. As far as that went, neither was Carolyn, but for a different reason.

"I'll just wait and eat when we get to Annie's tonight," she announced. "Manilla says she is preparing a most delicious meal."

The idea was contagious. If Carolyn would not eat, neither would Manilla. And of course, if she refused food, so would Babe and Cissy.

Oh well, Katie thought, it's too warm for us to be very hungry, anyway. Besides, Annie would have a good meal. She had grown to be an excellent cook, had Annie. For just one fleeting moment Katie let herself remember the first meal the Pierces had eaten at the Fosters'. The only reason they ate anything at all was to keep from hurting Mrs. Foster's feelings. Things were dirty and awful. Now the Foster house was as clean as anybody's. Mrs. Foster, a vast, good natured woman, had turned things over entirely to Annie, who did the cooking as she did everything else—with ease and energy and a great deal of skill.

Mr. Palmer seemed to realize that the day was too lovely to waste, that before long winter would be coming and keeping them all inside, so he let them play out a long time after he should have rung the bell. The children took advantage of this special treat, apparently relishing every minute of freedom, all the more because it was unexpected.

Billy and Babe Foster were having a "horse race." Each had found a tumble weed, rough and dry and airy looking, and had given them horses' names.

"Mine's Ginger," Billy announced, taking the name out of *Black Beauty*, which Mr. Palmer had been reading aloud to them.

"Mine's Jig," Babe announced, choosing the name of Herman's horse. All the children just about worshipped cowboys, and the best of the lot were Nick and Herman.

Billy and Babe placed the two round tumbleweeds side by side. They stood still, their hands behind them, waiting for a breeze to come along and move them. By and by it came, and off went the two tumbleweeds, rolling swiftly across the school yard. First Ginger, then Jig, was ahead.

"Whee—ee—" Billy yelled. "Get along, Ginger—"

"Jig—run—run—" Babe screamed, jumping up and down. The whole pack of children ran after the two jockeys and their "horses," all of them yelling encouragement to one or the other. It was every bit as exciting as a real race.

The weeds continued to roll along smartly, moved by a wind that came in little gusts, died down, stirred up again. Yells of delight greeted each puff; moans of disappointment came with its dying.

The wind had started up once more and Billy and Babe were off, screaming with glee, following their "horses." At that moment Hank came lounging over in their direction. One look at his face told Katie he was up to some sort of mischief—nothing in particular, just whatever came to hand first. He took a look at the children and started toward them.

"Hey," he said, "what yuh doing?"

As he spoke, he reached out with his foot to touch Billy's "horse." At the same time he tweaked the child's nose, none too gently.

"Now Hank—" Reilly said, plainly embarrassed by her brother's actions. Katie wanted to add her protest, but wisely refrained, knowing any word of hers would only serve to make matters worse. She kept silent, boiling with rage. The big bully, to come and interfere in a child's game.

"Don't!" Billy cried. The wind had started again and Babe's tumbleweed was off, rolling along at a good clip, while Billy's stayed behind, held by Hank's foot.

"Make me stop," Hank said, swaggering a little. He gave Billy's nose another tweak, this time strong enough to bring tears into the child's eyes.

"Hank, stop that!" Katie burst out, unable to restrain herself. "You ought to be ashamed of yourself, hurting a little child—"

"You mind your own business," he told her. And then he hurled at her the worst of all insults. "Teacher's pet," he taunted. "Figger to get in better by petting his kid. Let him fight for himself."

"Oh—" Katie choked, furious with him.

Hank turned back to Billy.

"Here," he said, holding his fist close to Billy's face. "Fight your own fights. Hit me—make me quit!"

As he spoke, he gave Billy's nose another twist.

And then an amazing thing happened. Billy, made bold by pain, or perhaps by Katie's protest, did just that. He doubled up his puny fist, hit Hank's outstretched paw.

"Well, the little squirt!" Hank roared. "Look at him. Do it again—"

And Billy did, while tears of rage and humiliation rolled down his baby face.

This time it pleased Hank to pretend that he was terribly hurt. He started to run, looking back in mock terror to see if he were being followed. Amazingly enough, Billy did follow, bellowing with rage at every step he took. The other children watched, open mouthed. This was more exciting than a tumbleweed race, and certainly more unexpected. Billy, no bigger than a mosquito, was running after the school bully!

Hank was enjoying the experience more than anybody. He was laughing, running a few steps, waiting for Billy to catch up, going into another burst of speed when he was close. He was pretending to be scared, pretending to be badly hurt. He ran around the school house, came back from behind Billy, passed him. Just as he did so, he stuck out his foot and tripped the child. Billy fell headlong on the ground.

Hank did not stop, but ran around the school house again, whooping like a wild Indian. So engrossed was he in his fun that he failed to see Cy, running fast as an antelope, rounding the corner of the school house from the opposite direction.

Mr. Palmer had just stepped outside the door to ring the bell. Katie suspected he had realized what was going on outdoors and had decided that the best way to stop it was to bring the children back into the school room. Too late the running boys saw him. Both swerved, trying to avoid hitting him. In doing this they missed him, only to encounter a greater difficulty. They collided with each other head-on, with such force that the sound of their collision echoed all over the school yard. The impact sent Hank staggering back. But Cy came out even worse. He stumbled a step or two, and then fell to the ground, his head hitting the stone foundation of the building, his arm crumpled up under him in a grotesque way. There was a snap—sharp and sudden, like a stick breaking.

"Cy, Cy—" Reilly screamed, running to him.

Katie followed her. Cy was lying very quiet, his body in a funny, twisted position. His eyes were closed; he seemed scarcely to be breathing. "Oh, Cy!" Reilly was sobbing wildly now. She knelt beside him, trying to get him to his feet.

"Don't touch him, Reilly," Mr. Palmer ordered.

He was still carrying the bell, but he put it down now and knelt beside the prostrate boy. The children formed a silent, white-faced ring around the two. At the edge of it was Hank, either too dazed by the impact or too frightened by the result of it, to come to his brother's side.

Mr. Palmer put his fingers on Cy's wrist, leaned over, put his head against his chest. Then he straightened up.

"Get some water, Hank," he said quietly.

There was authority in his voice, a quality which Hank seemed to recognize at once. He moved faster than Katie had ever seen him move before. In a few moments he was back with the dipper full of water. Mr. Palmer took it from him, dashed a little on Cy's face. The boy began to sputter, shook his head slightly.

"Hey—" he said weakly, and tried to rise.

"Lie still a minute," Mr. Palmer told him. "Take it easy."

Cy, too, seemed to recognize authority. He lay quietly, closed his eyes once more. His face was pale. Nobody said a word. They were all bound by the terror of the moment. In a few minutes Cy opened his eyes again. This time he made an effort to sit up. Mr. Palmer put his hand under the boy's shoulder. Cy winced, but he did not refuse the aid.

"Think you can stand up?" Mr. Palmer asked.

"Yep—"

He stood, but his face went even whiter and small beads of perspiration broke out on his forehead. He slumped against Mr. Palmer. One arm—the right one—dangled, crooked and funny looking. Katie had never seen a broken arm, but she knew this was one.

Mr. Palmer knew it, too. "Your arm's broken, Cy," he said. "We're going to have to take you home and get a doctor to set it for you. Dr. Kennedy's in Amarillo, isn't he, Katie?"

And then Katie remembered about Dennis. "He's out at the Ranch, seeing his aunt," she said. "That's a lot closer than Amarillo—maybe not ten miles away."

Even as she spoke, she was thinking how wonderful it was to be a doctor, to be able to come when people needed you. Dennis had chosen the good work, all right.

Mr. Palmer turned to her gratefully.

"That makes it much better. Hank, do you want to ride to the Ranch for Dr. Kennedy?"

Hank looked at him, something like defiance in his face.

"Ain't got no horse," he said—which was true. The Adams children walked to school—four miles, and home again—each day.

"Take mine," Mr. Palmer said. "In the meanwhile, I'll try to get him home. Manilla," he said, turning to the girl, "do you think you could walk home if I borrowed your spring wagon to take Cy home in?"

"Surest thing you know," Manilla answered promptly. "We can make it easy. Ain't more'n three miles."

"All right," Mr. Palmer said, "that's settled, then."

He took off his coat, made a pallet of sorts in the bed of the wagon. Reilly ran to get her own coat—very thin and shabby—and spread it out also.

"Can I go with you, too, Mr. Palmer?" she begged. She looked at him with pain and entreaty in her face—an apology for the way her brothers had acted, gratitude for the thing Mr. Palmer was doing. He caught this and said kindly, "Of course, Reilly. I was about to ask you if you would. I'll drive, and somebody ought to sit in the back with him."

Reilly ran to the wagon, forgetting her dinner pail in her haste. She got into the back with her brother, lifted his head gently, put it into her lap. Mr. Palmer started to follow her, then turned to Katie.

"Katie," he said, "I'll leave it all to you. Get things picked up and straight in the school room, and dismiss the ones who are left. Lock the door, and take the key with you. And will you let Billy go with you to the Fosters?"

"Yes—" Katie told him, feeling all solemn and quiet with the responsibility that had been thrown on her shoulders.

Mr. Palmer got up on the seat. He slapped his lines across the broad fat back of the Foster horse. The wagon moved off.

"Goodby," Mr. Palmer said. And then, over his shoulder, he called, "Thank you, Katie."

The little group of children stood a moment, watching the wagon, and then they filed back into the school house.

The room seemed very quiet and strangely lonesome. Actually, there were only a handful left. Three Fosters—Manilla, Cissy and Babe; two Pierces; Billy and Meg. Seven in all. Inside the room they seemed to rattle around eerily, like the Pierce children when Mama was gone.

They all filed disconsolately to their seats. Things had happened so fast, they still weren't quite able to grasp them. One minute they had been out there watching a tumbleweed race, and the next everything had broken loose. Nobody found it in his heart to say it was all Hank's fault, even while they were thinking it was too bad for Cy to have to suffer for his brother's meanness. Hank had been teasing Billy; Hank had run into Cy, knocking him down. Perhaps they were remembering the look on Hank's face when he rode Mr. Palmer's horse off to get the doctor. Remembering that, they knew he was being punished now, and plenty. Instead of saying these things, though, they just sat still, looking at Katie. She had been left as their leader; they turned to her for guidance.

Katie looked around her uncertainly. "Well," she finally said, "I guess we might just as well go home."

"Oh, dear," Manilla lamented, "it's the day for art! Ain't we going to have art?" She had started to add "Katie," but hesitated, apparently feeling that, under the circumstances, that would be presumptuous on her part.

"My goodness," Katie was thinking, "they all act as if I were a real teacher!" It scared her, just thinking about it.

"Couldn't we just draw a little while?" Carolyn asked politely. Even she was showing Katie a deference usually reserved for people like the teacher or the traveling preacher.

Katie thought hard. It couldn't be more than two o'clock, a good two hours before time for school to be out. Annie certainly wouldn't be looking for them yet. True, the Fosters would have to walk home this evening, but that would take little longer than the fat Pierce horse needed to make the trip. There was no real reason why they shouldn't draw a while, if they wanted to.

"All right," she agreed, "we'll have the art lesson."

Even as she spoke, she knew it was exactly what she wanted to do, had hoped they could do.

"Oh, goody!" Manilla exulted.

"Thank you, Katie," Carolyn said primly.

They got out the paints and crayons, the pencils and drawing paper. Katie made up her mind that, since there were so few today, she would draw something herself. She decided she would try to paint Carolyn, bending so intently over her art work. Long ago she had done a silhouette of Melinda, using washing blueing for paint, a piece of wrapping paper for paper. Now she had real paints, real drawing paper. It ought to be fun. She put on a few strokes, looked at Carolyn—a few more, another look. The picture was growing under her very fingers.

She was both delighted and amazed to see how

much it looked like the child. The same grave, dig-
nified expression. The little tilted nose. The long,
straight, soft hair. Katie took another look at her subject, glanced back at the painting, and felt the intoxi-
cating delight that comes with artistic creation.

"Why Katie!" she was surprised to hear Meg ex-
claiming. So engrossed had she been that she was
unaware of anyone else in the room save herself and
Carolyn. "Katie—you've drawn Carolyn! How pretty.
Draw me, too!"

Katie laughed with pleasure. "All right," she said.
"Sit still—I'll do you, too."

"Me, too," Manilla begged. And all the others
chimed in, "Me, too. Draw me, Katie—."

One by one the pictures grew . . . Manilla's . . .
Meg's . . . Billy's. As each new one was finished, the
children screamed with delight. Katie's fingers fairly
flew. It seemed to her she was in a world all by herself.
Even the children whose faces she drew were not quite
real to her. They were, instead, merely something to
capture and put on paper. Lights and shadows; sheen
of hair, shine of eyes. Lift of eyebrow and shape of
nose. As each one was finished, the children would
cry, "Oh, Katie—that's me! How wonderful!"

Katie was working on Babe Foster's picture, when
suddenly it occurred to her that the room seemed dark.
She looked up quickly. It was nothing but a temporary
shadow. A cloud was over the sun. She went back to
her work.

Babe was finished. She turned to Cissy.

She was only half-way through when uneasiness

struck her. It was nothing she could quite put her finger on. Then she realized that the room was dark, almost like late evening. She put down her picture, rushed to the window. She looked out and guilt and fright caught at her heart.

The sun was gone. Her first thought was that she had stayed so long it was night.

"Put your paints and things away quickly," she said. "It's late—time we went home."

While they were obeying, she went back to the window. This time she knew it wasn't evening. A cloud had rolled up across the horizon. It was black, and it was big. There were swirls of white foam on it, and at the edges, a green and eerie light. It rose, a dark and angry curtain, blanketing the whole sky.

"Hurry," Katie urged. "I'll help you."

Bad though the storm might be, she had promised Mr. Palmer to leave the room in order, and that she would do.

They were still putting things away when the wind hit. It came, a sudden burst of force and sound, out of a great stillness. Then, as quickly as it came, there was stillness once more.

"Katie!" Carolyn quavered. "What's wrong?"

Katie did not answer. She did not know what was wrong, save that it was some sort of a storm. What kind? A cyclone? Not this time of the year. Then she remembered the suddenness with which the blizzard had hit, that first winter they came to the Panhandle—so suddenly that it caught Papa away from home. And it caught the Bad Men, too, and they sought refuge in the Pierce dugout. It had been just like this—a sudden, icy blast, screaming down upon them after a warm and summer-like day.

A blizzard! They still told tales, out here on the plains, of men and cattle who were caught in one and froze to death before they could get to shelter.

The wind hit again—this time with greater force. There was a stillness, and then the wind again. By now it was even stronger, and it did not stop.

Katie walked to the door, opened it. A sharp edge of coldness came through. Yes, it was a blizzard, all right.

"I want to go home." Cissy Foster began to cry.

"All right," Katie said. "We'll go. Get your wraps."

Their wraps! Not one of them had worn more than the lightest of coats. Katie should have known this was a "weather-breeder." Mama would have known, maybe, but Mama hadn't been there to tell her.

The children donned their wraps obediently. Together they went to the door. Katie opened it. The icy wind blew against them; the angry sky looked down on them.

"Oh, Katie!" Meg whimpered. "I'm scared."

Katie didn't answer. She couldn't. She was too scared herself.

All her life Katie had been afraid of storms. It was stupid and childish of her, she knew, but she couldn't help it. In summer, when lightning and thunder came, she always went to her room, crawled up in her bed and tried to drown the sound by burying her head in her pillows. In winter, when the wind was blowing wild and untamed across the miles of prairie, she crept close to Mama. The others laughed at her, but that never helped a bit. She went on being afraid and shrinking back from storms.

Now she was really afraid, for, even at the very beginning, she could tell this was no ordinary storm. Here was something the likes of which had never hit before. The black cloud had blotted out most of the light; the wind was screaming like a demon turned loose. And, already, snow was beginning to fill the air.

Of course, what she ought to do was to rush back to the Fosters, arriving there before the storm hit. Three miles to go. She tried to calculate in her mind the time this would take. Meg and Billy and Babe—they could ride Cleveland. She and the others could walk.

She opened her mouth to tell the others the plan. And then another blast of wind hit, sending bits of snow and icy spray against the window panes. And suddenly she knew she could not risk taking these children out in the storm.

"Katie!" Babe screamed. "What are we going to do!"

They all turned to her, those children. They fixed their eyes on her because she was the biggest, the one Mr. Palmer had left in charge. She had to decide now, for all of them.

If they went out into the storm, they would probably freeze to death. They might get through to the Foster's, but it was a risk. Even if it were not for the cold, they might lose their way in the snow, which was beginning to come down very thick and fast now.

If they stayed in the school house, they might freeze to death, too. It would be hours—maybe days, before people could get to them.

"What are we going to do?" Carolyn asked. Her voice was frightened, scarcely audible.

And Katie made up her mind.

"We are going to stay right here," she said.

The Fosters began to cry, all except Manilla, who looked as if she wanted to.

"Don't cry," Katie told them. "We'll be all right here. Just as soon as it's over, they'll come for us. Stop crying now, hear me?"

She spoke with a confidence she was far from feeling. *Who* would come for them? Not Papa or the twins, for they were in Amarillo. Nor yet the Foster men, or the Cartwrights, for they were there, too. Mr. Palmer, maybe? No—he had no more than reached the Adams' place by now, driving as slowly as they must go. Besides, he would be sure that they were all at Fosters, for had he not told them to go as soon as he left?

Annie? That was foolish even to consider. No woman, not even Annie Foster, could brave this blizzard. Anyway, Annie didn't know Mr. Palmer wasn't with them. She wouldn't worry overmuch, thinking he had kept them at school because the blizzard was too bad to venture through, knowing he was capable of looking after them.

A gust of wind shook the windows, like a child shaking a rag doll. Katie shuddered at the force of it. Billy saw her and, sensing her fright, began to whimper his own fear and terror. Seeing him, Katie knew that the luxury of fright—at least, of showing it—was not for her.

"Don't be afraid, Billy," she said, as steadily as she could. "We're perfectly safe here. Just as safe as if we were at Annie's."

He quieted down, either because he believed her, or was too polite to express his doubt.

Chapter 10

KATIE HAD TOLD Billy not to be afraid, and even as she spoke, panic swept over her. The children were huddled around her; outside the wind was howling, shaking the windows as if it, too, wanted to come inside and join them. The darkness was already creeping in, by now the light was almost gone.

Here she was, responsible for these children, with no one else older, or even her own age, to turn to for help or advice. Wildly she wished that Reilly had stayed, even though she knew the girl would only have looked to her for everything, almost as completely as the younger children were doing. But there were only the small ones left, and she herself must find courage she did not possess, resourcefulness she had never known.

"It's getting cold, Katie," Meg whispered. She shivered a little, and in the dimming light her small face looked drawn and pale.

The room was indeed growing colder. The day had been so warm that Mr. Palmer had allowed the fire to die down. Katie went to the stove, opened the door and looked inside. There were only gray ashes. A fear more chilling than the cold seeping in from the outside swept over Katie. What if the fire had gone out entirely, leaving not even a single bit of live coal? She had no matches, and without them how could she start a fire? And without a fire—! She pushed the thought resolutely from her.

Slowly, with infinite care, she raked the dead ashes away. And finally she saw it—one live coal, buried among the ashes. So small it was, she was almost afraid to breathe lest she extinguish it forever.

There were a few sheets of waste paper in the coal bucket, sitting next to the stove. She took these out, tore them into shreds, put them over the spark. They caught, burned up brightly and, even as she looked at the flame, it died down.

She should have remembered to have the splinters of wood ready to catch fire from the burning paper. Was the spark still left? She had used all the paper in the bucket; she looked around her for something else. She ran for her tablet, tore out a few sheets. She got some pieces of kindling from the box Mr. Palmer kept behind the stove. First she put in the paper—her precious tablet paper, which Mama always cautioned the family to use carefully. After what seemed like an eternity, a flame shot up. She put on some small splinters of wood. They caught.

Now she knew she must put on more kindling and then, very carefully so as not to extinguish the fire, she must put on small pieces of coal. Easily—slowly—.

Never was there a more beautiful sight than that coal bursting into cheery flame. She put on another piece, this time with less fear. And as she did so, she was conscious of the children standing behind her. They must have known how much depended on what she had been doing; they must have held their little breaths, all the while she worked.

"Oh, Katie," Billy said, his voice shot through with wonder and relief, "Oh, Katie—you built a fire!"

He walked close to the stove, held his small hands out to the comfort of it.

She had made a fire. But that would not last forever unless there was fuel to keep it going. She looked at the coal bucket; it was not even half full. She must bring in extra coal; before the storm got worse, she must do that. She remembered Mama had made them bring in fuel that other time the blizzard hit. Before long it would be so bad that she would not dare to go outside, even to make the short journey to the coal shed and back. She must act quickly, if she were going to act at all.

She went to the coal bucket, dumped its contents on the floor. She started toward the door, carrying the bucket with her.

"What are you going to do, Katie?" Carolyn asked thinly.

"I'm going to get some more coal."

Carolyn looked at her strangely—as if she wanted to cry and was restraining herself with only the greatest of effort. Finally she spoke.

"Katie," she said, "if you are going for coal, I am going with you. It is my bounden duty to go." She set her jaw as she finished speaking, and every line of her face, of her body, showed determination to carry out her intentions.

Katie was opening her mouth to say no, it was too cold for Carolyn. Then something came to her. They were in this thing together, she and Carolyn were. They, and all the others. Maybe she was the oldest, and because of that, responsible for them; but she in turn must have help from them if they were to come through this safely—not with the big chores, like bringing coal, but with a far more difficult thing, that of keeping their own courage high. Maybe giving them something to do would help here.

"All right, Carolyn," she said, "we'll carry coal together."

"I'm going, too," Manilla said sturdily. And all the others chimed in, "Me, too—me, too."

Manilla could be useful, yes, Katie decided. But she must not let those other small ones outside now. She thought quickly of a way to keep them inside. There were some things she could allow, some she must prevent.

"No," she said to the youngest children, "you must stay here. I tell you what you do—pull the chairs close to the stove. Bring the lunch pails in from the cloak room."

Strange that they should take her word for things so instantly. Even as she spoke, they began to obey. All but Manilla, standing stubbornly by, knowing those small errands were not for her.

"Manilla," Katie said, "You bring in a bucket of water. We will get thirsty tonight."

She picked up the coal bucket, and then, followed by Carolyn, went out into the cold. Behind her she could hear, rather than see, Manilla following with the water bucket.

They might as well have left their light coats off, for all the good they were against the cold. The wind blew through them as if they were made of tissue paper. By now it was coming in gusts so strong that Katie and Carolyn had to brace themselves against it, as if it were a rude hand, tugging at them. They filled the bucket, went back to the school room.

Once inside, Katie looked at what they had carried in, at the small bit she had dumped on the floor. It was a mighty little, she decided, weighed against the terrible cold outside, against the time they might have to spend here before help came. Quickly she made up her mind. She dumped this load on the pile already there and started out to the shed once more, Carolyn trailing her in silent loyalty.

Two more trips they made, and as they struggled back this third time, Katie knew she had gone just before it was too late. By now, the force of the wind was much greater than it had been, even so short a while back as their first trip. And the snow was coming down so thick and fast it was all the two sisters could do to see the outlines of the school house as they struggled toward it.

Katie closed the door behind her, locked it. She walked over to the stove, threw in a lump of coal. It was as if the locking of the door had made the children realize their situation.

"Katie," Meg cried, "I want my Mama. I don't want to stay here all night by ourselves!"

"We have to stay, honey," Katie said, trying to comfort her. "We're all right. By morning, someone will come for us."

She spoke with a confidence she did not feel. As a matter of fact, she wanted to wail, too, and cry for Mama. What was it like to stay alone, with no grownups to protect you? Long ago, the Pierce children had done this when Manilla Foster was ill and Mama had gone to help out. But Melinda had taken the responsibility at that time. Was Melinda scared half to death then, Katie wondered? Perhaps, but she had acted so sure of herself that Katie had taken courage, had even gone to bed and slept the night through. She found herself wishing now that she had stayed up with the others, had learned how children conduct themselves in time of emergency.

Outside the wind howled louder, fiercer. Spats of snow hit the window panes, coming so fast it was impossible to see outside. The cold, too, was increasing. If they stayed close to the stove, they could manage, though. Thank goodness there had been that one small live coal left in the stove! What if—Katie shuddered a little, pushed the thought from her. There were enough real problems to face without borrowing any. She turned to the children.

"Keep on your coats," she directed. "Your caps, too, if you wore them."

Any wraps they might have would be only the lightest. Warm as the morning was, they would not think of heavy coats. What they had, they were wearing, though, all except Manilla Foster who stood, blue with cold, and coatless, close to the stove.

"Manilla," Katie asked sharply, "Why didn't you put on your coat when you went for water?"

"Didn't wear one," Manilla admitted apologetically. "Annie told me to, but I didn't."

"Oh—" Katie was taken back. A wrap, even a light one, would help. If the children were protected a little more against the cold, she wouldn't have to keep so much fire going. And the smaller the fire, the longer the fuel would last.

"I ain't c-cold," Manilla declared, vainly trying to still the chattering of her teeth.

If only there was something for Manilla to put on. Frail as she was, she might get sick from exposure. Katie looked around her, saw the flag hanging behind Mr. Palmer's desk. Action was almost as quick as thought. Katie walked to the front of the room and took it down from its place. She shook it, and a smell of dust filled the room. Then she folded it, making a three-cornered shawl. This she took back to Manilla, while the others watched, round-eyed.

"Wrap this around you," Katie said.

"Oh, Katie—" Manilla's shocked voice filled the room. "Ought I?"

"Go ahead—it's all right."

Manilla still hesitated, evidently preferring death to disloyalty.

"Manilla," Katie told her sternly, hoping she would find the right words, would overcome the child's reluctance without diminishing her respect for her country's symbol, "Manilla—it's like—like a soldier, coming to your rescue if the Indians were here. Put it on!"

Since Katie felt that way about it, Manilla seemed to have no further doubts. She wrapped the flag around her thin shoulders.

Katie, seeing her, resisted an impulse to smile. It was slightly ridiculous to see Manilla Foster, hunched close to the stove, wearing the flag. The little ones looked at her uncertainly, as if maybe they should stand up and sing the national anthem. But Manilla stopped shivering, and a little color came into her face. Watching her, Katie knew her idea had been all right.

The wind lashed the room. It shook the schoolhouse to its very foundations, as if maybe it would send it rolling across the country like the tumbleweed "horses" the children had been playing with at noon. Noon—only a few hours away, but a world away in time.

Hearing the wind, Billy began to whimper a little. Softly, as if he didn't want to make any trouble, even when he was no longer able to control his fear. The sound tore at Katie's heart. Up until now she had been able to do the necessary things—start the fire, get the coal, send Manilla for water, find a wrap for her. But this new thing, this panic among the children, she wasn't sure she could meet, for by now Billy's fright had caught the hearts of the others, and all four of the small ones were crying.

It was a panic in which Katie would have liked very much to join; could have joined with good reason, for she knew better than any of them the dangerous nature of the situation in which they were placed. The storm could last a couple of days. These Texas Panhandle blizzards had been known to drag out their fury that long. But it also could be over by morning—the worst of it, that was. In the meanwhile, they were indoors, and there was coal and water. They would not really suffer. All she could do now was to keep the others from fear. As much as she could, she must. She saw them looking at her, her own fears mirrored in her face. Inspiration came to her.

"Let's play a game," she suggested.

"What?" they asked. But their faces brightened a little, and the whimpering stopped.

Once when the Pierce children were out bone gathering, they had thought that they saw Indians. Actually, it was only bear grass, whose tall spikes they had mistaken for the feathers on war bonnets. Melinda had said then that they must play a game, pretending not to notice. And they had played. Now there was real danger, not fancied. And Melinda was not here to keep them going—only Katie, who had never had enough courage even for herself, and who must now find it for all of them.

"I," she began, and then hesitated, trying to think of something that would be both active and easy. "I think follow-the-leader would be good. Like this— just do what I do—"

Do what I do, Katie was thinking. That's the way it's going to be. From now until help comes, that's what they'll do. For a moment the thought made her dizzy, and then she pushed it aside, knowing that she, as well as the children, would be better off if she kept busy.

She went to the middle aisle. "Follow me," she ordered. They fell in line docilely, looked to her for further instruction. She started to walk; they walked after her. This was slow, not much fun, really. She broke into a run; there was the sound of running feet following her. My goodness, the Pierce children were never allowed to run in the house. The very daring of it gave Katie a sense of excitement. That, and the exercise, started her blood rushing through her veins, made her feel better. And, as she might have known, the children's spirits soared with her own growing confidence.

They ran up and down, around and around. Finally Katie circled back to the stove.

"Let's rest awhile," she suggested.

They sat down once more. The light was very dim by now, almost gone entirely. For the first time Katie remembered that night would bring darkness. A long, endless time of darkness as well as cold. Against the cold she had a weapon; the darkness would have to be endured.

"I'm hungry, Katie," Carolyn said timidly. It wasn't like her to be timid about anything. But the growing darkness, the wail of the wind outside, the strangely unfamiliar schoolroom, now that they were alone in it at a time when they had never before been in school, all had combined to frighten the child.

"Well, go get your lunch boxes—" Katie began. And then something else came to her. If they were here for a long time, they mustn't eat all their lunch at once. They must save it for breakfast tomorrow, and maybe even for dinner. Perhaps even beyond that.

"Manilla," she asked, "did you have any of your lunch left?"

"Two fried pies and a couple of biscuits and meat," Manilla said. "Annie fixed more than I wanted."

"And the others—Babe and Cissy—"

"We carried ours in the same bucket," Manilla said. "That's what we had left."

"And you, Meg?"

"I didn't have a thing left, Katie. I was just real hungry today."

One less than she had hoped for!

"I got a boiled egg," Billy put in. "I don't like 'em very much, and I left mine. And a couple of apples."

At least that was something.

"I tell you what we'll do," Katie said, thinking fast. "Carolyn and I will get our lunch boxes and we'll all have a picnic right here."

A picnic! That promise, for the moment, diverted them from thinking of their own lunches.

"I'll get our boxes, Katie," Carolyn volunteered.

She was gone only a moment, and when she came back, she looked excited and important.

"Guess what, Katie," she said, "Mr. Palmer's lunch box was there. And Reilly's and the boys'."

Mr. Palmer's was fine. But Katie couldn't face the prospect of eating anything that came from the Adams' place. She'd have to be a lot hungrier than she was now to do that!

"I'll get mine, too," Billy offered.

Katie thought quickly. It would be better, she decided, to eat less food, more often. "No," she said, "Carolyn and I will have the picnic now. A little bit later you and Manilla can have one. Won't that be fun?"

"Sure," Billy agreed.

Katie opened her own lunch box. She divided the

bread, the meat, and the cookies into six parts, then put them on a desk. "Come on and help yourselves," she said.

They filed by, each helping himself. To their everlasting credit, they did not make even one remark about the smallness of the portions.

"It's like a party," Carolyn said, "a very elegant party."

The wind caught at the corner of the schoolhouse. This was not a party. It was a hard and dangerous time.

"Eat your lunch," Katie told the others. "I have to put more coal on the fire."

Only Carolyn eyed her sharply. She had noticed that Katie hadn't counted herself in the division. She followed her sister back to the stove.

"Katie," she said softly, "here—eat some of mine. I don't want all of this. Honest, I don't."

Katie started to say she wasn't hungry, that Carolyn must eat it herself. And then she remembered something. Even now she wished she had stayed up that night to help Melinda. Maybe afterwards, Carolyn would like to feel she had really helped.

She took a bite of each of Carolyn's portions.

"Thank you, Carolyn," she said. "That was very sweet of you."

The night wore on. The wind continued to howl. The darkness was complete, save for such times as Katie opened the stove to put in more coal.

"I'm cold, Katie—"

"We'll run around the schoolroom again. Only,

this time take off your coats. You won't need them while you are exercising."

Around and around they went, carefully, so as not to bump into a desk.

"I'm hungry, Katie—"

"We'll get your lunch box this time, Manilla— yours and Billy's."

"How'll we know ours?"

"I'll open the stove door, so you can see."

They brought the lunch boxes; Katie made the division. This time she included herself, not wanting to stint Carolyn, who would certainly offer part of her portion if Katie failed to keep any for herself.

"I'm sleepy, Katie—"

"Sit in the back desks and put your heads down. Maybe you can sleep a little—"

They made their way to the back desks, tried to do as she had told them.

"My goodness, Katie," Manilla Foster complained, "it's like sleeping on a high, hard rock."

Katie was aware of Carolyn, standing close to her.

"I'll sleep after a while," she said. "I'm not a bit tired, Katie, really I'm not. I'll stay here with you. You aren't going to sleep, are you?"

"Not for a while, Carolyn. I want to keep the fire going."

"I'll help," Carolyn told her.

"That will be fine, Carolyn," Katie said, feeling a quick shame, remembering that she had thought she would have no one to turn to, no one to help her. She had lumped Carolyn in with the other little ones. Carolyn wasn't acting like a baby at all.

"I couldn't get along without you, Carolyn," Katie said quickly.

"Oh, Katie—thank you. Thank you, Katie—"

Katie couldn't see Carolyn, but she was pretty sure there were tears of pleasure in the child's eyes, even as she felt tears pricking at her own lids.

That's sisters, Katie thought. They stick together. They don't have to be grown-up before they start. I guess they are just born sticking together.

Katie woke suddenly from what was really only a half-doze. She jumped up quickly; the room was very cold. Maybe she had let the fire go out! She threw open the stove door; no, there were plenty of glowing coals left. She put on a little kindling, though, and then some more coal. The fire blazed. Warmth filled the cold room.

The children stirred. And someone coughed—a quick, hollow sound which cut straight through Katie's heart. What if one of them got sick! She pushed the thought from her.

They lifted their heads; they stood up.

"I'm cold—" Babe said.

"I'm hungry—" Meg added.

"Let's play follow-the-leader again," Katie told them.

Without question, they stumbled into the aisle. The exercise seemed to do them all good. And, miraculously, once they were back in their places around the stove, Katie noticed something she had been too occupied to see before.

It was getting light outside, even though not much

more than a grayness, where all had been completely black before. The wind had died down, and morning was coming.

Morning was coming, but the light that came into the room was a strange grayed down whiteness. It was not so much light as a feeling of being in a white bowl—sides, top, bottom, closing down on them. Katie looked toward the windows, trying to see the reason for it. And then she knew.

The snow was banked up against the windows, almost to the top of them. A solid wall of whiteness, drifted hard against the panes. Carolyn had followed Katie's glance.

"My goodness, Katie," she marveled, "we're in an igloo!"

"What's an igloo?" Meg asked.

"A snow house," Carolyn explained with lofty con-descension. "They make it out of—well, out of snow!"

"We're in an igloo," Billy chanted. The others joined him, thinking this some sort of adventure. Only Katie did not join. She could see what this meant.

If the snow lay that high, they were indeed in a snow house. And that meant they could not get out. And they needed to, because there was only a little coal left. Enough for one more replenishment if she were reckless; two, if she were careful. And there were only the Adams children's lunches left. Coal for two more times; food for possibly two lunches, if they ate lightly. This—and outside the snow lay deep and high.

Katie thought hard. Should she let the children eat now, or save the food for later.

"I'm hungry, Katie," Billy said.

"I tell you what," Katie suggested, "why don't we run around the room first, and then I'll tell you a story, and then we'll eat."

So they ran around the room, and as always, felt the better for the exercise. Then Katie gathered them close to the stove and began a story. It was all about princes mounted on white chargers who went about slaying ogres and dragons. And there was a princess, too, high up in a tower, waiting for the rescue.

In a way, she thought, she was a princess. She was in a tower, imprisoned by a cruel, wicked dragon, which was snow. The ogre—cold—was out there, too, waiting to grab her. She put more into the telling of the story than she realized, for suddenly she looked at Meg, to see tears were running down her little cheeks.

"Oh, Katie—" she begged. "Go on—go on quick and get the prince there!"

"Oh, honey, don't cry," Katie said. "He got there and saved the princess. Now let's eat again."

Katie opened the Adams children's lunch pails. She was surprised to see that they were clean inside, very clean. But they were also sparse. Reilly had one by herself, the boys shared the other. In each was an identical lunch.

Some cornbread, spread with molasses. Some fat meat.

Just that, and nothing more.

Suddenly Katie remembered how the Adams children always went off by themselves to eat. The other children thought they were being hateful. They weren't, not at all. They were ashamed to open their lunches before those more fortunate children who had hard boiled eggs and biscuits and fried pies and apples—maybe even, now and then, a piece of pull-taffy, or even cake or cookies. The others ate together, trading bites, discussing their own lunches. But the Adamses withdrew in pride and shame, eating their own cornbread and molasses and cold fat meat.

Katie divided the lunches evenly, not neglecting herself. She had expected the children to protest at the meagerness of the fare, but they said nothing. Perhaps, she thought, they are thinking the same thing I am. Perhaps they are feeling sorry for the Adams children, just the way I am.

Maybe embarrassment made Hank and Cy act the way they did. Maybe they really wanted people to like them, but didn't know how to go about making friends. Maybe they hated to wear ragged clothes, and walk to school when others rode, and stay off by themselves to eat their lunch. Katie ate her cornbread thoughtfully.

Katie put the scraps back into the lunch pails carefully, as if she were handling something very precious, as indeed she was. At best, this was their last meal. She would save it for late afternoon. Maybe by that time someone would come for them. And once more she remembered that no one knew they were marooned there. Wherever Mr. Palmer was, he'd believe them safe at Annie's. And Annie wouldn't be too concerned, believing that Mr. Palmer was with them and would look after them. No—Katie couldn't hope for rescue too soon; and besides, one look at those drifts outside the window made her know that rescue, even if people wished to do it, would not be easy.

Panic gripped her for a moment, then she brushed it aside quickly. She mustn't let the children know her feelings. She mustn't—she mustn't—

"Katie," Meg broke in on her thoughts, almost timidly, "I— I'm cold—"

"We'll run around the room a while," Katie said.

And so they ran around, back and forth, until they were breathing hard and fast once more, until their blood was circulating. And when they sat down, Katie went back to look at the stove. The fire was quite low; no longer could she delay putting on some coal, if she wanted it to catch fire. She put on all that was there. A very small portion it was.

There was no way of overlooking the truth any longer. The last bit of coal was in the stove. And the cold was creeping into the room—relentlessly, without mercy. It slipped in like some stealthy, cruel animal which could afford to takes its time, to wait, knowing that eventually it would have its prey. The children were aware of its coming, and a sort of terror seemed to be coming over them. Now they did not mention the cold, but their little faces were gray and pinched with it. They were careful not even to look into the direction of the stove, of the empty bucket.

But Katie was aware of their thoughts, more than if they had complained. What was she going to do?

Even with their wraps on, even if she kept the children moving, how long could they endure cold? Hunger seemed unimportant now. People had been known to go without food for a long time, and be little the worse for it afterwards. But all the terrible stories she had heard of people freezing to death came back to her now, flooding her with a panic she found it hard to push aside. All along her worries had been about what *might* happen. Now the thing had happened. They were marooned here, and there was no more fuel!

She looked at the children, knowing that, even if they got through the day, night would bring still greater cold, a cold that would give them no quarter.

"Katie," Billy said firmly, "it is getting cold in here. We need some more coal."

It was as if he had put into words the terror all of them were feeling. Suddenly Meg began to whimper, her fright too much to contain. And then Manilla, huddled by the dying fire with the flag of her country clutched around her, coughed. It was a deep, tearing cough, all the more painful because she tried so valiantly to suppress it.

That settled it. Katie would have to manage some way to get more fuel. But how, with the snow higher than her head between her and the coal shed?

There was only one way. She must shovel her way through.

The implement was easy to come by. A shovel stood in the corner behind the stove. Meant to be used in putting in fuel, taking out ashes, it was still large enough to serve as a snow shovel under ordinary circumstances. But this was certainly not ordinary. Still, it was the best that Katie had, and she would have to use it. She picked it up in one hand, took the bucket in the other. She walked toward the door.

"What are you going to do, Katie?" Carolyn

asked.

"I'm going for coal," she answered, and she wondered at the way she spoke, as simply as if she were going to walk out into a sunlit schoolyard and maybe look at some flowers blooming there. No hint of the fear that was hers.

"I'll go with you," Carolyn said.

"No—" Katie wasn't going to allow Carolyn out in this snow. That was final. She would do this thing alone. Strange, but Carolyn did not question her—not at all.

Katie opened the door, and there before her was a wall of whiteness. The wind had packed the snow solidly against the door, so solidly that, even with it opened, scarcely any snow came into the room.

"It's over your head," Carolyn wailed. "Oh, Katie—how can you get through it?"

"I'll try," Katie said, "I'll try—"

The next half hour was a nightmare to Katie—a nightmare set in whiteness, bound by cold, shot through with fatigue and terror and uncertainty. Little Katie Pierce, pitted against cold, against death itself, not only for herself, but for those others, those children left in her care. She put her shovel into the snow, lifted a bit of it, tossed it aside, high up over her head. It was like scooping water out of the ocean with a teaspoon. She couldn't do it. She couldn't—A bit of snow out of the way. A mountain still to be removed. A shovelful—another mountain ahead of her. Her breath was coming fast. Her arms were aching. She was trembling all over. But she kept on. A shovelful out of the way—another. . . . Another. . . . Another. . . .

And then something happened. Katie could not believe it. It was a cruel jest. It was like seeing a mirage when you are dying of thirst in the desert.

No, it was not a mirage. She had come to the edge of the drift. Before her the snow lay not more than a foot or so deep, between her and the coal shed.

The bitter cold was eating at her now. In spite of the exercise, it was numbing her, cutting through her light wraps as if she were dressed in the thinnest summer clothing. She stumbled on toward the coal shed, conscious as she went that she was the only spot of brightness in a world of white. Nothing was showing up in its true colors—grass or schoolhouse or yard or anything. All was white—all except herself, moving along in her red coat and hood.

She filled her bucket with the precious blackness of the fuel. She struggled back through the path she had made for herself, across the place where it became nothing more than a narrow tunnel through the deep drift. She went inside the room, put the coal on the fire. She dumped what was left on the floor and started back once more.

"I'm going with you," Carolyn said in a voice that was not to be denied.

"I'm going too—" the children all cried.

Katie tried to say no. But, why not? Now it was only a sort of game they would play—playing in the first snow of the season. Now they could go out if they wanted to, for, when they came back, warmth would be waiting for them.

"All right," Katie said, "you can all go. You can each

bring back a little coal with you."

Isn't it strange, Katie was thinking as they filed through the snow, that this time it seems like an adventure. No fright, no terror, no struggle. They might have been playing a game, in spite of the bitter cold. The first time she had gone, it had been no adventure, though; that first time was no game!

And now they were back in the schoolroom once more, but this time was different. A fire was burning; there was warmth. Katie would not let herself think of that other thing—that there was no food.

"What are we going to do now, Katie?" Billy asked.

"We'll play school," she said.

"Who'll be teacher?"

"I will," Katie answered. At any other time she would have trembled at her presumption.

They played school for fifteen minutes maybe, she couldn't tell. One lost count of time in a situation like this.

Suddenly Katie turned her head, listening. Did she really hear something? Or did she just wish it so hard that she thought she did? Across the distance she strained her ears; above the children's chatter she sent out her mind and heart to listen.

No—someone was coming! Horsemen. There could be no mistake. Katie began to tremble; her knees turned to jelly. She started toward the door, thought she could never make the trip. She could feel the children's eyes on her, the question in them. Was there—yes, there was! Katie flung open the door, letting in a great rush of cold and snow. And then she saw, just at the edge of the school yard, two men. They were so muffled up, it was impossible to see who they were. But there was no mistaking those two horses.

Nick and Herman, riding Jig and Jingo, were coming toward the schoolhouse.

There they were, just as Katie had promised Meg. The princes were coming to the rescue!

Chapter 11

"KATIE, I'LL SET the table for you," Dick offered. "Long as I'm home, I might as well help."

Mostly Dick fussed about having to do anything around the house. "Squaw's work," he'd grumble. But now he had offered, and Katie let him. He did it very nicely, too. When the meal was on the table, he and Bert ate it quietly, making none of the usual comments on Katie's cooking. After it was finished and the dishes washed, Bert asked politely, "Would you like to play dominoes, Katie?"

This was as amazing as Dick's offering to set the table. Neither of the boys liked playing dominoes with her. She was too slow about seeing combinations that would "make something" for her side; she got confused and threw away obvious plays. Sometimes she could beg them into it, but here was Bert offering when Katie hadn't even asked.

Ever since the blizzard they had been like this. Very polite, very helpful.

The blizzard had been such a bad one that Papa and the twins hadn't been able to come back from

235

Amarillo until Tuesday. Then they got the story of what had happened.

Part of it came from Nick and Herman.

"Got to thinking we ought to look in on your stock Friday, as well as Saturday," Nick said. "Storm started while we were at your place, so we holed in."

"Good," Papa said.

That's the way people did out here—stopped wherever a storm overtook them, whether it was with strangers or friends, whether people were at home or not.

"Next day, when things sort of cleared up a little, we knew we'd better be hitting for the Ranch. And I'll be dog-gone if we didn't see a bunch of kids playing out in the snow in the school yard."

"Yes sir-ee," Herman said. "And we moseyed over, just to see whether some kids had been caught there."

"And there they were," Nick grinned, "just having a regular picnic."

He made it sound very simple. Nothing about the struggle through the snow to fill the coal bucket, or the last bit of the lunches gone, even to the Adams children's cornbread and cold bacon. Katie smiled at Nick, grateful for his doing this. Even now, she couldn't let herself think too much about it.

"I think they didn't really want to leave," Herman teased.

Didn't want to leave! Katie had felt she couldn't get out of that schoolhouse fast enough. And yet she had been obliged to stay there with the children while Nick rode to Annie's for extra wraps and blankets. Herman stayed with her, keeping a fine hot fire going, joking with them to make the time pass. Before long, there was Nick back, laden with wraps and overshoes and so on until he looked like a huge, fat pack rat. Katie helped get the children into the wraps, and then the procession took off, "looking like a bunch of gypsies," as Nick said.

Certainly they made a motley-looking crew, so bundled up in wraps they could scarcely sit on their mounts. Katie and Carolyn rode Cleveland who, though stiff and hungry, had not really suffered because he had been in the shed. Then came Meg on her own little pony, who had also been inside the shelter. Cissy Foster was riding behind her. Nick took Billy in his arms; Manilla rode back of Herman who had Babe in his arms. When they finally got to the Fosters, Annie took them in, scarcely able to ask questions fast enough.

She could hardly believe what they told her— about Cy's broken arm, and how Mr. Palmer took him home, leaving the children by themselves because there was no other way to work things.

"My goodness," Annie marveled, "don't tell me you kids were in that schoolhouse all by yourselves! If I had known that, I *would* have been worried crazy. As it was, I felt bad enough. All I could do was tell myself Mr. Palmer would take care of you. And he wasn't even there!" Her voice trailed off, as if the wonder of it was too great for her even to contemplate.

A twinge of guilt caught at Katie's heart. She felt responsible for Annie's worry. Had it not been for her, they would have been safe at the Fosters' before ever the storm hit.

"It sure was lucky you didn't try to come here, Katie," Annie told her. "You would all have frozen to death on the way."

Katie could not bring herself to answer that.

"Katie was most resourceful," Carolyn said complacently.

Strange that, while they were shut in by the storm, Carolyn had not used any big words at all. Now that they were safe at Annie's, eating Annie's good food, warmed by Annie's good fire, she was once more talking big and important. "She made a fire," Carolyn went on, "and she carried in coal before the storm got severe."

"You helped," Katie said quickly. "And Manilla got in a bucket of water."

"Yes, but you told us to," Carolyn went on. "And," she added, "she divisioned our lunches. She made us play we were having a picnic."

"And when we got cold," Manilla added, apparently determined to get into the story, too, "she made us play games."

"It started our blood circulationing," Carolyn explained wisely.

"Looks like Katie sure saved the day," Nick remarked.

Katie flushed.

"You all helped," she said, "every last one of you."

Papa and the twins heard these stories, from Annie, from the cowboys, from Carolyn. Dennis, too, had his contribution to make when he stopped off on his way back to Amarillo. He and Mr. Palmer had been caught by the blizzard at the Adams' place and had to spend the night there.

"Oh, gosh!" Bert exclaimed. "That must have been pretty awful."

"I've seen better." Dennis grinned. "But there was no way out of it. Hank and I got to their place just as the storm broke."

Katie was remembering those lunch baskets and finding in her heart pity rather than blame for the Adams boys.

"How is Cy's arm?" she asked.

"It will get along fine. Clean break—no complications. When the arm comes out of the sling, he'll be as good as new."

Katie thought home had never looked so wonderful as it did when Papa came for her and Carolyn, taking them back. He had a good fire burning and things were neat and straight. He and the twins had cooked a big meal.

"But not as fine as you can cook, Katie," the twins said. They seemed a little embarrassed and ill-at-ease around her—as if she were a stranger they were meeting for the first time. She herself became embarrassed, just seeing how they acted. It had been like that ever since she got home, up until right now, when Bert was offering to play dominoes with her.

"Oh, Bert!" she cried, flushing with pleasure. "I'd *love* it. If you are sure you don't mind," she added hastily.

"No—we don't mind," he told her.

"I'll make some molasses taffy to eat while we

play," she offered.

"Sure," Bert said. No teasing, such as she had halfway expected, saying they didn't want their teeth pulled out.

She made the taffy, set it in dishes outside in the snow to cool. When it was cool enough, the boys brought it in, and the four of them started pulling. The twins were best at it—they would stretch the mass out and out until Katie couldn't see how it stayed together. Then they would slap it back smartly and start all over. Katie was no good at all at pulling, not even as successful as Carolyn. She got all tangled up and Dick obligingly helped her, again without the usual teasing. By and by the candy was hard enough to put on plates. Katie took a knife and rapped the back of it sharply across the lengths of candy, dividing them into pieces small enough to put into their mouths easily. Katie tasted one. It was wonderful—spicy and sweet, but not too sweet. It melted slowly on her tongue, tasting more delicious by the minute.

She put a big plate of the taffy on the table, and then the four of them sat down to play dominoes.

"Remember, Katie," Bert, who was her partner, spoke patiently, "if you have a five-four or a six-three, you play it. You can make something that way."

Katie, getting bothered as she always did, looked her dominoes over carefully. She did not see either of these, so got out a two-three instead. She started to play it.

"My goodness, the other way around, you little nin—" Bert stopped himself quickly. "If you put it the other way, you can make five, Katie," he finished quietly.

She hastily rearranged the number. The game went on. At the end, Katie and Bert were ahead. She had hoped this would make him want to play another game, but instead he said he thought that was enough for one evening and began to stack the dominoes into the box.

"Katie," he said, not looking at her as he talked, "how come you decided to stay there in the schoolhouse instead of trying to make it home?"

"It was so dark outside," she said hesitantly. "The cloud, I mean—"

"Sure, I know. But scared as you are of clouds, I would have thought you might have tried to make it to Annie's."

She didn't answer. How could she tell him that she had stayed because she was afraid of storms—that this one looked too black to venture out in. Her fear had kept her there. And there was something else. It was something no one had mentioned yet—the reason why she and the children were still at school when, had they obeyed Mr. Palmer's orders, they might have been safe at Annie's before the storm hit. Katie turned her mind from the thought—the remembrance of the cold and the scanty lunches and the fear.

"You were mighty smart, Katie," Dick told her gravely. He acted as if he were talking to a grown woman. No hint of teasing in his voice now.

"You sure were," Bert agreed.

Something kept coming back to Katie, after she was home—something she could not forget. Nights, after she had gone to bed, it danced before her; days, when she was working around the house. In a way, it helped to blot out the memory of the ordeal she had undergone in the schoolhouse. She remembered that with something between sadness and exaltation. Sometimes she felt she did not understand it at all; at other times, she was sure she knew exactly the meaning of it all, only she could not quite put it into words.

Annie had finished feeding the ravenous children, after they had got into the house. Nothing had ever tasted quite so good as Annie's food; nothing had ever looked so wonderful as that house; no one had ever seemed so beautiful as Annie, concerned and yet happy to have them back again. There was a richness, a content in just being where she was—a sense of safety, too, and happiness. Now she had sent the small ones off to bed, with hot bricks at their feet, and she and Katie were sitting at the kitchen table, talking like adults.

"Here," Annie said, pushing a piece of pie toward Katie. She reached for the coffee pot, poured a cupful. She lifted the cream pitcher, let the yellow cream flow into the cup. "Drink this," she said. "It will be good for you."

That was all it took to make Katie feel as grown-up as Annie herself.

"Now," Annie said, "tell me about it. Did you say Mr. Palmer took Cy home before noon?"

"No," Katie told her, feeling as if she were discussing another age, another world. "They left a little while before the storm came."

"You mean—" Annie broke in, "*he* went with Cy Adams in a spring wagon just ahead of the storm!"

"Yes—" Katie answered.

Annie jumped up quickly. Her face was pale, as if Mr. Palmer was the center of all her world.

"They may have been caught in it," Annie said. "Oh, Katie—if I had only known while Nick and Herman were here, I would have sent them—"

Then, even as she was speaking, Mr. Palmer himself walked into the room.

Annie turned quickly to face him. Her eyes were wide and dark; she seemed to sway a little on her feet. She looked at Mr. Palmer as if he were a ghost—a figure she had never expected to see again. He looked back at her, almost as strangely. They moved toward each other slowly, as if they were not really conscious of making any motion at all.

Then Annie stretched out her hands. Her face was glowing.

"Bill—" she said softly, her voice rich with happiness, with relief. "Bill—I thought—" Her voice died out into a whisper.

Mr. Palmer was reaching toward her. Just then there was a chorus of shrill yells from the bedroom and Bill and Sue came rushing out together.

"Papa—Papa—" they screamed. "You're here!"

Mr. Palmer turned slowly toward them. He looked like a man who was awakening from a dream. The children threw themselves upon him. He reached down and put his arms around them. Across their heads, he looked at Annie, and when he spoke it was almost formally.

"Now Miss Annie," he said, "tell me what happened."

Annie cleared her throat. It was as if her voice came from a long distance, and there was no brightness in her face at all. Instead, it was hurt and stricken—the face of a child who has been punished for something which was not her fault at all.

"You'll have to ask Katie," she said. "She was just getting ready to tell me—"

That was the thing Katie kept remembering. It was all very clear the day Annie came over to see how things were going, now that Katie was back home.

"Making out all right, Katie?" Annie asked.

"Yes, thank you," Katie replied. She wanted to ask Annie the same question, but someway she felt she knew the answer. Annie didn't look right at all. The hurt was still on her face—and a sort of hopeless look, as if maybe she had given up something she felt she never should have wanted in the first place.

"Have you seen Mr. Palmer?" Katie asked, not at all sure herself why she did.

"No—" Annie said. Then she added, "Now, Katie, you're big enough to catch on to things. You saw how I acted that day when he—when he walked in. I thought he had frozen to death, maybe, and I was just so glad to see him that I forgot myself. I ran to him like a ninny. I can hardly let myself think of it now—the way I acted, and all."

"I don't see why," Katie declared, honestly amazed.

"I'll tell you why," Annie said. "I was just throwing myself at him, and I'm not for the likes of him. Me—why Katie, I never have been to school a day in my life. And he's so smart. He's been to college, and all. He needs a—" Annie hesitated, as if she would not even let herself say the word that was so clearly in her mind. "He needs someone smart," she finished miserably.

"Annie," Katie said firmly, "you're smart. Smart as anyone I know. Smarter than most. And you're—" Katie hesitated, wishing for Mama or Melinda, or even Papa, who would know exactly what to say to Annie, to make her see what sort of a person she was. "You're wonderful, Annie," Katie finished lamely.

Annie laughed a little.

"That's just because you love me, Katie," she said. She was silent for a moment, and then she stood up, briskly and with purpose.

"Now I ought to be ashamed. I sit here talking about myself, and what I really came for was to cook up some things for you. Why, you must be worn out, after that time in the schoolhouse."

When Katie tried to protest, she said, "Now see here, Katie, I can't do enough for you. Remember—Manilla and Babe and Cissy were there with you. You saved their lives, too, and I'm grateful. Let's get at that baking now."

The house was clean and there was a smell of cooking in the air when Annie left. A cake—the spices filling the kitchen with richness—sat on the table. Beans bubbled in a pan, a roast was cooking in the oven. It felt like home; like a place some woman loved. And then it was that Mr. Palmer walked in.

"Why Katie," he said, "how good this all is. My, you've grown to be a fine cook and homemaker."

"I didn't do it," Katie said. "Annie was here. She cleaned the house and did the cooking."

"Oh, Annie—" Mr. Palmer said.

Funny, but his face looked just as Annie's had a little earlier. A little sad, very wistful—as if he, too, wanted something he knew he could never have.

"She's a fine person," he said.

"Yes," Katie agreed, wanting to say more, afraid to break the spell.

Suddenly he turned to her.

"You were there that day I came in, Katie," he said. "You are big enough to understand what was about to happen." They were almost Annie's words.

Katie sat still, waiting for him to go on.

"She's the finest person I know," he said softly. "I was, well, I was ready to tell her so—to ask her to marry me. And then, in rushed Billy and Sue, and all at once I saw things the way they were. Here I am, ten years older than she is. A man with two children, and not much of a job. What right have I to ask any young girl as fine as Annie to share that sort of a life?"

"That's the sort of life she's used to," Katie said, feeling as if maybe she was talking when she should remain silent. "I mean—looking after children and—well, people—"

"That's it," Mr. Palmer said. "I want to give her something better. She shouldn't have to look after others all the time. She deserves something better. She ought to have ease. She ought to have someone to take care of her."

"I think—" Katie hesitated, feeling as if all of Annie's future lay in what she was going to say—all of Mr. Palmer's, too. Perhaps she ought to keep quiet. Maybe she would only make things worse by talking. . . . She took a deep breath and went on, speaking softly, but with certainty. "I think that is the way Annie likes things," Katie said. "Doing for others, I mean. I think that is what makes her happy."

"How do you know?" Mr. Palmer asked sharply. "Maybe if she ever had things smooth and easy, she'd like that better."

Suddenly Katie was out of patience with him—and with Annie, too, for being so timid and so shy.

"Well," she said crossly, "the least you could do would be go ask *her* how she feels about it!"

Mr. Palmer looked at her strangely. He looked a long time. Then he laughed, a sort of quick, breathless little laugh.

"I'll do it, Katie," he said. "I'm scared to death, but I'll do it."

And off he went. Katie could hear the sound of his horse's feet, going off very swiftly in the distance.

Mr. and Mrs. Cartwright drove over to see Katie.

"My dear little Katie," Mrs. Cartwright said, leaning over to kiss her. "You saved Meg's life. When I think of what you did—" She got out her handkerchief, wiped her eyes.

"Oh, that's nothing—" Katie told her, then blushed furiously, thinking that she sounded as if she felt Meg's life was nothing! "I mean," she went on hastily, "I didn't do anything—"

And then she blushed again, realizing she hadn't helped things one bit.

"Didn't do anything," Mrs. Cartwright protested. "You shouldn't say such a thing. You made those children stay inside, out of the storm, and you kept a fire going, and you rationed the lunches. Why Katie, you were a heroine."

"You were a real smart girl, Katie," Mr. Cartwright told her. He turned to Papa. "You ought to be proud of her, Pierce," he added.

"I am," Papa assured him quietly.

"Anyway," Mrs. Cartwright went on, "all of us are pleased and proud—even those who didn't have children at school that day, so what we've decided to do, Katie, is to have a party honoring you for being so brave and saving the children's lives. It will be at the schoolhouse next Saturday evening, and everyone will come, whether they have children in school or not."

"A party—" Katie repeated. Parties were wonderful. She had been to only a few, and now here was one just for her. And then she remembered the conditions under which it was being given, and all the flavor went out of it.

"Oh, you shouldn't do that," she protested. She blushed again, remembering that she must sound as if she didn't want them to give a party. "I mean—" she said miserably.

"Oh, now you deserve it," the woman told her. "I must go and pass the word around."

She got up and went out of the house, followed by Mr. Cartwright, leaving Katie wondering what to do.

Tell the truth? Explain to everyone why she had

stayed at the schoolhouse when she should have been gone long before the storm struck? Admit that she got so interested in art, was so pleased with her own ability to draw the children, that she stayed on and on, oblivious of the passing of time? Explain that she stayed, not solely out of a desire to protect the children, but because of her own fear of storms? She had not been brave and foresighted, as these people were giving her credit for being. She had been first careless, then cowardly. And now they were planning a party to reward her!

She went around the house, very quiet, very thoughtful.

"Are you sick, Katie?" Papa asked. "You didn't take cold there in the schoolhouse, did you?"

"No, Papa," Katie said, not looking at him.

Papa was silent for awhile. Then he continued thoughtfully, "Katie, if there's something troubling you, you can tell me about it—if you want to, that is."

"Oh, Papa!" Katie fled to him, wailing. "Oh, Papa!"

She flung herself into his arms, and he patted her shoulder gently. He didn't say anything; he just let her cry. Finally she stopped, just a little.

"All right," Papa said, "now go wash your face and then sit down there in Mama's rocking chair and tell me what is wrong."

Katie went obediently and washed her face. She caught a look at herself in the mirror over the washstand. She looked awful—her hair all mussed, her dress twisted. She ran a comb through her hair, she pulled her clothes neat and straight. This done, she went back, sat down in the chair and took a long breath.

"It's the party," she told him, catching her breath in a little half-sob.

"I thought you liked parties," Papa said, obviously puzzled.

"I do," Katie admitted, ready to cry again. "It's the reason why they are giving this one. It's awful, Papa! I wasn't brave—I was scared. And before that, I was stupid, or we never would have been caught in the schoolhouse to begin with."

"Oh, I see." Papa pulled at his lip. "Now suppose you tell me all about it."

So she went back to the very first, to the reason why they had stayed so late at school after Mr. Palmer had told her to see that they went home. And how, when she had seen the cloud at last, she was afraid to go out into the storm it promised.

"That was it, Papa. I can't bear for them to give a party for me because I was wise and brave. I wasn't—I wasn't either one. It's the way I told you—I was just stupid first, and after that, scared."

Papa was silent a long time. Finally he began to speak, softly, as if maybe he was thinking the matter through as he went along.

"It isn't stupid to get so interested in something worthwhile that you forget the passage of time," he said.

Katie looked at him quickly.

"Nor is it bad to be scared," Papa went on. "I rather suspect that many of our greatest heroes—perhaps most of them—were scared half to death when they performed their heroic deeds. The point is, when the time came, you thought of others and not yourself."

Katie was quiet, considering his words.

"You rationed the food—you kept the fire going—you made the children exercise when they were cold. You kept their courage high. No, Katie—I am inclined to believe as the others do—you were a brave little girl. All the more so because you *were* frightened."

"But it was all my fault in the first place. I shouldn't have stayed when Mr. Palmer told me to see that the children went home as soon as the schoolhouse was cleared up."

"Yes," Papa admitted gravely, "that was wrong. But it is also wrong to keep on worrying about your mistakes."

Katie looked at him, honestly puzzled.

"You have to go ahead, Katie," he told her earnestly, "and do the best you can to correct the mistake. When you've done that, you must stop worrying about the matter, or feeling ashamed. That's being both weak and foolish."

"I wasn't any braver than the others," she told her father. "They did what I told them to. All night long, they did just what I said. They ought to have a party, too."

"Maybe they were as brave as you," Papa agreed. "But you were the one who had the foresight, and the judgment, to give the orders. You do have an idea, though. I think the party *should* be for all of them, as well as for you. I'll mention it to Mrs. Cartwright."

A happy light burst across Katie's face. A party for all of them, for every last one of them who saw that awful night through!

"Oh, Papa," she cried, "thank you!"

"And another thing, Katie," Papa went on gravely, "remember that gratitude is a lovely thing to give. Don't deprive these people of the privilege of showing it to you. Now I'll go see Mrs. Cartwright."

"Well, thank goodness, it fits fine," Melinda said.

She stood back to get a better look at the new red dress she had made for Katie to wear to the party.

"Annie wrote me what was going on," she had explained when she arrived, the day before, "and I remembered how nice you looked in my blue dress, so I just got some material and made you one like it. It's just fine, all but the hem. I'll run that up in a hurry."

"I'm going to look very pretty in my dress, too," Carolyn announced complacently.

Carolyn's dress was Katie's best, left over from last winter. She had outgrown it. Carolyn didn't mind inheriting it; on the contrary, she seemed very pleased.

"It makes me feel quite mature, Melinda," Carolyn explained gravely. "Just think—all you had to do to it was shorten it."

"That's right, Carolyn," Melinda assured her, threading her needle as she spoke. "You're growing up, all right."

Katie could understand how Carolyn felt. That's exactly how she used to react to getting one of Melinda's hand-me-downs—as if the simple act of slipping into Melinda's out-grown clothes gave her something of her older sister's status in the family. Across Carolyn's head she and Melinda exchanged amused and understanding glances, linking themselves together in an adult relationship entirely delightful to Katie.

"It was awfully sweet of you to make that dress for me, Melinda," she said.

"Oh, I wanted to. I had my own to go by and it wasn't any trouble."

Sewing didn't come easy to Melinda. Katie knew that very well. But she sounded as if she meant what she said—she really hadn't minded making that dress. Papa's words came back to Katie—maybe people did like doing things for others. Sometimes the kindest thing one could do was to accept kindness. It came to her that the people who were giving this party, and Melinda, who was helping in her own way, were the ones who were having the really good time.

And another thing. It wasn't easy for Melinda and Dennis to drive out here, just to bring the dress and go to the party. Katie hadn't expected them, but now that they were here, she didn't know how she could have seen it through without Melinda.

"I'm glad you came for the party, Melinda," she said.

"My goodness, Katie," Melinda declared, "I wouldn't have missed it for anything."

She was quiet a moment, and then she went on. "I guess I haven't told you yet, Katie, but I'm just real proud of you. All the time I have been wondering whether I would have got along as well as you did if I had been responsible."

"Oh, Melinda—" Katie's shocked voice cried out, rejecting the very idea Melinda had expressed. "Oh, Melinda—don't talk like that!"

She was too aghast to capture the full flavor of the compliment.

The evening of the party was perfectly beautiful, not really cold at all, and with a moon shining bright as day. It was hard to believe that a short two weeks ago a blizzard had lashed the land.

Papa hitched the team to the spring wagon and Katie and Carolyn, Dennis and Melinda rode with him. The twins decided they would rather go on horseback, which they did, sometimes riding ahead, sometimes dropping back to talk with the ones in the wagon. Katie, smoothing down the folds of her new red dress, felt a sense of adventure. Part of it was the dress, part was the new way Melinda had helped her loop up her curls, part of it was the beauty of the night. And over and above all was the knowledge that, at the end of the journey, something lovely awaited her. A mounting excitement took over so that she was almost giddy with it.

A lot of people had already arrived at the school house by the time the Pierces drove up. The yard was filled with buggies, wagons, buckboards and so on. And a great many riding horses were tied to the fence, proving that most of the boys had preferred, as had the twins, to ride horseback instead of coming with their families. Papa stopped the wagon. Dennis got out and helped Melinda to alight. Then Papa assisted Carolyn and Katie down, as carefully as if they had been grown young ladies.

Manilla Foster met them at the door.

"Oh, Katie," she said, "isn't it fun! A party for us,

like we was special."

Katie scarcely recognized the schoolroom, once she was inside. The desks had all been taken up and placed around the sides of the room, leaving the middle of the floor bare. Up on the platform, where the teacher's desk usually stood, was a long table, probably made of boards, although you couldn't see them, for it was all covered with a cloth. Annie Foster was there, placing plates and bowls on it when they were handed to her. Every few minutes someone came in with a fresh offering.

Mr. Palmer was at the door, greeting people and seeing that the food was taken care of. And, wonder of wonders, Hank Adams was helping him. Katie hardly knew him. He was very clean, and his hair was combed neatly, even if the part was slightly on the bias. But the thing that was changed most was his expression. He didn't look or act like a bully at all, just anxious to please, and maybe a little nervous because he was afraid of making a mistake. At that moment Mrs. Cartwright arrived with her hands full of dishes.

"Here, Hank," Mr. Palmer said matter-of-factly, "take this up to the table, will you?"

Hank took it and started toward the front of the room.

"Oh, ain't Hank doing *nice?*" she heard someone say at her elbow. She turned to face Reilly.

She was wearing the same red dress she had worn to the pie supper, and she was carrying the glove which, evidently, was her badge of correctness.

"Gracious sakes, Katie," Reilly said, "if you ain't gone and got a red dress, just like mine."

Katie's first impulse was to cry out that her lovely new dress wasn't anything in the world like Reilly's home dyed, ill-fitting one. But this she could not do; and did not really want to do. To Reilly, her own dress was just as lovely as Katie's, and Katie would not have things any different.

"Yes," Katie agreed, "they're both red."

"Ma and Pa come tonight," Reilly said proudly. "First time we have been able to get them out to anything."

She waved her hand toward a couple, sitting over in the corner. The woman wore a print dress; the man was clad in overalls. They seemed uneasy and unsure as to how they should act, but they were there and intended to stick things out, anyway.

"You come over here with me, Katie," Reilly said. "I want to introduce you."

Katie followed her.

"Ma, Pa," Reilly said, once they stood before her parents, "this is Katie Pierce. She's my best friend."

Reilly looked at Katie when she said it, a sort of hesitant pride in her face, as if maybe she was afraid Katie was going to deny her claim.

"Hello," Katie said shyly. Something prompted her to reach out and take Reilly's hand as she spoke. A great look of pleasure came over the girl's face. It was almost as if she were saying, "There, I *told* you so!"

Mrs. Adams' face lighted up. Even Katie could see her delight in the moment.

"Oh, howdy," she said. "Reilly's all the time a-talkin' about you. I sure am proud to meet you."

Mr. Adams was equally cordial—and equally

pleased. His eyes kept flicking back and forth to Hank, making his trips to and from the table, bearing the plates of food. In between these times, he would look at Cy, with his arm in a sling, the center of a small group of boys who were doubtless listening with avid interest to his details concerning the setting of the broken bone. It was the first time that Cy had ever had such flattering attention, and he was making the most of it.

Maybe that is what has been the matter all along, Katie was thinking. The Adamses just wanted to feel themselves a part of things and when they couldn't get the right kind of attention, they just went out for whatever they could get. Now here was Cy, holding the interest of the other children with details of his accident, and Hank helping Mr. Palmer, and Reilly claiming Katie as her friend. It was a proud time for the Adams family, all right.

Melinda made a rush up to Annie, standing by the table with the food on it. Annie looked positively beautiful. Her hair was combed softer than usual, and she had on a new dress, made fancy and pretty. She and Melinda threw their arms around each other.

"You look grand, Melinda."

"You look just too pretty for words, yourself, Annie."

Melinda pushed Annie off at arm's length to look at her again. She was right, Katie was thinking. Annie does look pretty—maybe even as pretty as Melinda. It wasn't the dress, or the way she did her hair, either. It was a sort of glow that seemed to cover each separate feature, so that there was a shining look about her.

"Now Annie," Melinda said, half laughing, half

serious, "go ahead—tell me—"

Annie pursed her lips up, looked as if maybe she wasn't going to say a word. Then she smiled, and it was like a light on her face. She leaned over and whispered a few words in Melinda's ear. Melinda looked startled, then delighted.

"You mean—?" Melinda said.

Annie nodded vigorously, and a soft and delicate flush colored her face. Then she leaned over to whisper something else.

"Oh, Annie!" Melinda exclaimed, and kissed her again.

Just at that moment, Mr. Palmer rapped for order, so everyone went down and found a seat, if he could, or just stood up as the men and boys were doing.

He said a few words of welcome, and told the crowd he thought it was a fine idea to have a school get-together. People needed to see each other, know each other better. He hoped everyone there would make it a point to meet everyone else. First they were going to have some games and stunts. They'd start off with charades.

Not a word about anybody's being brave. Not a word about the storm. Papa must have told him, and Katie felt a great relief. And yet, when the charades started, she noticed that the ones in charge were careful to choose those who had been in the schoolhouse the night of the storm. Every one of them was taken first, and given main parts.

She herself helped to act out "mis-under-stand-ing," standing under a chair which someone held over her head. She felt very pretty in her new dress; she was pleased that she was considered a "miss." It was the longest time before Papa guessed the word. And then there were tableaux—Columbus sighting new land, and Washington cutting down the cherry tree, and things like that. Manilla and Carolyn and Meg were seated in a group, to be the three little figures who "hear-no-evil, speak-no-evil, see-no-evil." Carolyn, her hands graceful and lovely across her lips, looked like a real statue. But Manilla, overcome by a wish to see how the act was going over, peeped through her fingers, which were supposed to be covering her eyes, and brought down the suppressed giggles of her audience.

Once these were finished, it was time for refreshments. Then it was that the honor guests really came into their own. All of those children who had spent the night at the school house, with Katie coming first and Billy bringing up the rear, were sent around the table ahead of the rest. There was no doubt, then, that the party was for them.

"Katie, do have a piece of my angel food," Mrs. Cartwright was urging her.

"Katie, I baked this vinegar pie because I knew you loved them," Annie told her.

It seemed that everyone there was anxious for Katie, and those who had shared her experience, to have the best. After them trooped the others. Laughing, pushing good naturedly, helping themselves. Even when everyone had gone back several times, it seemed as though there had scarcely been a dent made in the array of good things to eat.

"Say," Nick suggested, "why don't we dance a while,

and then come back and eat some more?"

The thing must have been planned in advance, for almost as soon as he spoke, someone pushed Mike Farraday out into the center. He was holding his fiddle, ready to start playing. Bub Foster said he'd do the calling.

"Get your partners," he yelled, above the squeaking of Mike's fiddle.

The boys began making their way toward the girls. The twins chose a homesteader girl apiece—two bright, merry looking girls with very dark eyes and curly hair. They were the Drummond sisters, someone said, and looked enough alike to be twins, although they weren't. Mr. Palmer led Annie out on the floor, and she looked even prettier than before. Mr. Foster got Mrs. Foster into the lineup. Nick and Herman also found a couple of girls—Katie supposed they must be some new families who had just moved in, for she had never seen them before. And, as soon as the suggestion had been made, Dennis and Melinda were ready.

Katie slipped over to the benches at the side of the room. Dancing was for the grown-ups, and suddenly she felt very young—as young as Carolyn and Manilla. She tried not to feel left out, tried to remind herself that things had been perfectly lovely until now, and that it was going to be fun to watch the others dancing.

"Want to dance?" someone was saying.

She turned, and there stood Bryan.

"I—I guess not—" she said diffidently. And then she felt she had been ungracious. Actually, she did want to dance, more than anything in the world. "I don't know how," she admitted honestly.

"Oh, come on—it's a square dance, and easy. Just follow me—"

She looked up, and there was Papa watching her. He nodded, just the least little bit. Katie stood up.

"All right—" she said.

"Form your circle—" Bub called.

Scrape, scrape went the fiddle. Bryan took her hand; they joined the circle that was forming. Whether by accident, or design, she wouldn't know, Dennis was on her other side. He took her hand and it gave her a sense of comfort to realize that he and Melinda were there at her side, helping her.

"Sashay round—" Bub said.

They began to circle around, slowly at first, then gaining speed. Katie was awkward and embarrassed, felt herself stiffening.

"You're doing fine," encouraged Bryan. "Just let go, and follow me—"

She took a few steps. Suddenly the tightness was gone and she felt light and easy. It was like flying; it was like being a bird in the air. The music got into her mind and heart. It was like playing the organ; it was like singing when all the notes came right.

Swish, swish went the women's skirts. Katie felt her own red dress billowing out as she made a turn. Her curls were loosened by the exercise, her cheeks pink. There was no time to straighten her hair; she wouldn't have done it had there been. There was too much joy in following the steps, in moving around and around the floor, a part of this group. She passed down the line, swinging with all the different men—Dennis, the twins, Mr. Palmer, and Mr. Foster who, in spite of his size and his age, was moving as lightly as a boy.

"You're doing fine," Bryan said, once she was back with him again. "I told you—"

It was quite late when the Pierce family finally started home. The twins were not with them—they had ridden home with the black eyed sisters. It was miles out of their way, but that didn't matter at all.

Carolyn, who should have been asleep long ago, was still wide awake.

"It was a most delightful party," she said. "You looked beautiful, Katie."

"Thank you, Carolyn," Katie told her. Her head was still spinning with the excitement of the evening. She thought she'd never be able to go to sleep, for sleeping would make her forget, for the time, all the lovely things that had happened.

"You did look nice, Katie," Melinda said.

"And you danced with exquisite grace," Carolyn went on.

"Say, Katie, you did dance well," Dennis told her. "You got right in there and kept time. I guess that comes of knowing music, and having a feel for time."

"Didn't Annie Foster look pretty?" Papa said.

"Yes—" Melinda agreed. And then she added, "There's a reason, and she said I could tell you. She's going to get married."

"Annie married!" Dennis said. "Who's the lucky man?"

"Mr. Palmer," Melinda told him.

"Well of all things!" Papa exclaimed. "I guess I shouldn't be surprised, but I am."

Katie said nothing. But something warm and happy welled up in her heart. It was as if the happiness of the evening had been rounded out now and was complete.

No, not quite. If only Mama were here to talk to about it. Then it *would* be complete.

Chapter 12

IT WAS ALMOST as if the strength of Katie's wishing had brought Mama back. On the Monday after the party, a letter came from her. Papa had it when Katie and Carolyn got home from school.

"A letter from Mama, girls," he said. "I waited for you before I read it."

Katie threw down her books and wraps. Carolyn ran to him crying, "Let me see—let me see!" Papa opened the envelope and took out the letter enclosed.

"My dear ones," he read.

They were Mama's dear ones—Papa and the twins, Carolyn and Katie. Across the miles her words were coming to them. Letters were magic things, Katie was thinking. You put down little marks to tell what you wanted to say and across the distance you reached out to your loved ones, who got your message. What if people could neither read nor write! It was wonderful you could go to school and learn these things.

"Mother is much better," Papa read on. "In fact, she is so much better that I am coming home—"

"Coming home!" Carolyn cried. "Oh, Mama is coming home!"

"Coming home—" Katie echoed. Even when she said it, she could scarcely make herself believe it.

Mama was coming home! The thought ran like quicksilver through all their days.

"We'll have to get the house very clean," Katie said.

"Oh, gosh," Bert groaned, "almost I wish Mama had stayed in East Texas."

"Why Bert Pierce," Carolyn reprimanded him, "you don't wish any such of a thing. You are only exaggerated."

"Oh, sure—" Bert grinned at her. "Here, Katie— I'll take the mattresses out and beat them."

And he did.

"Now, Katie," Dick said, looking at her out of the corner of his eye, "do you think it's exactly honest to scrub things up and make Mama believe you kept it this way all the while?"

Another time, ages ago before she had learned how to take the twins' teasing, she might have been hurt by what he said. But now she only smiled at him without even attempting an answer, and for her forbearance she had her reward.

"I was only teasing, Katie," Dick told her. "You kept things fine—just real nice. Now if you want me to, I'll wash the windows on the outside for you."

Which he did.

With so much help about the house, Katie could turn her attention to cooking something good for Mama.

"I believe I'll make a vinegar pie," she said.

"And you might cook up a batch of beans," Bert suggested slyly.

And again, she only smiled at him.

Mama came home on Saturday, which made it very nice because there was no school that day, so Katie had plenty of time to finish getting things ready.

It was mid-afternoon when Dennis and Melinda came driving up with Mama. Katie saw them a long way off, Dennis' team trotting smartly across the prairie. Her heart rushed out to meet them, hurdling the distance between, beating so strongly that she knew Mama must hear it. Mama was in that buggy— Mama was coming home after having been gone for months!

They were all out of the gate before Dennis ever halted the team. Mama was jumping out of the buggy almost before it stopped.

"Oh, Mama!" they all cried, running toward her. And she ran to meet them, lightly as a girl would run.

Then they had reached her and she was kissing them all, beginning with Carolyn. After that she stood back and looked at them. Then she kissed them all a second time.

"You look fine," she said. And then—"Carolyn, Katie, you've both grown *inches*. I'll have to start letting those dresses out, right away."

"I'm getting quite grown-up," Carolyn told her complacently. "In fact, I am almost a young lady. If Katie would only hurry and get married, I would be Miss Pierce."

They all laughed at that, and then they went into

the house. Katie noticed that the twins wanted to be close to Mama just as much as she and Carolyn did.

When Mama went inside, she looked around as if she could not see enough of it, this house she had been away from for so long. She seemed to be feasting her eyes on things.

"It looks grand," she said, "so clean and nice."

"It ought to," Dick grumbled. "I got blisters on my hands from scrubbing."

"And I can't even straighten up, my back is so tired from carrying mattresses around," Bert told her.

"Katie let everything get in a mess," Bert said. "And then, just before time for you to come, she made Dick and me get things clean." He grinned when he said it, and of course Mama knew better.

"Why Bert," Carolyn protested indignantly, "it is not right to tell such—such *prevaricators*. Katie kept things very nice."

"Of course she did," Mama said. "I knew—all along I knew she would."

And suddenly it all seemed worthwhile to Katie —the big pans of beans and the uncertainty and the dread. Mama had depended on her, had believed she would not fail. And, for the most part, she hadn't disappointed her.

Supper that night was like old times. Once more the entire family sat together around the table, linked in love and happiness. There was chicken and potatoes, and, of course, beans—and for dessert, the vinegar pie.

"You didn't make this yourself, Katie?" Mama

marveled.

"Oh yes she did," Carolyn broke in. And then she added thoughtfully, "It's a great deal better than the first one she made."

That awful first pie! The memory of it still had the power to make Katie blush.

"Why Katie," Mama said, honestly amazed, "I couldn't make as good a one."

The statement, Katie knew, was, as Carolyn would say, "an exaggerated," but it was one that made her very happy nevertheless.

By the time the family reached dessert, they had begun to try to fill in the gaps of the time that they had been separated.

"How's your mother getting along?" Dennis asked with professional interest.

"The bone's knitting fine," Mama told him. "She's getting along all right. We found a good woman to stay with her, for a while, at least."

"She'll make out all right," Dennis declared. "The worst is over now."

"She gets awfully lonesome," Mama said. "She hated to see me leave. But of course, she knew I had to come back here."

"Maybe Melinda ought to go down and stay with her for a while after Christmas," Dennis suggested.

"That might be an idea," Mama agreed. "She needs someone."

"Of course I'll go, if she needs me," Melinda said.

The household fitted back into the old routine with scarcely a ripple. Mama took the lead, Katie helped. It seemed almost a dream that she had, only lately, done all these tasks for the family. It looked so easy when Mama did things; Katie still remembered what an ordeal each separate chore had been until she mastered it, after her fashion.

"Katie," Mama said, "Papa has been telling me how well you got along. You did a fine job."

She and Mama were washing dishes while Carolyn made doll clothes. Katie looked at Mama gratefully, but did not answer.

"He told me about the storm, and how you kept the children at school, and all that—"

Katie raised honest eyes to her mother's face. Some way it didn't seem so hard to talk about it now.

"Did he tell you—why I stayed?" she asked.

"Yes, he told me. But most of all, he told me what you did *while* you were there. That's what really mattered."

"Mama," Katie asked suddenly, "do you suppose I'll ever get over being scared of—of storms and things?"

"Probably not," Mama told her. "At least, I never have—"

Mama, afraid of storms! Afraid of anything! Mama, who had always acted like a rock to lean upon.

"You scared of storms!" Katie cried, astonished. "You never acted the least bit afraid, Mama."

"I tried to hide it," Mama said. "But I was, anyway. I was also afraid of snakes and scorpions and—yes, even water dogs."

Katie stared at her in open-mouthed wonder.

"And I hated the wind," Mama went on. "And the great distances out here. I used to lie awake nights,

wondering what I would do if one of you children got
sick, with no doctor closer than thirty miles."

"But you never told us—" Katie protested weakly.

"Of course not," Mama told her briskly. "People
don't go around discussing their fears."

Katie looked soberly at Mama. Wasn't it funny
that now, at long last, she felt adult around her mother.
Mama was talking to her the way she would talk to
another woman. A great joy flooded Katie's heart. To
think that Mama would tell her all the things she had
always kept secret before!

"Katie," Mama continued thoughtfully, "when I
left Grandmother's, I thought I'd have to come back
and tell you that you must give up the idea of going
back to Lewisville to school."

Give up the idea of going back to Lewisville!
Mama couldn't mean what she was saying. For six
years Katie had cherished the dream. Last summer
she was practically ready to go when Grandmother
had her accident. Katie realized she must stay at home
then. But she never once doubted that she would
go after Grandmother got better. Even when things
were the hardest, while she was trying to take Mama's
place, she would comfort herself with the thought that
next fall she would go back to East Texas and do all
the things she liked most to do. Katie was meant to go
back there to school. Melinda had said so when she
herself gave up the idea. Even Grandmother had realized this. It was not fair that she should have to give
up the dream which had nourished her for so long.

"Yes," Mama said, "I was sure you shouldn't go.
Grandmother is very weak and nervous. She couldn't

have the responsibility of a child. But now that I'm back, I see things differently."

She paused and looked at Katie thoughtfully.

"I think," she went on, "that you should go. More than that—I think you shouldn't even wait until next fall. It would be well if you could go right after Christmas."

"Right after Christmas—" Katie repeated incredulously. That wasn't more than a month away.

"Yes, for you've grown up, Katie. You won't be a responsibility for Grandmother. You'll be company for her. You'll help look after her."

Above the joy of Mama's words a thought was beating at Katie's brain. Wasn't it strange to think that the thing she had once looked upon as a privilege had now become a duty? But even stranger was the fact that she liked it better this way.

"Do you still want to go?" Mama asked.

Katie drew a long breath.

"Oh, Mama!" she cried. "Yes, Mama!"

Katie sat in the middle of the floor, a pile of books in front of her.

"I wish you'd go through them, Katie," Mama had said. "The ones you don't want to take, leave here. Maybe Carolyn can use them."

Maybe Carolyn can use them! First they had been Melinda's, and then Katie's. Now they would come to Carolyn. It was a sort of legacy, one you grew into and, in turn, grew out of. Katie opened one of the books to the fly-leaf and looked at the writing there.

"Melinda Pierce: Her Book."

And beneath it, "*Katie* Pierce: *Her* Book."

She had underlined two of the words, trying to emphasize the fact of her own possession. At the time she scarcely knew why she did it, but now she thought she understood. Always as a child she had followed Melinda, had been guided by her, had felt lost and uncertain without her. By putting emphasis on her own name, perhaps she had hoped to make of herself a little bit more of an individual than she had been before. Much as she loved Melinda, she was not merely her sister; she was *Katie* Pierce, an entirely different person.

She put the book—her geography—aside in a box which was to be left for Carolyn. And as she did so, she heard a knock at the door.

"I'll get it," Mama said, realizing that Katie was sitting with her lap full of books. She opened the door, and there stood Bryan Cartwright.

"Good morning," he said, very polite and nice. He looked neat and clean, as always, with his hair combed smoothly. And his face had that same merry look on it, as if he found life really a lot of fun. He had a box in his hand.

"Do come in," Mama said. And then, a little uncertainly, she added, "The boys are somewhere around the place."

"I'll see them later," he told her easily, not at all embarrassed. "It's Katie I came to see, really."

Even the twins, almost two years older than Bryan, would probably not have admitted so readily that they had come to see a girl. Katie started to flounder to her feet, feeling herself flush deeply as she did so.

"Oh," Mama said. And then, "Well, that's fine. You have company, Katie."

"Hello," Katie said, pushing some books aside as she struggled to rise.

"Hello—no don't get up. I'll just come over there."

He walked to where she was sitting and dropped easily on the floor beside her. "Oh, a history book," he said. "I always liked history." He picked it up, turned a few pages, reading a line here and there. Mama watched a minute, then slipped out of the room. Time was when Katie would have felt self-conscious and embarrassed at being left alone to entertain a guest—any guest, but especially Bryan. Now she felt very easy about it. Partly this was because he was acting as if it was just the most ordinary thing in the world for the two of them to be sitting here on the floor, surrounded by school books.

He looked at the book a few moments, and then he glanced up quickly. "Oh," he said, "I was about to forget what I came for. My mother says you're going away to school."

"Yes," Katie told him, "back to the Academy, near where Grandmother lives."

Wasn't it strange that now, as she told him, it didn't sound quite so wonderful?

"That's what my mother said. And she wanted to send you a present to take with you. She's awfully grateful about—well, about the way you acted during the storm. She says you saved Meg's life, and you did. That was just real smart of you, Katie," he finished quietly.

Something sang in Katie's heart—a gladness, a delight. It was so strong that she could not even make herself protest that she had done nothing much.

"Well, anyway," he said, "here's the present."

He handed her the box.

Katie took it, her hand shaking a little. A present, for her!

"Aren't you going to open it?" he asked.

She untied the ribbon and drew out a length of filmy white material, delicate as cobwebs. She looked at it glowingly. She was always moved by the sight of beautiful things, and this was lovely beyond description.

"My mother said it's called a fascinator," Bryan told Katie. "It's to put over your head when you go to parties—and things."

She still sat, holding it in her hands. Finally she brought herself back to reality. "Tell her I said, I said—" She hesitated, not finding words for her gratitude. "Tell her I said—thank you," she finally finished.

"Oh, that's all right. Say, why don't you try it on?"

Suddenly Katie felt a great daring, a wish to drape this bit of lacy stuff across her hair, even if she was wearing a print dress, with which it was certainly never meant to be worn. She looped it over her head and put one length across her shoulder, letting it fall down in the back. She had never worn a fascinator before, but some instinct told her how to do it.

Bryan looked at her, surprise in his face, and something else—an admiration, a different look from any she had ever seen there before. He even seemed a little embarrassed. When he finally spoke it wasn't about the scarf at all.

"What are you going to study?" he asked.

Strangely enough, with Bryan embarrassed, Katie felt a little more confident. She couldn't explain it; she just did.

"Oh, the same things we had here," she told him, "only more of them, I guess. And music and art. And—well, elocution, I guess." Now her voice trailed off uncertainly, for some way these didn't seem important as she mentioned them to Bryan—just girl studies, unimportant.

"That's good," he told her, regaining his confidence. "When you come back, those things will be fine. Right out here we can use them—all of them. Pretty things."

He didn't say *if* she came back. He was taking it for granted that she would. It was something she wasn't even sure about in her own mind. What if she got down to East Texas and liked it so well she wanted to stay? The country there had never ceased to call to her, ever since she came out here to the Panhandle. East Texas, with its gentleness, its green trees and flowers, its soft air. She couldn't stay, and leave the family, of course. But what if she wanted to so much that she'd never be happy in the Panhandle again?

"Say," he broke in on her thoughts, "you are going to write to me, aren't you?"

She looked at him quickly, ready to say of course she'd write to him, just as she'd write to Mama and Papa, Carolyn and the twins. But as she moved her head quickly, the length of the fascinator stirred a little, so that she was conscious of its softness, of its loveliness framing her face. And all of a sudden she had a wish not to answer right off.

"Will you?" he asked again.

For just a moment she hesitated, letting the new knowledge run through her mind and heart. She wasn't a child, to answer him with a child's forthright candor. She was Katie Pierce, almost sixteen years old, and she was going away to school and a boy was asking her to write to him. A delicious sense of power came over her, and a sweetness. She lifted her eyes and then, partly from shyness and partly because she just wanted to, she looked at him again, this time through her lashes.

"Maybe—" she said delicately.

And the funny thing was that something told her he didn't want her to promise for sure—not right away, he didn't.

"You just better," he said, looking very grown-up. "Now promise me you will."

"All right, I will," she told him—and knew that this time it was all right to promise.

"That's more like it," he said, getting up as he spoke. Katie stood up, too, the scarf still on her head.

"You look awfully pretty," he told her, his voice low and a little constrained. He held out his hand, and Katie took it.

"Goodby," he said. He turned to go, then hesitated a moment, as if he wished he could think of more to say.

"Goodby," Katie said, very low.

"Don't forget about writing."

"I won't. I promise—" And then, "And you'll write

to me?"

Suddenly he was himself once more—merry, at ease.

"Why, of course." He grinned. "How else do you think I could keep getting letters from you?"

He moved quickly now, toward the door. For just a second he stood there, still smiling at her. Then he opened it, went outside. He turned to look at her once more.

"Goodby," he said, over his shoulder.

"Goodby," Katie said. And again, "Goodby—"

The door closed behind him.

Katie was back to the books on the floor. She sat very still, however, not touching them. The scarf was still on her head. Once or twice she reached out to touch it, lingeringly, her eyes far away. Finally she took it off, folded it neatly and put it on the chair beside her. Then she went back to the books, handling them gently, absent mindedly.

One by one she picked them up, looked at the names on the fly leaf, put them into the box.

It was as if she were putting away a part of her life, she was thinking. Six years of living in the Panhandle. It was almost as if she could see, nestling there among the school books, a little girl with flying hair and blue eyes and pink cheeks—a little girl who was scared of everything, clinging close to her older sister, following the pattern set by her. She felt a sort of sweet sadness, knowing that she was leaving this little girl here, along with the school books.

And, even as she was conscious of the thought, another picture came to her, a foreshadowing of that new life which would be hers. Melinda would not be there for her to follow now. Nobody, not even Mama, would be there to tell her what to do. For the first time in her life she would be, not just Melinda's sister, not even Mama's daughter, but, first of all, *Katie Pierce: Herself.*

But, she thought honestly, she would be taking them with her, in a way. All the things Mama had taught her, all the things she had learned from Melinda. They would go with her. As far as that, all that the Panhandle had taught her, all she had gained from these books she was packing away. Those things were woven into her life, and she would take them with her, even though she was leaving their physical presence behind.

In a year or so she would be coming back. All along she had known she would do this, but now she had a deeper, more astonishing knowledge. She would come, not because she had to, but because she wanted to. This land, with its wide horizons had cast its spell over her. It had given her the finest opportunity any place could give a girl—the chance to grow up.

She picked up the book of fairy tales now, the last one that was left unpacked. She looked at the picture on the cover, the one of the Prince, remembering how she had used to be sure that some day she would meet him. She looked at it curiously.

And then suddenly a strange thing happened. The face became clear. Very clear indeed. Smooth brown hair, blue eyes, and a merry look about him—a good look.

Bryan Cartwright's face.

Something sweet and breathless swept over Katie,

sent her heart strumming up into her ears. The force of it set her trembling a little. She ran her hands across the cover, touching it gently, as she had touched the scarf. For a long time she sat motionless. At last she picked up the book, with a sweet and secret smile on her face, and started to put it into the box with the others, those outgrown school books.

Then she brought her hand back quickly, the book still in it. She got up and went to her room where her trunk was sitting, already half packed. She lifted the things already there and in the very bottom of the trunk, she tucked the book.

This one would not be left here; this one, she would take with her.

About the Author

Loula Grace Erdman, born in 1898 on a family farm in Missouri, was destined to pursue a lifelong career in both teaching and writing. The writing came early. Her first story sent to a publisher, at age fourteen, received a rejection, but with encouragement to continue. It would become Miss Erdman's practice to learn from her mistakes, to find out what readers looked for, and to continually improve her skills.

Although Miss Erdman eventually became an award-winning author with 17 novels, nonfiction, and many short stories, articles and essays to her credit, she "saw herself first as a teacher and then as a writer." * Even before she had received a college education, she taught in elementary schools. Later, in college, she made friends with a young woman from Texas. Her friend's mother, impressed with Loula Grace, found her a teaching position in Amarillo. Miss Erdman accepted the offer "providing that her younger sister could have a teaching job as well." The young teacher-writer, just like some of the characters in her own books, would come to adopt the Texas Panhandle as her own home. Over the years she taught elementary, then junior high levels, and finally college classes in creative writing at West Texas State College—making time for her own writing all along.

As she learned more about the early days of Texas in the Panhandle, Miss Erdman became fascinated

* This and other quotations are from an essay on Loula Grace Erdman in *The Handbook of Texas Online*.

by the untold stories of the first settlers—the "nesters"—and by the courageous role of the women. Of the homesteader she said, "The story of his stubborn courage has been overlooked." And she thought someone should speak for the ordinary woman in her personal relationships and in the real life dilemmas she faced. Miss Erdman's prize-winning novel, *The Edge of Time*, grew from extensive investigation into that era. Drawing upon this same research, she wrote *The Wind Blows Free*, for young people, and further traced the Pierce daughters' stories in *The Wide Horizon* and *The Good Land*. Another junior novel, *Room to Grow*, tells of one of the French families who helped to settle Texas. Books like these, whether novels for adults or youth, have been much appreciated by Miss Erdman's readers. Old-timers praised her accuracy, and new generations have felt that she understood well the every-day struggles of women and girls.

Miss Erdman never married, but contributed richly to her world and "came to regard her students and colleagues as her family," in addition to her own siblings, nieces and nephews. She died in 1976.

More Stories about the Pierce Family

The Wind Blows Free

While homesteading in the 1890's in the Texas Panhandle offers the prospect of something new to irrepressible little Carolyn, and unending adventure to the lively twins, Bert and Dick, it promises to be an ordeal of labor and isolation for Mama, Melinda and timid Katie. 14-year-old Melinda Pierce, the oldest child and most reluctant pioneer, is especially dismayed. She has given up her friends and happy town life, for this? Before long, however, Melinda is caught up in the compelling beauty of this land of wind and plains, with its adventures and with its gift of new friendship. She finds herself joining wholeheartedly with the other members of her family in their determination to answer the challenge of the Panhandle and make it home. This is the first of the three stories about the Pierce family.

The Good Land

Carolyn, the youngest of all the Pierces, is finally 15 years old. Despite what others may believe, she is no longer a baby! In fact, from her position at the tail end of the family, she sees more than anyone would think, including the sorrows of her sister Katie's stalemated romance. Carolyn would like to help! But help is a delicate matter; as it is in another case, with the new immigrant family, the Warrens, whose Papa so strangely guards his home against the neighbors and whose lonely daughter, Rowena, Carolyn would like to befriend. On top of everything else she must deal with her own anxieties about leaving home to go to high school in Amarillo. Will she find friends and be accepted? With *'scruciatingly* consistent effort, irrepressible, well-meaning Carolyn gets in and out of more than one difficulty, finds new companions, proves herself a true friend—not the least with the up-and-coming Jim Foster—and so brings the Pierce family tales of the Texas Panhandle to a satisfying close.

LIVING HISTORY LIBRARY

The Living History Library is a collection of works for children published by Bethlehem Books, comprising quality reprints of historical fiction and non-fiction, including biography. These books are chosen for their craftsmanship and for the intelligent insight they provide into the present, in light of events and personalities of the past.

TITLES IN THIS SERIES

Archimedes and the Door of Science, by Jeanne Bendick
Augustine Came to Kent, by Barbara Willard
Becky Landers, Frontier Warrior, by Constance L. Skinner
Beorn the Proud, by Madeleine Polland
Beowulf the Warrior, by Ian Serraillier
Big John's Secret, by Eleanore M. Jewett
Enemy Brothers, by Constance Savery
Galen and the Gateway to Medicine, by Jeanne Bendick
God King, by Joanne Williamson
The Hidden Treasure of Glaston, by Eleanore M. Jewett
Hittite Warrior, by Joanne Williamson
If All the Swords in England, by Barbara Willard
Jamberoo Road, by Eleanor Spence
Madeleine Takes Command, by Ethel C. Brill
Nacar, the White Deer, by Elizabeth Borton de Trevino
The Mystery of the Periodic Table, by Benjamin D. Wiker
The Reb and the Redcoats, by Constance Savery
Red Falcons of Trémoine, by Hendry Peart
Red Hugh, Prince of Donegal, by Robert T. Reilly
Shadow Hawk, by Andre Norton
The Small War of Sergeant Donkey, by Maureen Daly
Son of Charlemagne, by Barbara Willard
Sun Slower, Sun Faster, by Meriol Trevor

The Switherby Pilgrims, by Eleanor Spence
Victory on the Walls, a Story of Nehemiah,
     by Frieda C. Hyman
The Wind Blows Free, by Loula Grace Erdman
The Winged Watchman, by Hilda van Stockum
Year of the Black Pony, by Walt Morey